CH

THOOM! Something exploded outside the Astral Dome, big enough and near enough to make them all stagger. It was followed by more booms, and the sound of screaming.

"Crivens!" Fergus cried. "What now?"

THOOM. THOOM. THOOM. THOOM. Something was coming closer to the Astral Dome.

Gonzalo's raygun hummed, and Fergus's arms crackled with lektricity. Archie backed away, his wrists still handcuffed.

CRUNCH! Something metallic and snake-like punched through the ceiling of the Astral Dome, ripping off part of the roof. The thing curled inside like an octopus's tentacle and pulled, tearing out a huge chunk of ceiling.

Framed in the hole against the bright blue sky was a massive machine with a bulbous, seaweed-draped steel passenger compartment atop eight writhing mechanical tentacles. Stenciled on the side of the thing was a black flag with a white skull over two crossed swords.

"Pirates!" one of the cowboys on the arena floor cried. "Pirates from Galveston!"

BY ALAN GRATZ

The League of Seven
The Dragon Lantern
The Monster War

Ban This Book

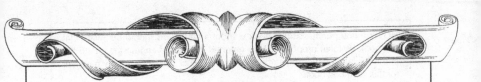

THE
MONSTER
WAR

A League of Seven Novel

ALAN GRATZ

Illustrations by
BRETT HELQUIST

A TOM DOHERTY ASSOCIATES BOOK
NEW YORK

This is a work of fiction. All of the characters, organizations, and events portrayed in this novel are either products of the author's imagination or are used fictitiously.

THE MONSTER WAR

Interior illustrations by Brett Helquist

Map by Jennifer Hanover

A Starscape Book
Published by Tom Doherty Associates
175 Fifth Avenue
New York, NY 10010

www.tor-forge.com

The Library of Congress Cataloging-in-Publication Data is available upon request.

ISBN 978-0-7653-3827-3 (trade paperback)
ISBN 978-1-4668-3852-9 (e-book)

Our books may be purchased in bulk for promotional, educational, or business use. Please contact your local bookseller or the Macmillan Corporate and Premium Sales Department at 1-800-221-7945, extension 5442, or by e-mail at MacmillanSpecialMarkets@macmillan.com.

First Edition: July 2016
First Trade Paperback Edition: June 2017

Printed in the United States of America

D 0 9 8 7 6 5 4

To my friends and superfans:

Finn Goldberg, Theo Henry, Josefina Houchard,
Charlie Marsh, Zoe and Ella Martindale,
Eli and Oscar North, Abby Ryner, Tristi Townsend,
Ian Veteto, Jack and Turner Weinmeister,
and, of course, Jo Gratz!

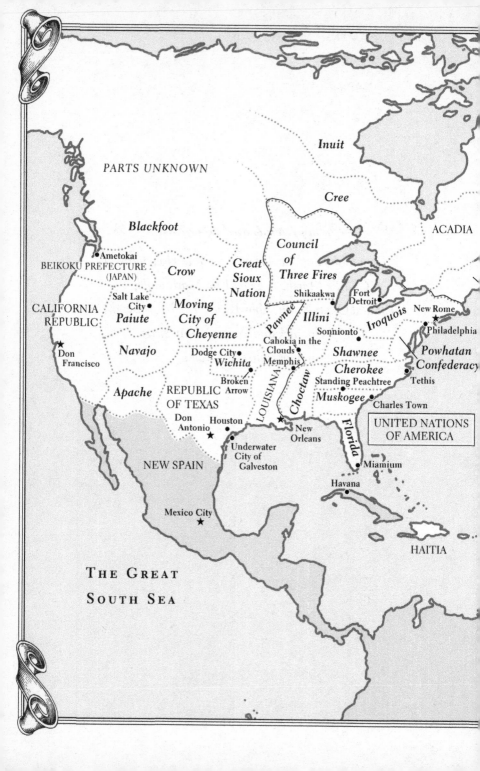

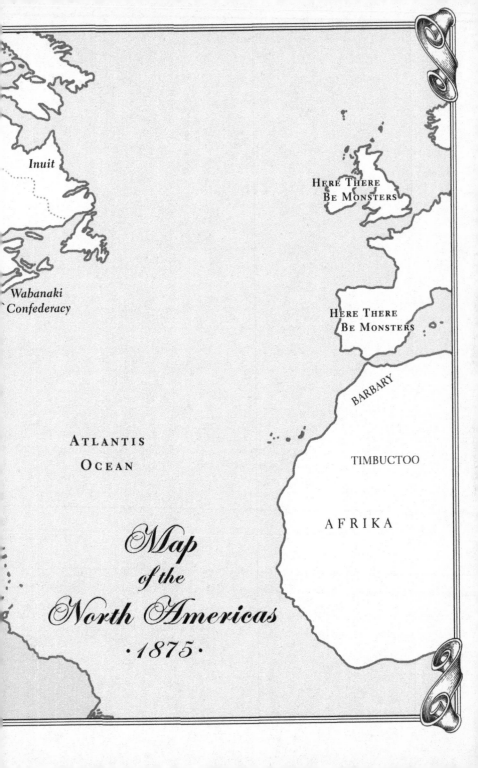

Inuit

HERE THERE
BE MONSTERS

Wabanaki
Confederacy

HERE THERE
BE MONSTERS

BARBARY

ATLANTIS
OCEAN

TIMBUCTOO

AFRIKA

Map
of the
North Americas
·1875·

THE
MONSTER
WAR

Thirty days hath September.
Seven heroes we remember.

Archie Dent knows there really are monsters in the world.

They're the Mangleborn—ancient, colossal, unkillable monsters who feed off lektricity. Trapped in prisons deep within the Earth, they sleep, whispering their dreamsongs to the weak-minded and waiting for humanity to rediscover lektricity. Each time we do, the Mangleborn rise to destroy civilization, and each time a new League of Seven must come together to put them back in their prisons. Every League is different, yet always the same: a tinker, a lawbringer, a scientist, a trickster, a warrior, a strongman, and a hero to lead them. Seven men and women with incredible powers from all parts of the known world who join forces to stop the Mangleborn from enslaving humanity.

Again and again different Leagues have saved the world, but only the Septemberist Society remembers. Founded after the last League of Seven defeated the Mangleborn, the Septemberists hoped to break the never-ending cycle of destruction by monitoring the Mangleborn in their prisons and working in secret to stop anyone from experimenting with lektricity. But the Septemberists have failed. The Mangleborn are rising again, and now the super-strong Archie Dent, raised by Septemberist parents to battle the Mangleborn and their deadly offspring, the Manglespawn, must put together a new League of Seven to stop the monsters from destroying the world.

If Archie doesn't destroy it first.

1

The chain that shackled Archie Dent to the boy beside him
rattled as the steamwagon bounced down a rutted road, and
they swayed into each other. Archie and his fellow prisoner sat
in darkness in the back of the covered wagon, surrounded by
the other children the kidnappers had taken from Houston's
back alleys. They were the forgotten—the children who wore
rags for clothes, ate scraps from trash bins, and slept outside.
They were orphans, with no families and no homes to go back
to. No one would miss them when they disappeared.

Archie wasn't worried about the chain around his leg. He
could rip it off whenever he wanted to. But the boy he was
shackled to looked frightened. He was a Texian about Archie's
age, and just as small, with light brown skin and dark black

hair. He had the same grubby, dirt-caked look of the other street children, but unlike the rest he wore proper denim pants, a cowboy shirt that used to be white, and a scuffed-up pair of brown leather boots. The boy stared straight forward, his eyes vacant and distant like so many of the others.

"Everything's going to be okay," Archie said.

The funny thing was, the other boy said the same thing to him at the same time.

Archie blinked. This homeless kid was telling *him* everything was going to be okay?

"Name's Gonzalo," the boy said, still staring straight forward. "What's yours?"

Archie didn't want to tell the kid his real name. Luis Senarens, the writer Archie and Hachi and Fergus had saved in the tunnels beneath New Rome, had published dozens of pulp adventures featuring the three of them battling giant monsters, and now he was famous. Gonzalo might have read one of Senarens's dime novels and give away who he was.

"My name's, um, Clyde," Archie lied.

Gonzalo turned his head at that, almost like he didn't believe him. But if he thought he was lying, he didn't call Archie on it. "Where you from, Clyde?"

"Philadelphia," Archie said, telling the truth this time.

"Long way from home," Gonzalo said.

"What about you?" Archie asked.

"Austin, originally," Gonzalo said. "Now kind of all over. You got parents?"

The couple who'd raised Archie, Dalton and Agatha Dent, lived just outside Philadelphia, in Powhatan territory. He'd thought of them as his parents for the first twelve years of his life, but technically Archie didn't *have* parents. Because he wasn't human. The thought chilled him all over again, and he longed for the solitude of the dark corner in his hotel room.

"I . . . I don't have any parents," Archie told him, which was true and wasn't true.

Gonzalo nodded. "I never once laid eyes on mine."

The steamwagon shuddered to a stop, and Archie tensed, ready to fight. But they were just picking up more children. They weren't wherever they were all being taken yet. One of the banditos who'd kidnapped them threw open the curtain at the back of the wagon to push more children inside. Bright sunlight lit up the darkness, and as Archie threw an arm up to shield his eyes he remembered doing the same thing this morning in his hotel room when Mr. Rivets had thrown open the curtains.

"Don't!" Archie had told Mr. Rivets, shrinking back into the shadows in the corner.

Mr. Rivets, Archie's clockwork manservant, tutor, and best friend, ticked softly as he studied his young charge. "It is time you got out of that corner, Master Archie. Cleaned yourself up. Had some food. You haven't eaten in days."

Archie twisted away from the light streaming in through the window. "Why should I?" he asked Mr. Rivets. "I don't need to eat. I don't even need to breathe. *I can't die.* I could sit here in this corner forever if I wanted to."

"Which would be an incredible waste, sir. It is time you re-joined the living," Mr. Rivets told him.

"I don't want to," Archie said. "I don't want to do anything." He'd told Mr. Rivets the same thing every day for a week, ever since they'd arrived in Houston. Ever since he'd learned the horrible truth about how he'd been brought to life. "Close the curtains. I belong in the darkness."

That's what he was, after all. A shadow. The darkest shadow of them all.

"There are matters you must attend to, Master Archie. If I were not now self-winding, I would have run down long ago. And you promised Miss Hachi and Master Fergus you would meet them here in Houston. They may be somewhere in the city as we speak, and we must warn them about Philomena Moffett and her Monster Army."

"I don't care. I don't want to see them. I don't want to see anyone ever again. I'm done. With everything."

"There is something else, Master Archie," Mr. Rivets went on, as though Archie hadn't said anything. "In my search for Master Fergus and Miss Hachi, I have discovered that children are being stolen from Houston's streets."

Archie lifted his head. "What?"

"Homeless children," Mr. Rivets said. "Taken by masked men with steamwagons. In broad daylight, no less. I interrupted one such kidnapping only this morning, and alerted the local authorities to the problem. But they are too taxed due to handling security for the annual Livestock Exhibition and Rodeo currently being held at the Astral Dome."

"The *what*?" Archie said. He shook his head and turned back to the wall. "No—I don't care. I don't want to know. It's not my problem."

"I see," said Mr. Rivets. "I apologize, Master Archie." His brass head with its metal bowler hat and mustache tilted as he thought. "There *is* one small matter at least that must be attended to. Your parents have sent us funds via pneumatic post, and the post office requires you to be there in person to sign for it."

Archie squeezed his eyes shut tight. "I don't care, Mr. Rivets!"

"May I remind you, Master Archie, that without these funds we shall be turned out of the hotel and onto Houston's streets, where, I can assure you, it is far brighter and hotter than your corner."

Archie huffed. *Fine.* He would go to the post office and sign for the blinking money. But that was it. He was coming right back here to this corner, this shadow. He wasn't taking a bath, or eating food, or sleeping in a bed. He was through pretending to be human. And he wasn't rescuing any kidnapped children either.

He was through pretending to be a hero too.

Archie had followed along in Mr. Rivets's shadow, brass goggles hiding the eyes he kept on the ground so he wouldn't have to see the brown-skinned, black-haired people of Houston staring at his pale white skin and snowy white hair. They walked for nearly half an hour through Houston's hot, dusty streets, until finally Mr. Rivets stopped. Archie looked up to find himself in a narrow dirt alleyway squeezed in between two wooden warehouses somewhere in Houston's maze of side streets. A dozen or so half-naked Texian children were playing some kind of game where they tried to bounce a rubber ball through barrel rings they'd nailed to the wall. Farther down the street, two dogs fought over a scrap one of them had dug out of an overturned trash can, and a pile of empty wooden crates looked as though someone might be living in them.

Archie didn't understand. Where was the post office?

"I would advise you not to fight at this juncture," Mr. Rivets said. "You should allow yourself to be captured instead. That way you'll be taken to the ringleaders of the operation."

"What ringleaders? What operation?" Archie asked. "What are you talking about?" Had Mr. Rivets slipped a cog?

The ground rumbled as two steamwagons backed into the lane, one from each direction. Texian men in brown leather pants, denim shirts, and white cowboy hats leaped from the covered beds of the wagons, rayguns in hand and bandanas covering their faces. *Kazaaack!* An orange beam from one of the pistols blew up the rubber ball, and the children screamed. They tried to run, but both ends of the street were blocked by the men and their steamwagons.

"All right, *chamacos!*" one of the banditos called. "No messing around now! Into the trucks nice and easy, and nobody gets hurt." One by one, the banditos snatched up the children and tossed them into the wagons.

"Mr. Rivets, what's going on?" Archie asked. But when he turned around the machine man was gone. "Mr. Rivets?"

And that's when Archie understood: Mr. Rivets had tricked him into getting captured by the kidnappers so he would have to save the other children.

2

Archie squinted in the bright light as more chained children were stuffed into the steamwagon with him and Gonzalo. If he'd wanted to, Archie could have broken their chains, crushed the kidnappers' rayguns in his fist, and punched every one of the banditos into the next alley. But knocking these men through a wall wasn't going to save all the *other* children they had kidnapped and were holding somewhere else, and these banditos would just be replaced by more men with bandanas and rayguns. Archie silently cursed Mr. Rivets with a few choice words the machine would have scolded him for using. Archie didn't want to be here. He didn't want to be *anywhere*. He wished he'd never been born—or whatever you called how he came into the world. Created. Sculpted. *Soaked with blood.*

Archie shuddered at the thought. This was it. The last time. He would ride this steamwagon to the banditos' headquarters and save these kids because he was here, but then he was done. And if Mr. Rivets wouldn't listen, Archie would wander off into the Texian desert, cross the border into New Spain, and disappear into the wilderness alone.

As to what the banditos were doing with the children, Archie had a guess. In his experience, it always came down to the Mangleborn, the giant prehistoric creatures that stirred every few hundred years to drive humanity mad and destroy everything they'd built. Some Mangleborn-worshipping cultists needed the children's blood for sacrifices, or wanted to turn them into hideous half-human/half-animal Manglespawn, or meant to feed them to some Mangleborn or Manglespawn. Archie shook his head. Whatever it was, he would stop it, and then he was done. For good.

Archie heard a roar outside the steamwagon as it slowed to a stop. *Here we go*, Archie thought. *A Manglespawn with a bat's wings and a bear's body. Or maybe a Mangleborn with a thousand snakes for arms and rooster legs for feet.* Archie popped his neck and got ready to fight.

"Sounds like a crowd," Gonzalo said. "A big arena. The Astral Dome, maybe."

Archie blinked. Now that Gonzalo mentioned it, it *did* sound like the roar of a crowd.

The bandits hooked a cattle ramp with covered sides to the back to the wagon and shooed the children out, two by two. As they passed from the steamwagon, Archie briefly saw the round, silver top of the Astral Dome, one of the Seven Wonders of the New World. The ancient coliseum dominated Houston's skyline.

"You're right," Archie whispered. "They're taking us into the basement of the Astral Dome!" He shook his head again. "Underground. It's always underground."

"What is?" Gonzalo asked.

"Nothing," Archie said. No reason to scare Gonzalo until he saw whatever monster it was these guys worshipped. That would be enough scare for a lifetime.

The roar of the crowd above was louder now, and came every few minutes. It was like they were right underneath the arena floor. Something thudded above them, shaking the stone ceiling and the walls, and the crowd roared again. What exactly did people *do* in a rodeo? The pens they passed in the hallways under the arena were filled with steamhorses and mechanical bulls. Did they race them? Fight them? Archie had no idea. There weren't a lot of rodeos in Philadelphia.

It took Archie a few minutes to notice that the lights in the passageways weren't gas. They glowed bluish-yellow from behind small orbs set into the walls.

"Are the lights . . . *lektricity*?" he whispered.

"You mean like lightning? No, I don't think so," Gonzalo said, his eyes still straight ahead. "I hear tell they glow the same way fireflies do. That's why they call it the Astral Dome. Roof's covered with them, like stars. It's ancient technology. Older even than the Romans. Ain't never dark inside the Astral Dome. Never hot, neither."

Gonzalo was right—it *wasn't* hot in here! Archie felt a cold breeze coming out of a metal vent, cooling the underground passage. "But how—?"

"Air conditioning," Gonzalo said. "Legend says the ancients had a way to cool the entire arena without ice, but ain't no one knows how to do that no more. Instead, they pack the bottom levels with ice and blow air over it and through the air ducts the ancients built."

So. Some kind of ice monster then, Archie thought. *Something living in the frozen depths of the Astral Dome. Or maybe it's the ice itself—a kind of living ice that gets inside you, turns you into a killer snowman.*

"In here, *chamacos,*" a bandito told them, pointing to a dark chamber deep inside the passageways underneath the arena.

Here we go, thought Archie. *Now we meet the monster.*

The chamber was lined with more of the mechanical bull pens Archie had seen earlier, but these pens were full of children. Mostly Texian, like Gonzalo, and all dirty and thin and ragged. Archie looked around for some sign of Mangleborn or Manglespawn, but there was nothing. Nothing but shabby, crying children, and smiling banditos.

"A good haul today, *jefe,*" one of their captors said. He gave Archie a push, and Gonzalo stumbled forward with him on their chain. "We even got a *gringo!*"

A redheaded mestizo man with a bushy red beard, black suit, and brown bow tie crossed the room to them. "So I see! He'll fetch a good price in New Spain." He lifted Gonzalo's chin to look at his teeth. "They all will! Put them in the pens."

"Procopio Murietta," Gonzalo muttered as they were led away.

"You know this guy?" Archie asked.

Gonzalo nodded. "He's wanted for murder, bank robbery, and cattle rustling from Texas to the California Republic, and everywhere in between. And now it sounds like child slavery too."

Was that really all this was? Banditos rounding up children off Houston's streets and selling them as slaves to ranchers across the border in New Spain who couldn't afford Tik Toks? Not that it wasn't awful and needed to be stopped. It was, and it did. But Archie had been so sure there would be some Mangleborn connection to it all. He couldn't believe it was just good old-fashioned bad guys.

All the better. Archie could wipe the floor with these banditos, free the kids, and be headed south for the border in no time. Archie planned out his attack. He could knock down any jail cell door they put him behind, but it would be better to move now, before they locked him away. Better to keep the other kids safe until he was finished with the banditos.

"We oughtta make our move before they lock us up," Gonzalo whispered.

Archie stopped in surprise, bringing Gonzalo up short on the chain that connected them. "Who, you and me?" Archie asked.

"No," Gonzalo said. "I weren't talking to you—"

Something big and wild roared deeper down in the Astral Dome's sublevels, shaking the ground like an earthquake.

"Órale! What was that?" said Gonzalo.

Archie was afraid he knew.

"The *cucuy* is hungry," Procopio announced. "We need tributes."

The prisoners in the pens cried out and retreated into the darkness.

"What's a *cucuy*?" Archie whispered.

"It's a kind of bogeyman Texian parents scare their kids with," Gonzalo said. "A monster."

"Right. Of course," Archie said. He'd been right after all. No matter what, things *always* came back to the Mangleborn.

Gonzalo looked at the floor. "This one of them creatures you were talking about?" he asked. "The ones causing all the trouble?"

Archie frowned. "I didn't say anything about monsters." He'd been thinking it, but he hadn't said anything about the Mangleborn. Before he could ask what Gonzalo meant, the redheaded bandito started rounding up children.

"Take these, and these, and these," Procopio said, passing over Archie and Gonzalo, "and feed them to the *cucuy*."

"Wait! Take me instead!" Archie and Gonzalo yelled at the same time.

Archie and Gonzalo looked at each other, both surprised the other had volunteered to go in place of a tribute. *Who is this guy?* Archie wondered.

Procopio frowned down at them, trying to understand why two children would want to be fed to a monster. "No," he said. "These two are too valuable. Put them in a cell."

The ground shook again as whatever it was in the basement roared.

"Get the others down there," Procopio said. "The *cucuy* is restless."

There was no time to lose. Archie snapped the chain binding him to Gonzalo and got ready to fight. "Stay down and you won't get hurt!" he and Gonzalo told each other at the same time.

"What?" they said together.

The banditos pushed the crying tributes into a chute, and they disappeared below. Archie didn't have time to figure out what Gonzalo was talking about. He stomped his foot on the floor with all his strength—the strength of a hundred men—and sent a ripple through the floor that knocked everyone in the room from their feet. At the same moment, an orange raygun beam crackled through the air, scorching the air right above where Procopio had been standing. If Archie hadn't knocked him to the floor, it would have hit him.

"*Alto!* Drop your rayguns! You're all under arrest!" yelled the woman who'd shot the oscillating rifle. She was Texian, with long black hair and dark eyebrows, wearing a brown skirt, blue denim shirt, and white cowboy hat. Archie's stomp had sent her to the floor with her partner, a Texian man with a wide nose and a broad, bushy black mustache, who wore a long brown leather duster and a black sombrero. Who were they, and where had they come from?

The fallen banditos didn't stop, and they didn't drop their rayguns. *Kazaaak! Kazaaak! Kazaaak!* Orange beams lanced out from every direction as the banditos fought the invaders, and Archie found himself in the middle of a raygunfight. Beams sent rock and dust exploding from the walls and knocked prison doors off their hinges. Children ran in all directions, the banditos sometimes using them as human shields. Archie spun, trying to decide who or what to hit first.

"Where's Procopio?" Gonzalo cried. He knelt on the floor beside Archie with something in his hand that looked like a turquoise statue of a coiled snake. Where had he gotten that from?

"We'll take care of Procopio!" the woman yelled, back on her feet again and shooting. "Go after the tributes!"

Gonzalo nodded and ran for the chute where the banditos had dropped the tributes to the *cucuy*.

"Wait!" Archie cried, still feeling lost. "Wait for me!"

Gonzalo jumped into the chute, and Archie threw himself in headfirst behind him.

3

Archie tumbled head over heels, banging against the walls of what must have once been a metal air duct for the ancients, until at last he spilled out into a dark room. He landed face-first on a floor of ice and slid and slid and slid, slamming into a stone wall beside what he took to be Gonzalo.

"You okay, Clyde?" Gonzalo asked.

Archie tried to stand and had trouble. The ice was slippery and hard to walk on, and it was pitch black to boot.

"Clyde? You okay?" Gonzalo asked again. Was Clyde here? Archie suddenly missed Clyde and Buster and Kitsune.

And Sings-In-The-Night.

Then Archie remembered—he'd told Gonzalo that *his* name was Clyde!

"Me? Oh. Yeah. I'm all right. How about you?"

"I'll live."

Archie helped Gonzalo to his feet.

"Where's the kids?" Gonzalo asked.

"I don't know. Unless you can see in the dark, I'm as blind as you are," Archie told him.

Someone whimpered on the other side of the room, and Archie and Gonzalo shuffled across to them on the ice, using each other for balance. It was the children. They were huddled together along the wall.

"Is everybody still here?" Gonzalo asked.

"*Sí*," said a small voice.

"No sign of the *cucuy*?" Gonzalo asked.

The mention of the bogeyman's name set some of them to crying again. Archie's eyes had begun to adjust to the dark a little, but he still couldn't see a thing. There wasn't a hint of light down here.

Back in the shadows with the other monsters, where I belong, Archie thought.

"Clyde, you stay here with the kids. I'll look for a way out and come back for you," Gonzalo said.

"Huh-uh. *You* stay here with the kids. It's better if I go alone."

"Ain't gonna happen," Gonzalo told him.

"You don't understand. You'll just get hurt," Archie said.

"And you won't?" Gonzalo asked.

"No, I—"

The *cucuy* roared somewhere off in the darkness, a sound that shook dust from the ceiling and cracked the ice under their feet. The children screamed and sobbed.

"*Don't move* from here, understand?" Gonzalo told them, and Archie felt him slip past him.

"Wait!" Archie said. He put a hand to the wall and slid along as best he could behind Gonzalo. The slippery floor was bad enough, but Archie hated being blind. Every faint breeze and every *tick* of cracking ice sent him spinning, trying desperately to make out a shape, a shadow, a silhouette in the inky darkness. He was completely lost.

Unlike Gonzalo. The Texian moved along with more confidence, and didn't stop and turn at every little sound.

There was an open doorway in the wall at the far end of the room, and a hallway that a little groping around told them went left and right.

"This way," Gonzalo said, heading right. "*Ándale.*"

"Whoa, whoa, whoa. This way," Archie said, heading left.

"We shouldn't split up," Gonzalo said.

"I agree. So let's go this way," Archie said.

"Look, I'm the one in charge here," Gonzalo said.

"*You're* the one in charge here?" Archie said. "Says who?"

"Says the Republic of Texas. I'm a Texas Ranger."

Archie had heard of the Rangers—they were the legendary police force of Texas, skilled trackers and raygunslingers who roamed from town to town, going wherever they were needed to keep the peace.

"Right," Archie said. "*You're* a Texas Ranger."

Gonzalo lifted Archie's hand to his shirt, where Archie could feel a round metal badge the size of a Texian five-peso coin. Inside the circle, Archie's fingers traced the cutout of a five-pointed star.

"We go right," Gonzalo said, and he moved off that direction.

Archie followed along blindly. "But . . . you were living on the streets."

"I was undercover," Gonzalo told him. "My parents are Texas Rangers too. They were the ones who came in shooting upstairs."

"That was your *parents*?" Archie asked. That was way cooler than Archie's parents, who spent all their time in libraries.

"They followed me in," Gonzalo said. "We been tracking Procopio Murietta for months. We thought he was running a child slave ring out of Houston, but we never could get close to him. Then all of a sudden he got more open about it. Lot of other criminals came out of the shadows too. Like suddenly somebody flipped a switch, and now all the bad guys are going loco."

Somebody *had* flipped a switch, Archie thought. Moffett had turned on the Dragon Lantern. Now she was marching east across the country with her Monster Army, stirring up the sleeping Mangleborn who drove the weak-minded to madness.

Gonzalo's voice came to him from the darkness ahead. "Thought we finally got Procopio today. Would have too, 'cept for that freak earthquake that knocked everybody over."

"Um, yeah," Archie said. "About that . . ."

"Turn left," a man's voice said, and Archie just about jumped out of his skin.

"Who's that? Who's there?" Archie spun, trying to see in the absolute darkness, and slipped and fell on the ice.

Gonzalo's hand found his and helped him to his feet.

"That's Señor X. He's with me," said Gonzalo.

"But I followed you down the chute! There wasn't anybody else with you."

"We need to hurry," Señor X said. "It's getting closer, and we don't want to meet it here."

"What's getting closer?" Archie asked.

"*El cucuy,*" Gonzalo said.

"You mean, you believe the bogeyman's really down here? You've seen things like this before?"

"Nope," Gonzalo said. "But Señor X has."

"Right. The imaginary Señor X."

"I'm not imaginary, kid," Señor X said. "I'm as real as you are."

Archie followed along, straining his ears and his eyes for some sign of Señor X. Except for the voice, there was no evidence whatsoever that anybody else was with them. Maybe it was Gonzalo. Maybe he had a split personality. Whoever he was, Señor X kept telling Gonzalo which direction to go, and Archie kept following them.

"How does he know where the *cucuy* is?" Archie asked.

"I'm right here in the room if you want to talk to me," Señor X said.

Archie sighed. "All right. I'll play. *Señor X*, how do you know where the *cucuy* is?"

"Ever heard of infrared scanners?" Señor X asked.

"No," Archie admitted.

"Then why don't you shut up and let me do the driving."

So. In addition to being invisible, Señor X was a jerk.

The labyrinth-like passageways they traveled beneath the Astral Dome reminded Archie suddenly of the catacombs beneath the Septemberist Society's headquarters, and he remembered that day not so long ago when he'd been pretending to be Theseus, chasing the minotaur-like Lesool Eshar across the Afrikan plains. How simple things had been then—and what a fool he'd been to think chasing after mountain-sized monsters would be fun. Fighting the Mangleborn was a serious, dangerous business.

"It's here!" Señor X cried. "The *cucuy* is in the room!"

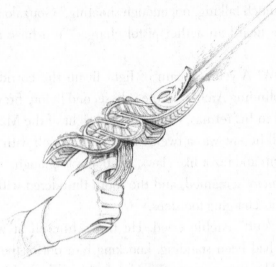

4

Something snuffled a few yards away, and Archie put his hands out blindly. He still couldn't see a thing!

"Where? Where is it?" Archie called. His super strength was going to be pretty useless if he couldn't see the *cucuy* to hit it.

"Is this one of them things you were telling me about, Señor X?" Gonzalo whispered. "One of them Mangleborn?"

"No," Señor X said. "It's a Manglespawn. The child of a Mangleborn and an animal. In this case, a human animal. And really, seriously ugly."

"How do you know about the Mangleborn?" Archie asked. "Who *are* you?"

"How do *you* know about the Mangleborn, kid?" Señor X asked.

"Too much talking, not enough shooting," Gonzalo said.

Archie heard an aether pistol charge. "You have a raygun?"

ZaPOW! A yellow beam of light lit up the corridor in answer, blinding Archie. In the split second before fireworks exploded in his retinas, Archie caught sight of the Mangle-spawn. All he saw was a twenty-foot-tall werewolf with short black horns and razor-like claws, but that was enough.

The *cucuy* screamed, and the room thundered with the sound of its charging footsteps.

"Look out!" Archie cried. He threw himself at where Gonzalo had been standing, knocking him out of the way. *Thwack!* The *cucuy*'s razor claws hit Archie and sent him flying across the room, where he thudded into the wall.

"Stay down! I'll protect you!" Archie and Gonzalo yelled at the same time.

ZaPOW! ZaPOW! ZaPOW! Gonzalo's raygun blasted the screaming *cucuy* again and again, without having to take time to recharge between shots. Archie's eyes started to clear, and in the staccato light from the raygun Archie could see the little Texas Ranger moving around the room, shooting again and again with that strange thing he'd been carrying up top. It worked like a raygun, but it didn't look like any raygun Archie had ever seen before. It was turquoise blue and shaped like a slithering snake, carved all over with lines and spiraling fili-grees like the gargoyles on ancient Aztek pyramids. Its tail stuck up at the back like the fin on a raygun, and its horned head belched aether rays out of its frog-like mouth. Gonzalo wielded it with calm, practiced ease, keeping the big hairy Manglespawn at bay like he saw monsters just like it every day.

Archie worked his way back across the icy floor to Gonzalo. "I thought you said you'd never seen a Manglespawn before!"

"I haven't," Gonzalo answered.

"How is that boy standing?" Señor X asked. "That hit from the *cucuy* should have broken half the bones in his body."

"I'm right here if you want to talk to me," Archie said to the air.

"Scanning," Señor X said. "Twisted pistons—he's the Jandal a Haad!"

The words hit Archie harder than a steamhammer. *Jandal a Haad*. Suddenly he was the broken little boy hiding in the corner of his hotel room again, a monster who feared the light of day.

"What's that mean? Jandal a Haad?" Gonzalo asked, still shooting at the *cucuy*.

"The Lemurians called him Tezcatlipoca. The Mountainheart. Enemy to Both Sides."

"Not helping," Gonzalo said, dodging a swipe of the *cucuy*'s claws.

"He's a monster, just like the *cucuy*. Worse than the *cucuy*. He's made out of stone. Super strong. Practically invulnerable."

The raygun. It was the *raygun* that was talking.

Señor X was a talking raygun.

"I'm—I'm not a monster," Archie said halfheartedly.

"You ever kill anybody?" Gonzalo asked without looking at him.

"N-no," Archie said.

Gonzalo's raygun lit up, hitting the *cucuy* again, but Gonzalo wasn't even looking where he was aiming. His face was turned to Archie, his eyes looking right through him.

"You're lying," Gonzalo said.

The raygun laughed. "If there's one thing Gonzalo sees, it's the truth. Always. You can't lie to him, kid. But G-man, I gotta warn you: I don't have anything strong enough to take down the Jandal a Haad. Not even on my highest setting."

Gonzalo rolled out of the way of another charge from the *cucuy*. "You're not taking this thing out either. It won't die."

"The Jandal a Haad can do it," Señor X said.

"My name is Archie. Archie Dent," Archie said quietly.

"Well, I knew it weren't Clyde," Gonzalo said. He backed away from a swipe of the *cucuy*'s claws, still shooting. "Can you do it? Can you beat *el cucuy*?"

Archie felt himself drifting away, reliving the moment Philomena Moffett had told him where he'd really come from. What he really was.

A bright yellow raygun beam hit Archie in the face, snapping him back to reality. He turned angrily on Gonzalo.

"Archie Dent," Gonzalo said, "*can you beat el cucuy?*"

Archie blinked. Hachi and this guy would get along great. Hachi . . .

"Archie!" Gonzalo cried. The *cucuy* was backing him into a corner.

"Yes. Yes! I can beat it. But I need light. I can't see it to hit it."

"One skylight, coming up!" Gonzalo yelled.

ZaPOW! A massive yellow beam erupted from the mouth of Señor X, exploding the roof. *KaTHOOM!* The raygun bored its way through sublevel after sublevel like a drill—*KaTHOOM-KaTHOOM-KaTHOOM*—until it burst through the arena floor and the wonder of the Astral Dome's ancient gasless lights streamed down on them.

Now that there was light, Archie saw that Señor X was right: the *cucuy* was seriously ugly. The only part of it that wasn't covered with fetid, bloody, matted fur was its callused and wrinkled face, which seemed like it was all forehead and teeth.

The *cucuy* lunged for Gonzalo.

"Oh no you don't!" Archie cried. He grabbed the hair on the *cucuy*'s butt and yanked.

Archie came away with two big handfuls of hair, and the *cucuy* howled.

"Um, sorry," Archie said.

The *cucuy* turned and charged him, but Archie met it with his fists. WHAM! WHAM! WHAM! He beat the *cucuy* back into the wall, hitting it again and again. But it wasn't going down. Archie grabbed the thing's big hairy legs and pulled its feet out from under it. *Thoom!* It slammed into the ground. Archie dragged it in a circle, building up speed until he was spinning it around.

"You like eating little kids, huh?" Archie said. "Well let's see how you like eating dirt!"

Archie launched the *cucuy*. It smashed through the floor above them as it spun, and the next floor, and the next floor, tearing an even bigger hole than the one Gonzalo had shot to let in light. The *cucuy* stopped short of the glowing ceiling and fell back to earth, slamming into the floor three flights above them with a boom.

"Whoa," said Archie. "I didn't meant to throw it *that* far."

"The *cucuy*'s on the arena floor," Señor X told them. "It's down, but it's not out."

"We gotta get up there lickety-split!" Gonzalo said.

Archie clapped the dust off his hands like a job well done. "Why? I got rid of it, didn't I? The kids are safe."

"Archie," Gonzalo said, "there's sixty thousand people up there watching the rodeo!"

5

Three floors above, Archie and Gonzalo could hear sixty thousand people scream.

Archie closed his eyes and cursed himself. *What kind of blinking flange tosses a Manglespawn into a crowded arena?*

"Can we climb the rubble?" Gonzalo asked.

"What? No," Archie said. "Look at it. We'd barely reach the next floor."

"It's a straight shot up from where you're standing," Señor X said.

Gonzalo nodded. "Archie—grab on."

"What? Why? Can you fly?"

"Nope," Gonzalo said. "But Señor X can."

Gonzalo pointed the serpentine raygun at the ground and yelled, "Repulsor ray!"

A spreading, circular blue beam erupted from the raygun's mouth—WOM-WOM-WOM-WOM—and Gonzalo started to lift off the ground.

"Whoa! Wait for me!" Archie cried. He threw his arms around Gonzalo's shoulders, and they were off. WOM-WOM-WOM-WOM-WOM. Gonzalo held the raygun pointed straight at the ground, and the blue repulsor beam lifted them higher and higher, faster and faster. The top two floors flew by and they burst into the bright light of the auditorium like a Roman candle.

Gonzalo cut the power to the repulsor ray and Archie's stomach did a somersault as they fell toward the arena floor. Archie screamed and squeezed his eyes shut, but at the last moment Gonzalo clicked on the repulsor ray again, and they landed as gently as though they had just stepped down off a stair.

"Thanks, Señor," Gonzalo said coolly, like he did things like that every day.

Archie opened his eyes and saw the inside of the Astral Dome for the first time. It was the biggest building Archie had ever been in. An entire Philadelphia city block could have fit in there, seven-story buildings and all. The round, arched ceiling glowed with the artificial lights of the ancients, but the cool breeze reminded him why this was truly one of the Seven Wonders of the New World: the dome's air-conditioning was keeping it a good thirty degrees cooler inside than out. The Astral Dome's round walls were ringed with three levels of yellow, orange, and red seats, and the tens of thousands of people who had been sitting in them scrambled like ants for the exits, trying to get away from the *cucuy* that prowled the dirt floor howling at them.

"*Damas y caballeros,*" an announcer somewhere said through speaking trumpets arranged throughout the stadium, "please move to the exits in a calm and orderly fashion!"

"Yeah, right," Archie muttered.

"We need a plan," Gonzalo said.

"I don't suppose that gun of yours has a freeze ray too, does it?"

"Nope."

"Then the plan is I punch the *cucuy,*" Archie said. "Hard."

"Yeah, well, you punching it and throwing it through the roof didn't slow it down, Jandal a Haad," Señor X said.

"*My name is Archie Dent,*" Archie told the raygun.

"Maybe we can all stop worrying about names until we take this thing down, *sí*?" Gonzalo said.

The *cucuy* slashed its razor claws through a metal gate, and a mechanical bull came charging out, followed by a steamhorse without a rider. The *cucuy* caught the rampaging bull and ripped it apart, spraying the arena floor with broken pieces of brasswork while the steamhorse scampered away.

"That was a thousand-pound mechanical bull it just ripped up," Señor X said.

Gonzalo didn't seem to be watching. His eyes were elsewhere. "That's it: I'll rope it."

"And then what?" Señor X said. "You can't hog-tie the *cucuy.*"

"No, but Archie can," Gonzalo said. "Or choke it until it passes out while you and me keep it away from the stands."

"You can lasso that thing?" Archie asked.

The *cucuy* tore into the stands, getting closer to the mass of people still trying to get away.

"Sounds like I better!" Gonzalo said. He put two fingers in his mouth and gave a piercing whistle, and the brass steamhorse galloped over to him. "*Hola*. May I ride you, *amigo*?" Gonzalo asked the horse. "I'm gonna try to rope that *cucuy*."

"Rope that thing?" the horse said. "You're crazy."

"The horse talks?" Archie said.

"Course it does," Gonzalo said. "Don't steamhorses talk where you're from?"

"No! And neither do rayguns!"

Gonzalo put a foot in the stirrup of the steamhorse's leather saddle and hitched himself up. "What's your name, *amigo*?"

"Alamo," said the horse.

"Well, that oughtta be easy to remember," Gonzalo said. "I'm Gonzalo, and this here's Señor X."

"Hey," said the raygun.

"How do," said the horse.

A talking raygun and a talking horse. Archie shook his head. It was the craziest blinking thing he had ever seen—and that was saying a lot.

Gonzalo grabbed the lasso hanging on the side of the steamhorse and unwound it. "Be ready," he told Archie.

"You're awfully cool for a guy about to try to lasso a Manglespawn," Archie told him.

"Why shouldn't I be?" Gonzalo said.

"Are you kidding?" Archie said. The *cucuy* was ripping out rows of seats and hurling them at the crowd. "Are you blind?"

"Yes," Gonzalo said, his eyes focused a few feet above Archie's head.

"Wait—*what?*" Archie said, but Gonzalo had already kicked the sides of Alamo and was galloping off toward the *cucuy*. Gonzalo had to be kidding, right? He couldn't really be blind. But the more Archie thought about it, the more it made sense—the way Gonzalo was always looking off in some other direction, the way he understood sounds better, the way he handled the darkness of the labyrinth so well. He hadn't blown a gasket when he'd seen the *cucuy* either, not like most people would. Because he *hadn't* seen it, not then, and not now. And whatever he did need to see, Señor X was there to tell him about.

Archie watched as Alamo swung Gonzalo in close behind the *cucuy*, and the blind ranger looped his lasso around the Manglespawn's head as easily as roping a fence post—all while looking off in the wrong direction.

"Hold up a minute, rodeo fans!" the announcer boomed. "Looks like we've got a new contestant, and he's roped himself a mean one!"

The people who hadn't squeezed out of the stadium turned to watch, their fear overcome by fascination. Gonzalo tightened the rope around the *cucuy*'s neck and backed Alamo away, pulling the Manglespawn away from the stands. It roared and sliced the rope connecting it to Gonzalo with its claws, but the ranger had its attention. Gonzalo drew his turquoise raygun and shot it in the face, which only made it angrier.

"Archie! You're up!" Gonzalo called.

Archie waited until the *cucuy*'s back was turned and jumped on it, landing just above the thing's skinned, callused bottom.

"*Uck*," Archie said, and he started to climb. But the *cucuy* knew he was there. The big shaggy beast jumped and twisted and kicked, trying to throw him off.

"Whoa! That is one bucking bronco!" the announcer cried. "And who's that snowcap riding him? He sure looks like that Archie Dent, hero of everybody's favorite dime novels!"

Archie heard the crowd roar like they had when he was in the dark passageways below. Why weren't they running? They were as crazy as Gonzalo, who was riding circles around the *cucuy* and peppering it with raygun blasts.

Archie kept climbing until he had the rope Gonzalo had looped around the *cucuy*'s neck.

"He's got the bucking strap, *muchachos y muchachas*! Now, does this white-haired snowball stand a chance in hell?"

Archie tightened the rope, and the *cucuy* roared. It shook and writhed, swiping at him with its razor-sharp claws.

"That *cucuy*'s trying to shuck him like an ear of corn, but our boy's sticking to him like a burr on your britches! Three seconds! Four seconds! Five seconds!"

Archie didn't have any idea why the announcer was counting the seconds, but he squeezed the rope tighter and hung on, his legs flailing in the air.

"Six seconds! Seven seconds! *Eight seconds!*" the announcer yelled, and the crowd went wild. "Ride 'em cowboy! Let her buck!"

Archie could feel the fight going out of the *cucuy*, and he gave the rope one last yank. *Snap!* The rope broke and Archie went flying. He heard the crowd gasp as one right before he hit the hard-packed dirt floor with a thump.

"Well, that just goes to show you, *mijos y mijas*," the announcer said, "there ain't a bull that can't be rode, or a rider that can't be throwed."

Archie lifted his head in time to see the *cucuy* fall to its knees, its ugly, twisted face blue. Its eyelids fluttered, and it fell flat on its face, shaking the whole building. *THOOM*.

Fireworks went off on the ceiling—indoor fireworks!—and Archie flinched. The audience in the stands clapped and cheered, and Gonzalo rode over to help Archie to his feet.

"Ladies and gentlemen, your All-Around Cowboy Champions, Archie Dent and the Raygun Kid!"

"Well if that don't beat all," the steamhorse said.

"Why'd he call you a snowcap?" Gonzalo asked. "Is your hair really white?"

"Yeah," Archie said. "Are you really blind?"

"Blind as a bootstrap," Gonzalo said. "Have been since the day I was born."

Archie suddenly remembered the story of a long-ago League of Seven he'd watched with John Otter during a Cherokee circle dance. One of the dancers had worn a blindfold and carried a talking stick: the League's Lawbringer. Archie felt the lektric tingle of discovery. Gonzalo was the sixth Leaguer!

Archie's excitement wilted like a flower in the hot Texian sun. He didn't care who the sixth Leaguer was. Or the seventh. He wasn't going to be part of any League of Seven. Not anymore. The *cucuy* was finished and the kids were saved. He was done.

Cowboys with ropes had come out onto the arena floor and were circling the *cucuy* to tie it down when it groaned, then growled, then started to push itself up.

"You gotta be slagging kidding me!" Archie cried.

The *cucuy* was on its hands and knees when—
KaZAAAAAAAAAK!—neon blue lektricity coursed through
its matted hair. It lurched and thrashed, howling in pain,
and hit the ground again with a thud, out for good this
time.

Archie knew only one person who could throw lektricity
around like that—

"Ladies and gentlemen," the announcer said, "please welcome that Lektric Cowboy, that hero of *The League of Seven
versus the Giant Snake of New Orleans*, that Genius in a Plaid
Skirt, Fergus MacFerguson!"

"*Kilt*," Fergus said.

Archie ran to where the tall, gangly redhead stood behind
the *cucuy*, all thoughts of not ever wanting to see him or
Hachi again gone as soon as he saw his old friend. Archie had
never felt so happy to see anyone in his entire life. He skidded
to a halt in front of Fergus, suddenly feeling childish for running over. What was he going to do, hug him?

"Does everybody read those dime novels?" Fergus asked.

"How'd you find me?" Archie asked.

"Are you kidding? I just listened for the 'boom' and went
the opposite direction everybody was running." Fergus grinned
and pulled Archie into a playful headlock, tousling his hair.
"Crivens, white! I think you've gotten even shorter since you
went away!"

Archie pushed him away stronger than he meant to, and
Fergus staggered and almost fell.

"Sorry! Sorry!" Archie said.

"It's all right," Fergus said, righting himself and balancing with more grace than Archie had ever seen him have. At least since a meka-ninja had sliced the tendon in his right heel, hobbling him. "I've got some new tricks up my kilt," Fergus said.

Fergus hiked up his blue plaid kilt and showed off his new knee brace. Gone was the clunky (but still amazing) leather-and-steel harness he'd cobbled together at Kano Henhawk's house. In its place was an even more amazing lightweight brass-and-fabric harness lined with ultrathin gears and servos. They clicked and whirred softly as Fergus held up his hands like a magician and raised his leg without touching it. He'd built himself a brand-new, completely automated knee!

"When did you make that?" Archie asked.

"Let's just say I've had a fair bit of time on my hands while Hachi's been gone."

Archie felt the temperature in the air-conditioned Astral Dome drop twenty degrees. What would Hachi say when he told her he was the reason her father was murdered?

"She's not with you?" Archie asked.

"Nae. New Orleans was *crazy*—do I have a story to tell you!—but in the end she found what she was looking for: the names of every one of the people who did that business to her da and her village when she was little. She left me behind when she went after them, and I haven't heard from her since."

Archie sighed with relief. At least he wouldn't have to drop that bomb today. Maybe he wouldn't *ever* have to. Maybe once Hachi took her revenge on the last of the people who'd killed all the men in her village, she wouldn't care anymore why they'd done it.

Right, Archie thought. *And maybe I'm going to move to Texas and become a mechanical bull wrestler.*

"Listen, Archie," Fergus said, suddenly serious, "that isn't all we found out in New Orleans—"

Gonzalo rode up on Alamo and hopped lightly to the ground.

"Ah, Gonzalo, let me introduce you to Fergus MacFerguson. Fergus, let me introduce you to Gonzalo, his talking horse Alamo, and his talking raygun Señor X."

Fergus put his hands up. "Aye, I think I just met the raygun."

Archie turned to find Gonzalo pointing Señor X right at them.

"Gonzalo, what's going on?" Archie asked.

"Now that one monster's down for the count, it's time to take care of the other one," Gonzalo said. The hum from the serpentine raygun in his hand rose in pitch as it charged with aether. "Archie Dent, aka Jandal a Haad, you're under arrest for murder."

6

Fergus dropped his hands. "Whoa, whoa whoa. You're arresting Archie for murder? You can't be serious."

"Dead serious," Gonzalo said.

"Nae nae nae," Fergus said. "First off, Archie's a hero. He just helped you take down this hairy, ugly beastie, for cog's sake! Second of all, Archie's never killed anybody—not anybody that wasn't already a monster, or trying to kill him first."

Archie grimaced. He loved Fergus for defending him, but if his friend knew the truth, knew what had really happened at Chuluota when Archie was born, he wouldn't be standing up for him right now.

"Fergus—" Archie started, but Fergus cut him off.

"Nae. You're not a criminal, Archie. And I'm not letting this wee cowboy arrest you, whether he's a real Texas Ranger or not."

"I'm real enough," Gonzalo said. "And so is this raygun."

"And how do you plan on capturing him, anyway?" asked Fergus. "Archie's walked away from a ten-thousand-foot fall before. You think that raygun is going to do anything but tickle him?"

"Archie Dent, Señor X says you're a monster," Gonzalo said without looking at him. "That true?"

"Yes," said Archie.

"Archie!" Fergus said.

"I'll ask you again—you ever kill anybody?" Gonzalo said.

Archie had told Gonzalo no before, but the ranger knew he'd been lying. Even if you didn't count all the people he'd killed who'd become Manglespawn and all the bad guys who'd attacked him first, there were the hundred men of Chuluota that had died to create him. It wasn't just Archie's hands that were covered in blood—it was his whole body. He'd literally been soaked in the blood of the men who'd been murdered to make him.

"Yes," Archie said. "I'm responsible for the deaths of one hundred men at Chuluota, and lots more people who were killed there besides."

"Have you slipped a cog?" Fergus said. "That's ridiculous!"

"No, Fergus. You don't understand. *I'm* what Blavatsky and Edison and the others were making in Florida. I'm the reason Hachi's dad was killed."

"I know!" Fergus said. "I know all about that!"

Archie frowned. "You do?"

"Aye, and so does Hachi. Blavatsky told us everything after

she died." Fergus paused, realizing how strange that sounded. "I'll explain later. Anyway, it's not your fault that all those people were killed. How could it be? You weren't even born yet!"

Archie shook his head. It wasn't a dark corner of a hotel room where he belonged, he realized that now. He belonged in jail. Someone had to pay for what had happened to all those people, and it was going to be him. He put his hands out.

"I'll come quietly," he told Gonzalo.

Gonzalo pulled a pair of handcuffs out from under his shirt and latched them onto Archie's wrists.

Fergus threw up his hands. "This is clinker, Archie. Total clinker."

"It's the right thing to do," Archie said. "I don't deserve to have a life. Not when all those people lost theirs to create me."

THOOM! Something exploded outside the Astral Dome, big enough and near enough to make them all stagger. It was followed by more booms, and the sound of screaming.

"Crivens!" Fergus cried. "What now?"

THOOM. THOOM. THOOM. THOOM. Something was coming closer to the Astral Dome.

Gonzalo's raygun hummed, and Fergus's arms crackled with lektricity. Archie backed away, his wrists still hand-cuffed.

CRUNCH! Something metallic and snake-like punched through the ceiling of the Astral Dome, ripping off part of the roof. The thing curled inside like an octopus's tentacle and pulled, tearing out a huge chunk of ceiling.

Framed in the hole against the bright blue sky was a mas-sive machine with a bulbous, seaweed-draped steel passenger compartment atop eight writhing mechanical tentacles. Stenciled on the side of the thing was a black flag with a white skull over two crossed swords.

"Pirates!" one of the cowboys on the arena floor cried. "Pirates from Galveston!"

One of the thing's tentacles snaked inside, snatched up a steamhorse, and lifted it into its hold. The cowboys on the arena floor drew their rayguns and fired, but the octopod's hull was too thick.

Gonzalo tied a rope to Archie's handcuffs and swung up onto his horse. "Time to ride."

Fergus grabbed Archie's arm. "Oy, hold on there, cowboy. There's a blinking ten-story-tall mechanical octopus attacking Houston. We need Archie!"

"He's under arrest," Gonzalo said. He backed Alamo away, tugging on the rope.

Fergus pulled Archie the other direction. "I thought you were a ranger! You ought to be out there rangering!"

"First I secure my prisoner," Gonzalo said, giving the rope another tug, "then I come back and fight the pirates."

Fergus yanked Archie back, the servos in his new knee brace matching Alamo's strength.

"Guys, stop!" Archie said. He shoved Fergus away and snapped Gonzalo's rope, sending them both staggering away. "*I'm* the one who decides whether I stay or go, and I say—"

KA-*THOOM!* An enormous chunk of ceiling fell on Archie, and everything went black.

7

"Archie! Hey, Archie! Wake up."

It was Fergus. Archie felt him shaking him awake. Archie put a hand to his head where the rockfall had hit him, but of course there wasn't a lump there. There wasn't even a scratch. The unexpected blow had knocked him out for a few minutes, but hadn't done any real damage to him.

As Archie came to his senses, he realized he wasn't in the Astral Dome anymore. He was in a considerably smaller, darker dome made of thick red-painted steel. For some reason the sunlight that came in through the round windows was wavy and dappled, and then Archie saw a shark swim by.

We're underwater, Archie realized.

Fergus and Gonzalo helped Archie to his feet. They stood

among a small group of men and women at the side of the round room, guarded by seven-foot-tall men with long black hair in ponytails, who wore nothing but loincloths and seashell necklaces. The guards' gray skin was covered everywhere in swirling black tribal tattoos that rivaled the thick black lines of Fergus's tattoo-like circuitry, and their noses were pierced with bones. In their frog-like webbed hands they held long-handled tridents, and fishnet hung from their belts.

In the center of the room stood an empty throne cut from coral, and at its feet lay an enormous mound of gold and silver and Texian pesos. Beyond the mountain of treasure were more of the same tall gray people in various states of undress, and all covered with the same strange swirling black tattoos. Some wore swords, others knives, and others leaned on harpoons. They stood around a long wooden table, eating, drinking, and laughing as they toasted each other with tankards of ale.

"Welcome to the Underwater City of Galveston," Fergus said. "We've been captured by pirates."

"You couldn't stop them?" Archie asked.

Fergus held up his soggy sleeves. "They shorted me out with water cannons, and they took away the cowboy's raygun. And his wonderhorse."

Gonzalo stood still, his eyes unfocused on anything in particular. "Karankawans. A fierce Texas coast tribe," he said quietly. "And there's twice as many of them as there are prisoners."

"Yeah," Fergus said. "*And* they're all armed, and we're not. We can all see that."

"He can't," Archie said. "Gonzalo is blind."

"He's *what*?" Fergus said. "No way."

Archie nodded, and Fergus waved a hand in front of Gonzalo. The ranger didn't blink.

"What kind of parents let their blind kid become a Texas Ranger?"

"All my brothers and sisters are rangers," Gonzalo said. "Why shouldn't I be one too just because I'm blind?"

"Right, of course," Fergus said, throwing up his arms. "Look, it doesn't matter. We've got bigger problems. Archie, look at the lights."

The lights? Archie looked up at the ceiling, where bluish-yellow glass domes glowed, filling the room with light. Those couldn't be gas lights. Archie had only seen lights like that before in one place: Atlantis Station.

"Are those—?"

"*Lektric lights,*" Fergus said. "Sensed it the minute I got inside. And it's not just lights, Archie. Lektric heat, lektric motors, lektric *ships*. The whole city is wired with the stuff!"

"But . . . but how? Why didn't the Septemberist Society find out and stop it?"

"I dunno," Fergus said. "Maybe because *it's underwater and run by pirates*? It's not like we got here by invitation, you know. It doesn't matter. Lektricity like this, it could wake any Mangleborn that happens to be sleeping nearby. We've got to shut it down. You start cracking skulls, and me and the blind ranger here'll go for the generators."

Archie shook his head and held up his handcuffed wrists. "I can't. I'm Gonzalo's prisoner."

"This again?" Fergus said. "Slag it, Archie! If you haven't noticed by now, we're *all* prisoners of some pirate king!"

A deep conch shell blew, and the pirates and prisoners got

quiet. A tall tattooed Karankawan man strode into the room, surrounded by more half-naked guards. The man they protected was dripping wet like he'd just come from a swim, and had on nothing but long canvas shorts, a jewel-encrusted gold crown, and a rope fishnet with sparkling glass floats, which he wore over his shoulders like a royal cape. One of his guards handed him an ornate silver trident, and he sat on the coral throne.

"His High Exaltedness, the Great Leo de la Mer, Pirate King and Lafitte of the Underwater City of Galveston, welcomes you to the Maison Rouge," a Tik Tok servant announced, and Archie was startled to realize he knew the voice.

"Mr. Rivets!" Archie said. It was! Mr. Rivets, covered in sea slime, stood beside and behind the throne, acting as the pirate king's court steward.

"Be quiet, you," a guard warned Archie.

What Mr. Rivets was doing here, Archie didn't know, but he was glad to see him again. Even if it *was* Mr. Rivets's fault he was in this mess to begin with.

"Before His Royal Highness deals with his prisoners, are there any who would speak or petition the Lafitte?" Mr. Rivets asked.

"What's a Lafitte?" Archie whispered.

"Jean Lafitte was the first pirate king of Galveston," Gonzalo told them. "You want to be the boss around here, you call yourself the Lafitte."

A teenaged Karankawan girl stepped forward, and the gallery of drunken pirates hooted and moaned. She was tall and thin like the rest of her tribe, but she wore a more modest sleeveless sea-green top and a matching short pleated skirt. Her long black hair had seashells woven into it, and her gray skin was covered with the same swirling tattoos as the rest of the pirates. But unlike the others, she wore a crystal clear, diamond-shaped gem right in the middle of her forehead, and she carried a harpoon whose metal hook glowed with a green aetherical flame. Archie and Fergus recognized that green aetherical flame, and they shared a knowing look. It was the same green flame Edison had bathed Fergus in when he'd turned him into a human computer back in Florida.

"And now there's *that*," Fergus whispered.

The Karankawan pirates were less impressed by her than Archie and Fergus, and they roared like the sea when the pirate king rolled his eyes and slumped back on his coral throne.

"And what has the brilliant and beautiful Martine come to tell us today, I wonder?" the Lafitte said. "No, don't tell me. Let me guess!"

Martine tilted her head and waited.

"Wednesdays are blue, which means clear sailing," the Lafitte guessed.

"No," Martine said. "Wednesdays are red." She tilted her head the other way. "And what color the day is has nothing to do with weather patterns."

The Lafitte slapped his tattooed forehead dramatically, clowning for the gallery. "Right! Of course! How silly of me. Let me guess again. Let me guess again. Using a mathematical formula no one else understands, you have discovered a way to make fish swim backward!"

The girl blinked and lifted her chin, reminding Archie of a blue jay he'd watched in his backyard. "There is no mathematical formula that would allow a fish to swim backward," she said.

The pirates guffawed, and the Lafitte closed his eyes and nodded, as though he couldn't believe he'd been so stupid. He was making merciless fun of her, but she either didn't understand, or didn't care. Archie didn't know for sure, but it seemed like she didn't understand.

"Do you wish to continue guessing, or may I tell you?" Martine said.

"Oh, please," the Lafitte said expansively. "Please do tell me, Martine. I can't wait to hear it."

"The Deep Ones are rising," the girl said.

The Lafitte's eyes went wide, and he looked to the pirate gallery, who burst out laughing again. "Oho! *The Deep Ones are rising.*"

Archie and Fergus looked at each other worriedly. What the girl called "Deep Ones" sounded suspiciously like Mangleborn.

"Based on my pattern of behavior," Martine said over their laughter, "that should have been your first guess."

"Your 'pattern of behavior?'" the Lafitte said, drying his eyes. "Do you mean, Martine, the fact that you have come here to my court *every day for the past month* and said *the exact same thing?*"

"Yes," Martine said. She tilted her head. "That is the pattern of behavior to which I refer."

"And what has been *my* pattern of behavior each time?"

"To laugh," Martine said. "And to do nothing."

"And to tell you that the Deep Ones are myths. Legends. Monster stories Karankawan mothers tell their children to make them go to bed at night." He wiggled his fingers like tentacles. "'Go to sleep, or the Deep Ones will rise and gobble you up!'"

The pirates laughed again.

"The Deep Ones are real," Martine said. "They sleep in the trenches at the bottom of the ocean, where not even the giant squid can go. I've seen them."

That quieted the room. The pirates fidgeted and looked away, sticking their noses in their tankards. They might believe the Deep Ones were just stories their parents told them to make them behave, but secretly they were all a little scared they might be true.

Lafitte smiled. "No submarine can go that deep. The pressures are too great."

"Mine can," Martine said.

The pirates clearly believed that if anyone could design a sub to go that deep in the ocean, it was this girl. The room was silent for a moment before the Lafitte cleared his throat.

"Martine, my dear, you are a genius," the Lafitte said. "No one here will deny it, least of all me. And I will let you come in here every day for the rest of my life and tell me the Deep Ones are rising if you keep designing wonderful machines like those octopods for us."

She designed those lektric octopus machines? Archie's eyes went wide, and Fergus looked impressed. Gonzalo frowned.

"Which you would never before have used to attack Houston so brazenly, were it not for the influence of the Deep Ones," Martine said.

The Lafitte spread his arms wide over the treasure at his feet. "And just look what our brazen attack has won us! Gold! Silver! Money! Tik Toks! Prisoners to ransom!"

"A temporary boon," Martine said. She tilted her head again. "There is a 95.6 percent chance this attack will cause the Texas

Navy to come for you, and an 82.1 percent chance they will destroy Galveston and everyone in it."

"Let them come!" the Lafitte bellowed. "We will destroy *them*!"

"This belligerence you feel is a direct result of the Deep Ones stirring," Martine said. *She talks an awful lot like Mr. Rivets*, Archie thought. "Can't you feel them nudging your brain? Making you wilder? Angrier?" Martine asked. She lifted her head like Edison used to, as though listening to some far-off sound on the wind. "Can't you hear the arithmetic in their song?"

"She's right," Fergus said loudly. "There's more of them rising other places. And all this lektricity isn't helping anything!"

A guard whacked Fergus in the back of the head with the butt of his trident, knocking him to the floor. "Quiet, you! No one wants to hear what you think."

Fergus stood back up holding the back of his head. "You can fight back any time now, Archie," Fergus whispered.

Archie sighed and looked away. He didn't deserve to be a hero. Not after all those men had died for him. He couldn't enjoy the strength their warm, living blood gave him while they lay cold and dead in the ground.

"Enough, Martine," the Lafitte said, less genial than he had been with her a moment before. "You have delivered your daily prediction of doom and gloom. Return to your ship."

Martine bowed and left the room, and the surly Lafitte called for the prisoners to be brought forward.

"Great," Fergus muttered. "She gets his pistons all twisted, and now we get to deal with him."

Mr. Rivets spoke again. "His High Exaltedness, the Great Leo de la Mer, now invites any of his prisoners willing to join his pirate crew to swear an oath of loyalty to him."

"Just in time to fight the Texas Navy, it sounds like," Fergus whispered.

The Lafitte found a few takers who enthusiastically swore, on pain of death, to fight for the pirate king and the Underwater City of Galveston. But Archie, Fergus, and Gonzalo weren't among them.

"Are there no others who would swear loyalty to His Royal Highness, and thus go free?" Mr. Rivets asked, looking straight at Archie.

Archie, Fergus, and Gonzalo still said nothing.

"No one else then?" Mr. Rivets asked. "Anyone? Are you sure?"

"They're sure," the Lafitte growled. He waved his hand. "Take them to the bathyspheres."

"Uh . . . ," Fergus said as they were led away.

"What?" Archie asked. "What's a bathysphere?"

"It's a . . . a small powerless sphere on a cable explorers use to visit the deepest parts of the ocean," Fergus explained. "Only, I don't think we're going to be doing a lot of exploring." He looked back over his shoulder as they were led away. "Maybe we should have lied and said we were with the pirate king after all."

Mr. Rivets shook his head at them. "I'll just wait here for you then, shall I?"

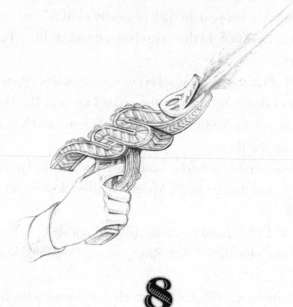

8

The bathyspheres the Lafitte kept his prisoners in were exactly as Fergus described them: small round metal chambers with a single window of fused quartz, which doubled as its door. They were steel gray, and covered all over with enormous bolts. The guards went around the room and threw switches set on the wall, and lektric winches lifted five dripping, seaweed-covered bathyspheres on chains out of open holes in the floor. A sixth chain spun up into its winch double-fast, its loose end *whack-whack-whacking* the ceiling before one of the guards shut it off.

"Oops. Chain must have broke," said one of the guards.

"There's one we're not getting back!" another guard said.

He peered down into the water. "Hope there wasn't anybody in that one."

The guards laughed as they loosened the bolts on one of the five bathyspheres that had survived being pulled up.

Fergus tried to get a spark from all the lektricity around, but he was still too wet. *"Archie,"* Fergus whispered.

Archie knew what Fergus wanted him to do. He wanted him to punch the guards, smash the bathyspheres, and get them out of here. It was true, Gonzalo and Fergus didn't deserve this, but he did. A bathysphere at the bottom of the ocean was even better than a prison cell.

When the bathysphere was open, Archie climbed inside without the guards even telling him to.

Fergus took a little more convincing, but the guards eventually wrangled him and Gonzalo in beside Archie. The guards screwed the enormous bolts back on the hatch with a lektric drill, and the three boys spread out on the curved bench that ran around the inside of the sphere to balance it.

Stale air hissed from a hole at the top of the bathysphere, and then their round prison dropped suddenly into the water, where it bobbed for a moment before sinking like a stone. Air bubbles burbled up past the foggy quartz window, and then all they could see were the twinkling lektric lights of Galveston's underwater domes against the dark black background of the sea.

Fergus immediately stood and examined the inside of the sphere, looking for some way out. But Archie knew there wasn't any. Not for Fergus and Gonzalo. Even if they figured out a way to open the bathysphere, they were still deep underwater—and dropping. If the water pressure didn't kill them, they'd surely drown.

Fergus threw his hands up as though he'd come to the same conclusion. "Brass, Archie," Fergus said. "This is just brass. You feel sorry for yourself and won't fight, so now we're all trapped in a wee metal ball at the bottom of the ocean. We could die in here before they remember to bring us up. *If* the chain doesn't break."

Archie hung his head and stared at his feet. He understood why Fergus was angry. But he couldn't be that person anymore. He couldn't be a hero.

Gonzalo didn't seem bothered by their situation in the least. He leaned back and whistled a little tune.

"You're awfully cool there, cowboy," Fergus said.

"I ain't worried," Gonzalo said. "Señor X will save me."

Fergus frowned. "Who's Señor X?"

"My raygun," Gonzalo told him.

Fergus looked back and forth between Gonzalo and Archie. "Your raygun is going to save you? What's it got, arms and legs?"

"No," Gonzalo said. "But Señor X will come for me, all the same."

Fergus shook his head and sat. "You're as crazy as this one is," he told Gonzalo.

"I want to hear about the hundred people you killed," Gonzalo said, his eyes looking in Archie's direction, but not right at him.

"He didn't kill those people!" Fergus said.

Gonzalo put up a hand. "I want to hear him tell it."

Archie sighed. He really didn't want to get into it all again.

He wanted to just disappear into the depths of the ocean and never come up again. "It's a long story," he said.

"You got somewhere else to go?" Gonzalo asked.

So Archie told him. About how he'd been carved out of stone and bathed in the blood of a hundred men and brought to life by the lektric sorcery of Edison and Blavatsky and the green fire of the Mangleborn buried at Chuluota. And then he explained about the Mangleborn, and the Septemberist Society, and the League of Seven, and how he couldn't be a part of it anymore after learning where he'd come from and how he'd been made.

Gonzalo stayed quiet the whole time. He sat and thought for a while after Archie was finished, and finally leaned over and unlocked Archie's handcuffs.

"What are you doing?" Archie asked.

"I'm letting you go," Gonzalo said.

"*Thank you*," Fergus said. "At least I'm not the only sane person here."

"But—but all those men. All the villagers who died that night—" Archie said.

"Died because somebody else killed them," Gonzalo said. "They're the guilty ones, not you."

"But I'm the reason they were killed!" Archie said.

"Just 'cause you put your boots in the oven don't make 'em biscuits."

"I don't . . . understand what that means," Archie said.

"It means that just 'cause you feel guilty over all them people dying don't mean it's your fault."

"See?" Fergus said. "Even a blind man can see you're not responsible for what happened."

"And you believe it?" Archie asked. "All of it? About the Mangleborn and everything?"

Gonzalo sat quiet for a moment. "Señor X told me some of it. He knows all about these Mangleborn you're talking about. Dealt with them in the long-ago past, best I can tell. And I know you're telling the truth."

"How?"

Gonzalo shrugged. "Just can. Got a nose for it. And if it's the truth, I gotta believe it all, tough as that might be."

"All right," Fergus said. "Now that Archie's free and you know what all this is about, maybe we can think about getting out of here."

Gonzalo leaned back again and closed his eyes. "Señor X'll get us out of here."

Fergus stood again. "Well, you'll forgive me if I don't hold my breath waiting for a *raygun* to come save me."

The bathysphere rocked, and Fergus had to put a hand out to keep from falling over.

"What was that?" Archie asked.

The bathysphere rocked again, the metal bolts groaning. Fergus kept his arms out wide and looked around without moving his head. "That's bad, is what that is."

"Did we hit bottom?" Gonzalo asked.

"No," Fergus said. "We may be at the end of the chain, but we're still swinging."

Thunk! Something struck a glancing blow to the bathysphere, and Archie saw a massive row of pale white suckers slide by the foggy quartz window.

"Did you see that?" Fergus squeaked. "Did you just slagging see that?"

"No!" Gonzalo said.

"A tentacle. A *big* tentacle," Archie said.

"With suckers as big as your head," Fergus said.

Archie looked up at Fergus. "That girl said the Deep Ones were stirring."

"Yeah. And there's a tasty lektric treat waiting for them in Galveston. We gotta get out of here," Fergus said, wild-eyed. "Archie, you can bust your way out, right?"

"Yes," Archie said. "But then what? I sink to the bottom, and you and Gonzalo drown."

"I *hate* the ocean," Fergus said.

Something growled in the water outside. There was no other way to describe it. They all froze, waiting for it to pass.

THOOM! Something batted the heavy steel bathysphere like it was a rubber ball, and it went spinning. Archie and Fergus and Gonzalo fell all over each other as the sphere tumbled and swung, the chain tethering them to Galveston groaning in complaint.

The bathysphere jolted again, coming to an abrupt stop. Suckers fixed themselves to the thick quartz window as a tentacle wrapped itself around the bathysphere.

Crick! Crack! Ping! Cracks opened in the steel walls of the sphere, spraying them with seawater.

"It's going to crush us like a walnut!" Fergus cried.

Archie spread his arms out wide to push the walls back, but he was too small, slag it. He couldn't reach both sides at the same time.

The Deep One was going to burst their bathysphere, and Fergus and Gonzalo were going to die.

The bathysphere suddenly lurched upward.

"Hey!" Fergus said. "Hey, that wasn't the Mangleborn! That was the chain!"

"Señor X!" Gonzalo said.

Archie still wasn't so sure about that, but *someone* was trying to pull them up. The Deep One held on tight though. The chain connecting them to the winch in Galveston screeched and groaned.

"We have to get it to let go," Archie said. "Fergus, you got any juice back?"

"Oh!" Fergus said. He rubbed his fingers and got a spark. "Yeah! Archie, pick him up!"

"What? Whoa!" Gonzalo cried as Archie lifted him off the bench with one hand, like picking up a doll.

Fergus put a hand to the metal wall and sent a jolt of lightning through it. *Kazaaaaaaack!* The Deep One roared and let go of the bathysphere, and they shot up through the water.

"Take that, you overgrown guppy!" Fergus yelled.

Sploosh! The bathysphere burst from the water back into the light of the brig, tossing them all to the floor. As they stood, they heard someone taking the bolts off the hatch. They all smiled and breathed a sigh of relief until the hatch fell away and they saw Gonzalo's raygun pointed at them by one of the Lafitte's tall, gray, tattooed guards.

"Hold it right there," the guard said. "Nobody gets out until you tell me where the treasure is."

"Treasure?" Fergus asked.

"This gun," the guard said, glancing at the serpent-shaped turquoise raygun in his hand, "this gun talks! It—it told me one of the prisoners knew where there was sunken treasure. That you?"

"That's me," Gonzalo said. "But I'm afraid there isn't any treasure."

Gonzalo started to climb out of the bathysphere.

"Stop, I said! Stop!" the guard said, backing away. "I'll shoot!"

Gonzalo hopped out of the bathysphere, and the guard pulled the trigger.

Click!

The raygun didn't fire. The guard blinked. He pulled the trigger again. *Click! Click! Click!* Nothing.

Gonzalo pointed to the mouth of the raygun. "There's your problem right there."

The guard turned the gun around to look at the barrel. *KaPOW!* The raygun shot him in the face. He flew across the room, slammed into the wall, and slumped to the floor.

"Ouch," Fergus said.

Gonzalo picked up his raygun as Archie and Fergus climbed out of the bathysphere.

"He made one big mistake," Gonzalo said. "He trusted Señor X."

"You're lucky he did," Señor X said. "Yours was the only bathysphere we could get to come up."

All the other winches had broken chains dangling from them. The Deep Ones had taken the rest.

Archie knelt by the guard. "Is he dead?"

"Señor X?" Gonzalo asked.

"Just stunned," the raygun said sadly. "One day you're going to have to let me kill someone."

"That day may come," Gonzalo said, "but not today." He spun the raygun on his finger and slid it into its holster with practiced ease.

"Where exactly did Señor X come from?" Fergus asked.

"And when did he fight Mangleborn before?" Archie asked.

"Thirty days hath September," Señor X said from his holster.

"Seven heroes we remember," Archie said automatically. "You're—*you're a Septemberist?*"

"Kid, I was a Septemberist before there *were* Septemberists."

"What's that supposed to mean?" Archie asked.

The floor beneath their feet shifted, and they staggered across the room.

"Later!" Gonzalo said. "The Deep Ones are done with the bathyspheres and they're coming for Galveston!"

9

An enormous pinkish-white tentacle slithered past one of the brig's small glass windows, and the room shuddered.

"We have to get out of here!" Archie cried.

"Where?" Fergus asked. "We're still underwater!"

"The girl," Archie said. "The one who told the pirate king about the Deep Ones. She has a ship! The king said so. She'll help us!"

"If she's even still here," Fergus said.

"Scanning," Señor X said. Gonzalo pulled him back out of his holster. "Got her," the raygun said. "She's still here. Eight domes over and down. She's on her ship. Leave this room and go right."

Archie held Gonzalo back. "Hold on! We have to get Mr. Rivets first! Señor X, do you know where he is?"

"I can't detect inanimate objects, kid. Not without some kind of tracker on them. You're going to have to leave him."

The city lurched again. Out the window, they saw one of Galveston's lektrified domes implode under a lobster-like claw the size of the Emartha Machine Man Building in New Rome. A massive air bubble burst from the busted dome like a mushroom cloud, casting off bodies and debris as it raced to the surface.

"No!" Archie said. "He'll end up on the bottom of the ocean! We can't leave him!"

"He's just a machine, kid."

"Says the talking raygun," said Fergus.

"Where's the main hall?" Archie asked. "That's where we last saw him!"

"We really ought to be getting to that submarine, G-man," Señor X said.

Archie looked imploringly at Gonzalo, then remembered the ranger couldn't see him. But apparently he didn't need to see Archie's desperation to understand it. "Main hall first, Señor," Gonzalo said. "Plot me a route."

The raygun sighed. "Okay. Go five steps forward and turn right."

"What's that expression about the blind leading the blind?" Fergus said. He and Archie followed Gonzalo into Galveston's maze of domes and the round metal passageways that connected them. There were guards and pirates all through the city, but none of them cared about Archie, Fergus, and Gonzalo anymore. They'd seen the things that were rising from the deep, and were driven insane by them. Some of them fought each other to get on board submarines. Others looted store-rooms for supplies. Some of them sat along the round domed walls and cried. One room was on fire, and Señor X had to re-route them. Another room was flooded and sealed off, and Señor X rerouted them again.

"You know, if every steamhorse had something like that raygun on the dash, nobody would ever have to get stuck in traffic again," Fergus said.

"If every steamhorse had one of me, we wouldn't need driv-ers anymore," Señor X said.

Archie ached to go faster, but Gonzalo walked through Galveston like he was out for a stroll in the park. It had to be because he couldn't see, and again Archie thought about what an incredible handicap that must be. Archie had never thought about how much information he got from his eyes. He didn't know how Gonzalo did it, even with Señor X's help.

"I thought you said not to trust Señor X," Archie said.

"I don't," Gonzalo said.

"This is why I hang out with this kid," Señor X said. "He's smart."

"Where'd you get that thing, anyway?" Fergus asked again.

"Found him," Gonzalo said simply.

Trustworthy or not, Señor X got them to the main hall. A handful of pirates were there fighting over the treasure they'd taken from Houston, and the Lafitte still sat on his throne, rant-ing to no one in particular about how the Deep Ones were still just a myth.

All that mattered to Archie was that Mr. Rivets was still

there. He ran across the room and hugged the machine man, then pushed him away.

"Mr. Rivets, you lied to me! You told me you were taking me to the post office, and you got me kidnapped instead!"

"Yes, sir. I felt it necessary to get you involved somehow," Mr. Rivets said. The machine man stood taller. "It was my first ever lie. How did I do?"

"Mr. Rivets can lie?" Fergus asked. "Since when?"

"Long story," Archie said.

Something went *boom* near the main hall, and water rushed in from one of the doorways.

"One we don't have time for," Señor X said. "We gotta go."

"Yeah, no offense, Gonzalo," Archie said, "but we're going to have to move faster than a brisk walk."

"Got it covered," Gonzalo said. He put his fingers in his mouth and belted out an ear-splitting whistle, and a steam-horse came galloping through one of the passageways.

"Wondered where you'd got to, boss!" the steamhorse said. Gonzalo swung up onto his back.

"Hey, I don't want to freak anybody out," the steamhorse said, "but I think the city might be sinking."

"A talking steamhorse," Fergus said, clearly impressed. Gonzalo helped Fergus climb up. "His name's Alamo."

"Well, that ought to be easy to remember," said Fergus. Gonzalo held out a hand. "Archie?"

"Mr. Rivets is too slow to keep up, and too heavy to ride," Archie said. "I'll carry him." Archie picked up the thousand-pound machine man and threw him over his shoulder.

They made a strange parade, the two boys on a talking steamhorse, guided by a talking raygun, followed by a small boy carrying a Tik Tok over his shoulder. But hardly anyone noticed. There wasn't anyone *left* to notice. Everywhere they went, the city had been looted and abandoned or destroyed. Lektric wires that lined the corridors crackled and popped.

"That tall lass was right about the Deep Ones," Fergus said. "And about the city being destroyed."

"It's good to see you at long last, Master Fergus," Mr. Rivets said from Archie's shoulder.

"You too, Mr. Rivets."

"And how is Miss Hachi?"

Fergus gave Archie a look over his shoulder. "She's been better. Not that I've seen her in a while."

"I hope that we are soon reunited," Mr. Rivets said.

"Yeah, Mr. Rivets," Fergus said. "Me too."

Archie missed Hachi too, but he didn't share their desire to see her again anytime soon. Just the thought of her sent him back to that corner in his hotel room.

"There it is!" Señor X announced. "She hasn't left yet!"

"That's a submarine?" Archie asked.

They'd run into a large glass dome with row after row of what looked like swimming lanes, but which Archie realized at last were submarine berths. The submarines entered from below, rising up into the dome to sit atop the water and unload along the long metal docks. All the lanes were empty save the last, which held something that looked more like a giant squid than a submarine. It was made of metal and riveted all over, but it was painted red like a squid. The main body of it was long and cone-shaped, with a pointed fin at the front like an arrowhead. Toward the rear of the cone was a huge glass window that looked like the thing's giant eye. But what really made the submarine look like a squid were the massive mechanical tentacles that swarmed out the back of it, picking crates up off the dock and loading them into a hole where the squid's mouth would have been.

"Crivens," said Fergus. "It's beautiful."

Archie couldn't agree. But beautiful or ugly, it was their only ticket off the sinking city of Galveston. He didn't see a door anywhere, so he set Mr. Rivets down and ran to the window, jumping and waving his arms. "Hey! Hey in there! Let us in! Please! Help!"

The others started making noise with him. Archie was about to start pounding on the hull when the tall, gray, tattooed girl appeared in the window. She moved as slowly and deliberately as Gonzalo did, but could clearly see them. She tilted her head and stood staring at them.

"Hey!" Archie yelled, not sure how much she could hear through the window. "Help! We need a ride! We know all about the Deep Ones! We've been fighting them on land too! Please, let us in!"

The girl tilted her head the other direction and kept studying them, and Archie was reminded again of a bird. The ship's tentacles finished loading the last of the crates, and the girl left the window. In a moment, the ship began to hum.

"She's not going to let us in," Fergus said.

"G-man, point me at the hull. I'll blast our way in," Señor X said.

"Forget that," Archie said. "I'll just punch my way in."

"And what good's a submarine gonna be with a hole in it?" Gonzalo asked them.

Crick-crack! The pinkish-white tentacles of a Deep One had found the glass dome overhead, and were squeezing it. Water sprayed from a dozen cracks, and the metal struts that supported the dome groaned.

"It'll be better than a glass dome with a thousand holes in it!" Archie said. He swung a fist at the hull, but it moved away from him. No, wait—*he* was moving away from *it*. Archie looked down and saw one of the ship's tentacles had wrapped around him, and was lifting him into the air. Everybody else had been picked up by tentacles too, including Alamo and Mr. Rivets.

The tentacles carried them toward the submarine's "mouth," where the crates had been loaded in. The girl was bringing them inside! The tentacles set them down gently in a cargo hold and retreated outside as a heavy door closed and bolted behind them. Glowing green lights along the floors flickered on so they could see, and the ship shifted and rumbled. They were moving.

"Now what?" Archie asked, his voice echoing in the big round metal cargo room.

"I suggest we seek out our host and thank her for her hospitality," said Mr. Rivets.

The door from the cargo room led to another large room dominated by two huge round windows like the one they'd seen from outside. The ship had already sunk below the waterline and left the Galveston dock behind, and as the submarine descended into the murky depths they got a slow, close-up look at the body of the Mangleborn attacking the dome. First came the massive tentacles, twisting and writhing with a life all their own. Then its tail, segmented like a lobster and finned like a flying fish. Then its scaled, barnacle-encrusted thorax with its pulsing gills, and then, at last, its long, hideous head, like a fanged horse. The thing's eyes followed them as they drifted down past it, mesmerizing everyone but Gonzalo.

"The Hippocamp," said a monotone voice behind them, and they all jumped. It was the Karankawan girl. She had come into the room from the front of the ship, and stood very still in the dark, her hands at her sides.

"The Hippocamp? You mean those nice, friendly sea-horses in the old Greek stories?" Fergus asked.

"There's only one," the girl said seriously, "and it's not friendly."

"Yeah," Fergus said. "I can see that."

The submarine moved away, and the Hippocamp didn't follow.

Archie let out the breath he didn't know he'd been holding. "It's ignoring us."

"I think it's more interested in destroying Galveston," said the girl. "Lights."

Lights like the ones in the cargo hold flickered on around the room, giving everything a greenish glow. Every other inch of the wall that wasn't giant windows was lined with shelf after shelf of books—two stories of them, all held in place with leather straps. Ornate brass walkways on the second floor were accessible by twin spiral staircases at opposite ends of the room.

"It's a library," Señor X told Gonzalo.

"A big library," Fergus said in awe. "There must be thousands of books here."

"Three thousand, nine hundred and one," the girl said. "I read a lot."

Archie introduced himself, and everyone else.

"My name is Martine," the girl said.

"Thanks for saving us," Archie said.

"You're welcome," Martine said. She tilted her head toward Fergus. "In the Lafitte's court, you said you knew of other Deep Ones that had risen."

"Aye," Fergus said. "We've fought a few of the land-based variety. But never anything like these beasties."

"The Deep Ones must be stopped," Martine said, staring out the window. "Even the one I'm looking for."

"What Mangleborn are you looking for?" Archie asked.

Something flashed out in the water, and Archie saw another Mangleborn right outside. Where the Hippocamp had been horse-like, this one looked more like an eel with a spiked, turtle-shell back. It twisted in the water, and with a kick of its stubby webbed feet it came shooting at them.

Martine disappeared through a door.

Archie and Fergus shared a glance, then hurried after her, with Gonzalo trailing casually behind. Archie followed Martine through a low engine room (where they lost Fergus, who couldn't help but stop to look around) and on into the cockpit of the ship. Martine sat in a swiveling red leather chair and studied a broad, curving panel of glowing green instruments and readouts. There were buttons and switches, levers and wheels, and dozens of gauges and dials. There were even some displays the like of which Archie had never seen before, with glowing green numbers and ghostly images that refreshed every time a green spinning line passed around in a circle.

The one thing there *wasn't* was a window.

"How can you see what's out there?" Archie cried. "There's no window!"

"I don't need to see outside," Martine said. "Not with my eyes."

Archie heard Gonzalo give a grunt of approval as he climbed into the small room.

"Well, *I'd* like to see what's going on!" Archie told her.

Martine pressed a button, and the roof over their heads slid back over a thick rounded window just in time for Archie to see the huge turtle-eel snapping at them.

Archie ducked and screamed, but Martine turned the steering column and pressed on pedals, and the submarine twisted and dove out of the way. Archie looked back through the window and saw the Mangleborn chasing them. He ducked again, but this time Martine swung them up and around like a swallow doing a flip, and they ran upside down along the monster's twisting, coiling back for a long moment before swinging down and around its belly and through its legs.

"I take it back," Archie said. "I don't think I want to see outside after all."

"It's called Yacumama," Martine said.

Archie was scared to death of it, but Martine piloted the submarine with the same expressionless calm she used when talking to them. No matter how the serpent coiled and twisted trying to catch them, she always managed to steer out of its way.

"How do you do that?" Archie asked. "Like you know what it's going to do?"

"I do know," Martine said. "The Deep Ones operate within predictable parameters."

Was she saying she actually understood the Mangleborn?

Martine pushed the steering column forward, and they dove around the Mangleborn's snapping jaws. Martine flipped another switch, and the ship's tentacles came to life, wrapping around the Yacumama's legs and tail. The Mangleborn kicked and thrashed, but Martine's squid-sub held fast.

"Tie it in a knot!" Archie told her.

Martine tilted her head, considering the idea.

"What kind of knot?" Martine asked. "A butterfly knot? An overhand knot? A square knot? A figure-eight knot? A slipped buntline? A clove hitch? A half hitch? A sheepshank? A monkey's fist? A hammock knot? You can't just say 'Tie it in a knot.' There is no 'knot.'"

Archie was incredulous. Of course there was such a thing as a knot! "A knot's a knot!" Archie told her.

"No, it's not," Martine said.

Archie wanted to pull his hair out.

"A square knot," Gonzalo said.

Martine nodded. "I will tie the Yacumama into a square knot." She took control of the tentacles, and Archie watched out the window as she twisted and pulled on the Mangleborn, tying it into a knot. When she finished she let go of the Yacumama and it sank, thrashing and squirming, into the dark abyss from whence it came. They were free!

Fergus hurried into the cockpit. "You guys! You won't believe what this thing runs on! It's not steam-powered, *or* lektric-powered. It's—"

Ka*FWOOM*.

The submarine rocked as something exploded in a fiery ball a few fathoms above them.

Ka*FWOOM*.

Another explosion went off on their starboard bow, and alarms rang out in the cockpit.

"What is it?" Archie cried, searching the window above them and seeing nothing. "Is it another Mangleborn?"

"No," said Martine, quickly making adjustments to her controls. "It's depth charges. We're being attacked by the Texas Navy."

A giant pinkish-white tentacle covered the window above them, and the submarine lurched.

"And the Hippocamp," Martine said.

10

KaFWOOM! Another depth charge went off, rocking the submarine, but that was the least of their worries. The Hippocamp had wrapped around Martine's submarine, and was dragging them down.

Martine pushed a button. *BWAAAAT.* Whatever it was sounded like Buster's raycannon going off, and the sea all around them flashed green. The Hippocamp roared, but didn't let go, squeezing the hull even tighter. More alarms went off.

"That was my biggest gun," Martine said in her even monotone. "Unless we can shake the Hippocamp, it will crush *The Kraken*'s hull in seven minutes."

"You have an aether cannon?" Archie asked.

"That's what I'm telling you," Fergus said excitedly. "The whole *ship* runs on aether!"

"That's impossible," Archie said. "Aether comes from the Mangleborn. It uses a . . . a different geometry," he said, remembering the phrase Tesla used. "That's why nobody can do anything but make guns out of it. No one understands it."

"I do," Martine said.

"Can we maybe figure that out later?" Señor X asked. "If she's right, we've got approximately six minutes and twenty-seven seconds left before that sea monster cracks this tin can."

"What about the tentacles?" Gonzalo asked.

Martine wrangled the controls. "The Hippocamp is stronger."

"Let's throw the Jandal a Haad at it," Señor X said. "He can keep it busy while the rest of us get away."

"*Archie*," Archie said. "My name is *Archie*."

"Nae," said Fergus. "That beastie'll just swallow him."

"Which is exactly what we want it to do," said Gonzalo.

Everyone looked at him like he was crazy, but he didn't notice.

"The raycannon couldn't pierce the Hippocamp's hide from the outside," Gonzalo said. "But if it's anything like an armadillo, it's squishier on the inside."

"What, you want me to swim out there with a raygun, get swallowed, and shoot it up from the inside?" Archie asked.

"Not just any raygun," Gonzalo said. He pulled Señor X from its holster with a flourish, spun it in his hand, and held it out to Archie grip-first.

"Oh, no," Archie and Señor X said together.

"I'm not getting swallowed by any fish," Señor X said. "I knew a guy once who did that, and it did not end well for him."

"And I'm not going in there with a raygun that can just decide he's not going to shoot."

KaFWOOM! Another depth charge went off, but much farther above them now. The Mangleborn was pulling them down.

"Five minutes, twenty-one seconds," Martine said.

Gonzalo put the serpentine raygun in Archie's hand. "Señor ain't gonna leave you hanging, 'cause if he does, he'll be stuck in there with you," Gonzalo told Archie. "And you ain't gonna get stuck in the belly of a whale, because Archie can't be et. Plus, you finally get to kill something."

"You can't kill a Mangleborn," Archie and Señor X said at the same time.

"Then mess it up some," Gonzalo said. "All that matters is that thing lets us go!"

The Kraken strained and shuddered against the Hippocamp's crushing grip.

Archie sighed. "How do I get outside?"

Martine led him to an airlock on the underside of the ship. One of the Mangleborn's tentacles covered part of it, but Archie could squeeze through. Just looking at the pale, slimy thing made Archie shiver.

"Isn't there some other way?" Archie asked.

"Two minutes, fifty-eight seconds," Martine told him.

Archie looked at the turquoise raygun in his hand. "Do you trust me?" he asked the raygun.

"No," Señor X said.

"Good, because I don't trust you either," Archie told him, and he jumped into the water.

Sploosh! Archie hovered for a moment, the water swirling around him, and then he started to sink. He grabbed for the Mangleborn's tentacle, but it was too slimy and slippery. He was sinking fast, away from the Hippocamp's tentacles, but he was too heavy to swim. This wasn't good. Sinking to the bottom of the ocean wasn't going to help anybody!

KaPOW! Señor X fired without Archie pulling the trigger, hitting one of the twisting tentacles. The Hippocamp growled, and the tentacle shot out and snatched Archie up. *Quick thinking!* Archie wanted to tell the raygun, but he couldn't talk underwater.

The tentacle dragged Archie through the cold, dark water to the ugly head of the Hippocamp, and it studied him with its big glassy eyes.

Jandal a Haad, the Hippocamp growled in his head.

Archie raised the raygun at the big eye and squeezed the trigger.

KaPOW! Señor X hit the Hippocamp with everything it had, and the monster roared. Then it did exactly what Archie didn't want it to do.

It ate him.

The Hippocamp's razor teeth chomped on him, cracking and breaking on Archie's stone body. Archie fought to pull Señor X's trigger as the Mangleborn's tongue moved him around in its mouth, but the raygun shot without him. *KaPOW! KaPOW! KaPOW! KaPOW!* It kept shooting as the Hippocamp swallowed them, and Archie closed his eyes and tried not think about the fact that he was moving down a Mangleborn's slimy esophagus. It felt like the Hippocamp was thrashing and writhing from the raygun blasts, but that might have just been the muscles of its stomach tossing Archie around—if Mangleborn even had stomachs.

Jandal a Haad, the Hippocamp said. *Jandal a Haad and Xiuhcoatl.*

Archie frowned. What was a 'she-oh-co-at-ul'? Another name for the Jandal a Haad in some ancient language?

All at once Archie wasn't in the belly of a Mangleborn anymore—he stood beside a wide river, surrounded on both sides by jungle. He was himself, but he wasn't. He could see a tall, strong man in this dream, and he knew the man was him. This other-Archie had black and yellow bands painted horizontally across his face and arms and legs, and wore nothing but sandals, a loincloth, and a white feathered headdress. The other-Archie's right foot was gone, and in its place was a replacement made of obsidian. In his hands, he carried a tall spear and a shield so polished it was a mirror.

The other-Archie was joined by two others. The first was a jaguar-woman covered all over with yellow fur with black spots. Her face was a mix of feline and human, and her hands and feet were claws. She wore a purple blouse and skirt, decorated with images of the moon. Beside her was a brown-skinned man with the top half of his face painted black, wearing white leather armor and a leather helmet decorated with blue and green hummingbird feathers.

In his hand, he carried Señor X.

Tentacles rose from the river in front of them, and the

horse-like head of the Hippocamp emerged from the river, its fangs dripping.

"Huitzilopochtli, stay back and hit it with Xiuhcoatl!" the jaguar-woman ordered. "Tezcatlipoca, get in close and cut off some of those tentacles! I'll try to climb up it and put this bomb down its throat!"

Archie could feel the bloodlust welling up inside the other-Archie, the shadow Tezcatlipoca, as he charged out into the river after the Hippocamp. The other Leaguer, Huitzilopochtli—their warrior?—fired Señor X again and again. *KaPOW! Ka-POW! KaPOW!*

The Hippocamp smacked the other-Archie away, and he flew off into the jungle. He got up seething, hot steam coming off his body in the humid jungle air. Tezcatlipoca roared and charged back through the forest, bursting out of the jungle with his spear raised. He carved off one of the tentacles and batted another away with his shield, but there were too many of them. Tentacles beat at him and squeezed him and choked him.

Jandal a Haad, the Hippocamp said, the name echoing in the other-Archie's head.

Then the jaguar-woman was there, slashing at the tentacles that held him with her claws, and he was free. But Tezcatlipoca was mad, and he lashed out at the jaguar-woman and the tentacles with equal venom. His mirrored shield slammed her in the face, and she crashed into the water.

"Ix Chel!" Huitzilopochtli cried.

KaPOW! A raygun blast from Xiuhcoatl hit Tezcatlipoca in the head, and he roared. He threw his spear at his brother and missed. Ix Chel jumped on his back and covered his eyes with her claws.

"Tezcatlipoca! Try to think!" she cried. "We're not your enemies! The Cahuayoatl is your enemy!"

"I'll tear off your skin and wear it as a pelt!" Tezcatlipoca bellowed.

Jandal a Haad, the Hippocamp whisper-sang. *Necoc Yoatl. Enemy to Both Sides.*

Tezcatlipoca grabbed Ix Chel by the tail and dragged her to him, raising her high above his head, and started to pull her apart.

"Tezcatlipoca! Wake up! Tezcatlipoca!" Huitzilopochtli yelled, shooting him in the face again and again. *KaPOW! KaPOW! KaPOW! KaPOW!*

Something kept hitting Archie in the face, and he put a hand up to block it. *KaPOW! KaPOW! KaPOW! KaPOW!* It was a raygun. Señor X was shooting him in the face.

"Archie! Wake up! Archie!" Señor X cried.

"I'm awake! Slag it, Xiuhcoatl, stop shooting me!"

"Hey! I'm not the one who fell asleep inside a—wait, what did you call me?" Señor X asked.

"Where are we?" Archie asked. Everything was still dark and squishy.

"The upper intestines, I think. If Mangleborn have intestines," Señor X said. "What I want to know is, how do you know my name?"

"I—I saw you. In a vision. That's why I passed out. The Hippocamp showed me a vision of another League. An old one. And you were there. And I was Tezcat—Tezcat—"

"Tezcatlipoca," Señor X said, low and angry.

Archie floated in the alien goo of the Mangleborn's intestines for a long moment.

"I'm not him," he said.

"It's been more than seven minutes," Señor X said.

"What?"

"It's been more than seven minutes. We saved the sub, or the Cahuayoatl crushed it and they're all dead. But either way, we can get out of here now."

"Cahuayoatl. That's what Ix Chel called the Hippocamp," Archie said.

Señor X was quiet again for a few seconds. "It means 'Water-Horse.' Different people have different names for the same monster, you know. Like Jandal a Haad and Necoc Yoatl and Archie Dent."

"I get it," said Archie.

Señor X shot through the intestines to the Hippocamp's skin, and Archie punched his way out from inside. The dark, cold seawater was a welcome relief. At least it washed off the white goo that covered him.

The Hippocamp sank slowly in the water, its tentacles twitching like it was half-dead. Or maybe just asleep. Señor X had done enough internal damage to it to put it out of commission for a long time.

But where was *The Kraken*? Had the Mangleborn crushed it? Archie clung to the side of the Hippocamp, searching the murky depths for any sign of the ship. He was afraid if he let go he'd sink to the bottom, and he'd never be able to climb out again.

Señor X fired, scaring Archie, but his yellow beam lanced out like a beacon. Something small and green and glowing came toward them out of the darkness. Archie pointed Señor X at it, but the raygun didn't fire.

It was Martine. She swam through the water with the grace of a dolphin, her webbed fingers and hands pulling her along so quickly she was on top of Archie almost as soon as he saw her. The green glow came from the harpoon she wore on her back—the same one Archie had seen in Galveston, glowing with aetherical power. But Archie didn't understand—how was she able to hold her breath so long?

Martine put her long, slender arm under Archie's, made sure he was secure, and swam up and away from the Mangle-born. As they rose, he saw the flaps of skin on her neck that rose and fell with the currents.

Gills. Martine had gills that let her breathe underwater.

Martine was the seventh and final Leaguer. The scholar. The scientist. Martine with her gills and her aetherical submarine and her library.

They were a proper League of Seven at last: hero, warrior, tinker, scholar, trickster, lawbringer, shadow. Archie felt a thrill—he was a part of something that only came around once every few centuries. He was a member of an honest-to-goodness *League of Seven.*

And then Archie remembered why Leagues came together in the first place. Why the world only needed them once every few centuries.

People only got a new League of Seven when the world was about to end.

11

Gonzalo, Fergus, and Mr. Rivets were at the airlock when Martine dragged Archie and Señor X back in. Gonzalo took a rag to Señor X, and Mr. Rivets handed Archie a towel.

"That was *gross*," Archie told them.

"We're not out of the water yet," said Fergus.

KaFWOOM. The ship lurched, and Archie staggered to stay on his feet.

"More depth charges?" Archie asked.

"No," said Fergus. "Torpedoes!"

Martine left for the bridge at the same maddeningly slow pace as Gonzalo, and Archie and Fergus hurried ahead to look out the window. A few hundred yards away sat a long, steel-gray submarine with the red, white, and blue flag of the

Republic of Texas with its lone star painted on its side. Its name was the TSS *Zavala*.

As they watched, a torpedo hissed out of its gun ports and shot toward them through the water.

KaFWOOM. *The Kraken* rocked again from the explosion.

Martine slid into her seat and began flipping switches. With an easy turn of the wheel, she guided *The Kraken* away from *Zavala*.

KaFWOOM. *The Kraken* rocked again as *Zavala* shot it from behind.

Archie strained to look back through the window. "Aren't you going to fight?"

"No," Martine said. "The Lafitte brought this on Galveston. They're just doing their job. I'm not going to hurt innocent people."

"Innocent people?" Archie said. "They're attacking us!"

"What kind of pirate are you?" Fergus asked.

"A bad one, according to the Lafitte," Martine admitted. "But I see no reason to attack and steal from manned submarines when there are so many wrecked ships full of treasure on the ocean's floor."

KaFWOOM. Another torpedo struck *The Kraken*, and Archie slammed into a control panel.

"I thought you built all those octopod raiding ships for the Lafitte," Gonzalo said.

"Designed," Martine said as she twisted and dipped and rose, trying to evade the torpedoes that hissed by. "The Lafitte's engineers built them. And what they chose to do with them was his affair."

What the Karankawan pirates of Galveston were choosing

to do with them right then was to engage the Texas Navy. *The Kraken* dodged and swerved through a maze of octopod raiders, all wrapped around Texas Navy submarines like giant squid attacking sperm whales. The water thudded with exploding torpedoes and bubbled with burning raycannon beams.

KaFWOOM. A torpedo hit them from the side as another Texas submarine joined *Zavala* in pursuit.

"There's too many of them," Fergus said. The glowing, spinning scope Archie had been so fascinated with was filled with moving dots. "We'll never get out of here in one piece."

"There is a 73.7 percent chance that you are correct," Martine said calmly.

Archie was no scientist, but he knew enough to know those weren't good odds.

"Another Mangleborn!" Fergus cried.

It floated up from the depths like an airship rising through the clouds. Whatever this Deep One was, it was gigantic. Bigger than the other two they had just fought combined. It was a monstrous, yellow-orange, almost transparent gelatinous ooze that undulated like a jellyfish, trailing a mass of dangling tentacles.

"I—I see it!" Gonzalo cried. It was the first time Archie had heard him slip a gear. Gonzalo backed into the doorjamb and slid to the floor. "I don't know how, but I can see it!"

Martine steered straight for it.

"What are you doing?" Archie cried.

"It's not real," Martine said.

"What are you talking about, it's not real?" Fergus said. "Even Gonzalo can see it!"

Gonzalo held out a hand, as though he could reach out and touch the thing. "It's—it's beautiful," he muttered.

A Texas Navy submarine ran into the monster's tentacles, and lektricity crackled around it. The submarine slowed and listed, its tail end rising as it floated dead in the water.

And still Martine drove right at it.

"Turn, turn, turn!" Archie cried. Behind them, the Texas Navy subs that had been pursuing them broke off their pursuit.

"There is no Deep One ahead of us," Martine said.

The Mangleborn got closer, and closer, and closer, and Archie closed his eyes and braced for impact.

Nothing. He opened his eyes. The jellyfish monster was all around them, but *The Kraken* was still streaming forward. Gonzalo looked all around them in absolute wonder.

"We must be slicing right through it!" Fergus marveled.

"There is nothing to slice through," Martine said. "There is no Deep One here."

She was right—they passed through the glowing, gelatinous guts of the thing without splitting it or pushing any of it aside.

"How did you know?" Fergus asked Martine, still staring at the impossible thing all around them.

"It's not on the sonar scope," Martine said. She pointed to the spinning readout with the ghostly images on it. It showed all the dots of the fleeing Texas Navy and Galveston pirate ships, but not the gigantic Deep One that had scared them off. The thing looked real, *acted* real, but it wasn't really there. It was just an illusion. An illusion that even Gonzalo could see. . . .

"Kitsune!" Archie cried happily.

"Kitsune?" Fergus said. "What's a Kitsune?"

Collision alarms suddenly went off in the cockpit. *Clang!* *The Kraken* jolted as something slammed down on it and yanked it up out of the ocean. The submarine lifted into the air, and as the last of the water sluiced off the window they saw the big friendly brass face of a giant steam man. It whistled happily at them.

"Buster!" Archie yelled.

The Kraken's tentacles wrapped around Buster's big mechanical arms, and his happy whistle became a frightened whimper.

"No, don't!" Archie told Martine. "They're friends! They're the ones who made everybody see the Mangleborn so we could get away!"

Martine pulled *The Kraken's* tentacles away, and Buster sat them down on a long, thin stretch of sandy beach. The big steam man whistled and hopped around anxiously as they made their way out of the airlock, pouncing on Archie as soon as he was clear of the sub.

"Okay! Okay! Hi! Hello, Buster!' Archie said, laughing, as the giant steam man jumped up and down on him, driving him down into the sand. It would have killed anyone else, but Buster knew he could play rough with Archie. "All right! All right," Archie told the big brass steam man with the soul of a dog. "Off. Off!"

"Buster, heel!" Clyde called, and the giant steam man bounded over to the good-looking Afrikan boy in the UN Cavalry uniform who stood on a dune nearby. "Sit!" Clyde said, and Buster thunked his big brass bottom down on the sand, his tailpipe wagging furiously.

"Archie!" Clyde said, and the two shook hands enthusiastically. "Buster was so happy to see you, I just about couldn't get out, and that's a fact!"

"It's great to see you again!" Archie told him. He hadn't realized how much he'd missed Clyde and Buster. "How'd you find me?"

"When we heard there was a big ruckus, we figured you had to be right in the middle of it."

Archie sighed. "I'm not *always* in the middle of everything," he said. "Where's Kitsune?"

Clyde pointed up to Buster's shoulder, where the fox-girl sat watching them. Archie waved at her, and she waved back before hopping down Buster's arm.

"Mr. R!" Clyde called to Mr. Rivets. "What's the word?"

"It is most gratifying to see you again, Master Clyde," Mr. Rivets said. "And you too, Miss Kitsune," he said as the fox-girl landed softly on the ground.

"Thanks for the save," Archie told her. "The submarine getting caught in the jellyfish was a nice touch."

Kitsune grinned. "A good lie is all about the details."

"Glad to see you're still around," Archie said.

Kitsune put a hand to the pearl necklace she wore. "I made a promise," she said. "I may lie, but I never break a promise."

"Gonzalo, this is the real Clyde," Archie told the Texas Ranger. But Gonzalo was still too stunned from his vision of the jellyfish-like Mangleborn to speak.

Archie introduced everybody else, including Gonzalo's steamhorse.

"Alamo?" Clyde said. "Well, that ought to be easy to remember."

"Yes," Martine said. "The name has a pleasing yellow-gray-yellow-blue-white combination."

Everyone was quiet for a moment.

"No, he means because of 'Remember the Alamo.' What do you mean yellow and blue and all that?" Archie asked. Alamo was unpainted brass, like Mr. Rivets.

"Yellow-gray-yellow-blue-white," Martine said. "The letters in Alamo's name."

"The letters in his name . . . have colors?" Fergus asked.

"Of course," Martine said. "All letters and numbers do. Archie's is yellow-blue-green-pink-white-orange. A very angry and confused combination."

Clyde, Kitsune, and Fergus looked awkward, and Archie cleared his throat. Every one of them had seen him get angry and confused and lose his mind and become a monster.

"What's wrong?" Gonzalo asked, sensing everyone's discomfort.

"Nothin'," Clyde said, diplomatic as always. "Great to have you on the team," he said, holding out a hand to Gonzalo.

"He wants to shake your hand," Señor X told him.

Gonzalo found Clyde's hand and shook it.

"Talking raygun?" Clyde asked, clearly impressed. "Where'd you get that?"

"Found it," Gonzalo said simply.

"Helps you see, huh? I knew a guy once who couldn't see," Clyde said. "Took a raygun blast in the face at the Battle of Stony Lake in '63. Name was Cetanwakuwa. Man could *cook*. Didn't know it 'til they put him on galley duty after the accident. Said he learned to use his taste buds and sniffer better when his eyes went bad. Guess it's like Mrs. De-Marcus used to say, 'One door closes, another opens.' You can't see at all?"

Gonzalo shook his head. "Not until today." He turned and looked right at Kitsune, even though she'd been quiet for some time. "You do that?"

"Yes," Kitsune said. "I can put pictures in people's heads. Make them see anything I want them to."

"*Órale!*" Gonzalo gasped, and he dropped to his knees in the sand. He buried his face in his hands as tears streamed from his eyes.

"Stop it!" Señor X cried. "Whatever you're doing, stop! You're hurting him!" The turquoise raygun hummed with a devastating charge. "Gonzalo! Gonzalo, pick me up and point me at her! Gonzalo!"

Kitsune stared at Gonzalo like she was burning a hole in him.

"Kitsune!" Archie said. He grabbed her by the shoulders and shook her. "Kitsune, what are you doing? Stop it!"

Kitsune came out of her trance and blinked, and Gonzalo sobbed.

"I'll kill her," Señor X said. "Gonzalo, pick me up, and I'll kill her."

"No," Gonzalo muttered. "No. It's all right, Señor. I'm all right."

"I didn't hurt him," Kitsune said.

"Then why was he crying? What did you show him?" Archie asked.

"Just this," Kitsune said. "The beach. The ocean. Us."

"*Que hermoso es*," Gonzalo said, still crying. They were tears of wonder and awe. "The colors. I never imagined the colors. . . ."

"Okay," Archie told Kitsune. "But maybe you need to go a little easier on the visions with Gonzalo for a little while."

Alamo helped Gonzalo to his feet, and Clyde, ever thoughtful, changed the subject while the ranger collected himself. "So you're the famous Fergus Archie's always talking about," he said, shaking Fergus's hand. "Archie says you can fix just about everything but a broken heart."

"Aye, and I might be able to fix even that if you didn't mind it being brass and clockworks," Fergus said. "I don't suppose you'd be needing any help with your steam man, would you?" Fergus hadn't taken his eyes off Buster since he'd climbed out of *The Kraken*.

"Sure could use a tune-up," Clyde said. "We had to march a far piece to get here for the big meet-up, and fast."

Archie looked at all the amazing people gathered around him: Clyde, Fergus, Kitsune, Gonzalo, Martine.

"The League of Seven," he said. "We're the League of Seven. Seven heroes brought together to save the world." He didn't have to tell them what from—every one of them had seen or fought a Mangleborn or a Manglespawn, and knew what they could do. "Fergus is the Tinker. Kitsune's the Trickster. Martine's the Scientist. Gonzalo's the Lawbringer. Clyde's the Leader," Archie said. "And I'm the Shadow."

"I already have a job," Gonzalo said. "I'm a Texas Ranger."

"You can be both, G-man," Señor X told him. "Trust me. You belong with these guys. We both do."

Archie remembered the vision he'd had inside the Hippocamp, of Señor X in the hands of a League lost to the sands of time. How many Leagues had the raygun been a part of before?

"All right," Gonzalo said. "Me and Señor X are with you. I just need to send word to my parents that I'm okay first."

"They won't care that you're off chasing beasties?" Fergus asked.

Gonzalo shrugged. "It's what we do. We're Texas Rangers."

"Well, unless somebody's better at hiding than I am," Kitsune said, "I only see a League of Six, not a League of Seven."

"Your math is correct," Martine said.

"So where's number seven?" Kitsune asked.

The tattoos on Fergus's face rearranged themselves, and his nose suddenly flashed blue like a lektric light and buzzed, making them all jump.

"Speak of the devil," Fergus said.

"What in the Sam Hill is that?" Clyde asked, staring at Fergus's nose.

"When Hachi and I split up, I gave her a homing beacon, like the one that meka-ninja had that I kept hearing at Atlantis Station," Fergus said. "I told her to turn it on when she was finished . . . doing what she needed to do." He tapped the side of his nose. "Looks like she just turned it on."

Everyone but Archie stared at him like he was crazy.

"Thomas Edison turned Fergus into a kind of lektric computational device," Archie explained, as best he understood it.

It didn't seem to help.

"Where is she?" Archie asked.

Fergus turned slowly in the sand until the flashing light and buzzing sound got quicker. "East," he said.

"Well, that's specific," Kitsune said.

"All right, slightly east-southeast," Fergus said testily.

"How far?" Clyde asked.

Fergus shrugged. "Not sure. We'll find out when we get there.

"Some of us can ride in Buster," Archie said. "The rest of us can take *The Kraken*."

"Whoa, whoa, whoa," Clyde said. "The whole plan was for everybody to meet up in Houston so we could go together and head off Moffett's monster army."

"Moffett? *Monster army?*" Fergus said.

"The Dragon Lantern turns people into Manglespawn," Archie explained, forgetting that he hadn't brought Fergus, Gonzalo, and Martine up to speed. "Only some people, though. People who have some part of the Mangleborn in them already."

"Deoxyribonucleic Acid," Martine said, and it was her turn to be stared at again. "DNA. I have been studying ancient Mu medical textbooks about it. It's the genetic sequence all living organisms use to develop and function."

No one understood what she was talking about, but she didn't seem to notice.

"Mangleborn and Manglespawn have interbred with humanity for hundreds of thousands of years. It's likely that most of us have some latent Mangleborn chromosomes in our DNA." She looked at Kitsune. "Some of us more obviously than others."

"Says the girl who sees colors in letters," Kitsune mumbled.

"Your supposition is correct," Martine told Kitsune. "I too am descended from a human-Mangleborn union. I am an eighth-generation Deep One–human hybrid."

"Wait—so you're saying your great-great-grandfather got all kissy-kissy with one of those water beasties we just escaped?" Fergus asked.

"Great-great-great-great-great-grand*mother*," Martine said. "Yes. I have made the study of the Deep Ones my life's work. I would like to find the Mangleborn who made me what I am today."

"And then what?" Archie asked.

"Kill it," Martine said.

They were all silent for a moment. Martine was the only one who didn't look uncomfortable.

"Okay," Fergus said, trying to get back to the matter at hand. "So the Dragon Lantern can activate the wee bits of us that are Mangleborn and turn us into monsters. So what?"

"So Philomena Moffett has it," Clyde said.

"That's good, innit?" Fergus asked. "She's the head of the Septemberist Society. She's the one who sent you after it to begin with."

"No. It's bad," said Archie. "Twenty-five years ago, the Septemberist Society tried to make a new League of Seven using the Dragon Lantern on orphans. It went really, really badly. The kids turned into monsters."

"And Moffett was one of those kids," Clyde explained.

"You're saying Philomena Moffett is—"

"A woman with tentacles for legs and a sonic scream that can knock over mountains," Clyde said.

"Crivens," said Fergus.

"She joined the Septemberist Society to destroy it from within," Archie said. "Then she found out about the Dragon Lantern—"

"And had us go get it for her," said Fergus.

"Now she's marchin' east, using it on everybody she meets," Clyde told the team. "We have to go stop her. Now. Six of us is plenty. It's even more than we thought we'd have."

"All right," said Fergus. "I'll allow that all that is really, really bad. But are you saying we don't go get Hachi first? What if she's in danger? What if she activated her beacon because she needs our help?"

"There is an *army of monsters* marching across America," Clyde said. "I think that wins out."

"Well, I'm going after her," Fergus said, "monster army or no monster army."

"We shouldn't split up again," Kitsune said.

"She's right," Archie said. "We should *all* go after Hachi."

"Archie—" Clyde said.

"We *have* to get her, Clyde. We're the *League of Seven*," he told them all. "One two three four five six *seven*. There's a *reason* it's seven. It's always been seven, every time. Every new generation. We found five and six just in time," he said, nodding at Gonzalo and Martine. "And now it's time to get number seven. We need her. We need to be seven to beat Moffett."

Clyde was leader enough to know when he had a civil war on his hands, and how to stop it.

"Okay," he said. "Okay. We go get this Hachi person first. I just hope she's worth it."

Fergus put a hand on Clyde's shoulder. "She is, mate. Trust me. She is."

12

Archie could see the clearing over the tops of the trees from the cockpit inside Buster's head. The clearing near Orlando, Florida, where Thomas Edison had tried to raise a Mangleborn. The clearing where Archie had first met Hachi and Fergus just a few months ago.

The clearing where, twelve years ago, Hachi's father and ninety-nine other men had been murdered, and Archie had been born.

From ten stories up, the stone altar at the center of the clearing looked so small. So insignificant. And so did the girl sitting on the ground beside it.

Clyde stopped the giant steam man a hundred yards from the clearing.

"That her?" Clyde asked.

Archie nodded. It was Hachi all right. She still wore her long black hair in a braid, and the same brown skirt, blue shirt, and leather bandolier.

"She doesn't look like she's in danger," Clyde said from the pilot's seat.

"Nae," said Fergus. He sat behind Clyde in the drummer's chair that had once been Clyde's. "She looks like she's waiting for someone."

"You," Archie told him.

Fergus gave him a wan smile. "I hope she is. But I think it's you she'll be wanting to talk to first."

"Oh no," Archie said. Hachi knew the truth about what had happened here at Chuluota. The truth about *him*. He didn't want to face that.

"It's got to be done," Fergus said. "You've both got to get past this."

"And fast," Clyde reminded him.

Archie sighed. If he and Hachi were ever able to get past what had happened in this clearing twelve years ago, it wouldn't be fast. But Archie knew Fergus was right. They couldn't just go on like it had never happened. They had to be able to work together without always wondering what one was secretly thinking about the other.

"All right," Archie said. "I'll go."

Archie climbed down through the steam man's floors. Martine was busy examining the apparatus that launched aeronauts, and Gonzalo and Kitsune sat at the galley table talking while Mr. Rivets served them coffee.

"We found Hachi," Archie told them. "She's not in trouble. I'm going to get her."

Kitsune hopped on top of the table and peered out one of the gun ports, trying to catch a glimpse of her.

"You want somebody to ride shotgun?" Gonzalo asked.

"I think I better do this alone. But thanks, Gonzalo."

"Are you sure you wouldn't like me to come with you?" Mr. Rivets asked. "Miss Hachi and I have developed something of a rapport."

"No, that's okay, Mr. Rivets. Thanks."

Archie left the rest of the League behind in Buster and tromped through the jungle-like forest toward the clearing. It took him back to that night months ago when he'd walked this same path behind his parents, who were under the spell of Malacar Ahasherat. The Mangleborn was still trapped far below the surface, thanks to Archie, Hachi, and Fergus, but he could feel the Swarm Queen tugging at his brain.

Jandal a Haad, she whispered sleepily.

Archie tried to put the thought from his head as he stepped into the clearing. Hachi had to know he was there—if the giant steam man looming over the clearing wasn't obvious enough, Archie's clumsy crashing through the jungle would have told her he was on the way. She didn't look up until he got close.

"Hey Hachi," he said at last.

"Archie," Hachi said.

Archie looked around the clearing, trying to think of something to say.

"Did you have to wait long?" he asked lamely.

"Twelve years," Hachi said.

Archie had meant since she'd activated her beacon, of course. Hachi knew that.

Archie swallowed. "Did you—did you kill them all? The people responsible for the death of your parents?"

"All but one," Hachi said. She pulled a raygun out from behind her and aimed it at him.

Archie put up his hands in surrender, even though the raygun couldn't really hurt him. They both knew that. "Look, Hachi, I—"

BWAAAT! Hachi shot Archie right in the chest. The shot staggered him, more out of surprise than anything, and burned a huge hole in his shirt.

"Hachi—" Archie tried again.

Hachi stood and advanced on him, an aether pistol in each hand.

BWAAAT! She shot him again, scorching off another part of his shirt but not hurting him at all. She went back and forth with the rayguns, shooting one while she waited for the aether aggregator to fill on the other.

BWAAAT! BWAAAT! BWAAAT!

High above them, Buster whistled nervously and stirred, wanting to come to Archie's aid. Fergus had to be holding Clyde and Buster back.

BWAAAT! BWAAAT! BWAAAT!

Hachi kept shooting him, a look of pure hatred on her face. Archie put his hands up, more to protect himself from the blinding light than anything. His shirt was in tatters and his skin had scorch marks on it, but he could barely even feel the blasts. There was nothing Hachi could do to hurt Archie short of dropping a mountain on him or pushing him down a giant hole, and they both knew it.

"Hachi—" Archie said.

Hachi threw the rayguns aside and pulled out a long, curved blade like the one the meka-ninja had used.

Shing! Shing! Shing! Hachi slashed Archie with it—left, right, left again—hacking at him like she was trying to chop down a tree. Archie put his hands down and stood still, letting Hachi hit him. When her sword broke, she cast it aside with the raygun and pounded on Archie with her fists, finally collapsing into his arms, tears streaming down her face. He hugged her close, not wanting her to see his own tears.

"Why won't you die?" she whispered.

"I'm sorry," Archie told her. "If I could, I would. I would swap places with your father in a heartbeat."

"*You did*," Hachi told him.

Archie hadn't thought about it like that before, but she was right. The lives of one hundred men had been swapped for his. They had traded places. A one for one hundred exchange.

"I wish it had never happened," Archie said. "Any of it. I wish I hadn't been born. I'm sorry."

Hachi sniffed and pulled back. Now it was her turn to look away. "I know. I know it's not your fault," she told him. "It's just so hard not to hate you. You're the reason my father was murdered."

"I hate myself," Archie told her. "I don't want to live. I won't. I'll find a cave somewhere. A hole in the ground. The bottom of the ocean. I'll disappear, so the people who did this don't get what they wanted. I won't be their hero. I won't be anything."

"No, you blinking flange!" Hachi said. She tried to shove him in the chest, but Archie didn't budge. "No, you have to live! Don't you see that, you idiot? As much as I hate it, you have to live. Do you understand?"

"No," said Archie.

Hachi grabbed his shoulders. "You're all that's left of them. Don't you see? If you crawl in a hole somewhere, it's like they died for nothing. You have to live the lives that were taken from them. All of them. You have to live a life worthy of a *hundred* lives. You have to fight for all the people who died to create you. You have to be the best slagging person who ever lived. Otherwise you dishonor their memories. Promise me. You have to promise."

"All right," Archie said. "I—I promise." He looked at Hachi, bent and weak, so unlike herself. She'd been ruined by all this as badly as he had. "But I *am* an idiot, compared to you and all these other people. You have to help me," Archie told her. "You have to help me live the life the men of Chuluota should have had. You have to help me be the man your father would have been."

Hachi was crying again, and she didn't bother to dry her eyes. She nodded and leaned down, hiding her eyes in Archie's white hair.

Archie looked away, embarrassed, and saw the twisted wreckage of Edison's lightning tower in the clearing. The busted, abandoned equipment. The carved stone altar.

"Why did you come back here?" Archie asked.

Hachi stood up straight and wiped an arm across her eyes. "I had nowhere else to go," she said. She sniffed. "Nothing else to do. Now that I've gotten my revenge on all the people who murdered my father, I don't know what to do with myself. I almost didn't activate the beacon."

"You do have a place," Archie said. "In the League of Seven. We found all the others. You're the last one we had to collect. Me and Fergus, we told the others we weren't leaving without you."

Hachi gave a half-sob, half-laugh. "Fergus," she said.

"He misses you," Archie told her.

Hachi sniffed again. "I miss him too."

"Come on," Archie said.

Hachi held him back. "Archie—about the League. I found something else out when I tracked down all the people who'd been here that night twelve years ago. *They were working for the Septemberists.*"

"What?" Archie couldn't believe it. "But—Edison, Blavatsky, they weren't Septemberists. The Septemberists worked *against* Edison."

"They hired them, Archie. Edison and Blavatsky and the others didn't know where the money came from, or how they'd been brought together. But think about it—who else would know just the right bad guys to bring together except the people who were keeping an eye on them?"

"But—but why?" Archie asked.

"To make you," Hachi told him. "To make the superhero who would anchor their League."

Suddenly it all made sense. Why *wouldn't* the Septemberists fund a secret group to create him? They'd done the same thing twenty-five years ago at Dodge City—built a secret facility to try to create a new League of Seven. Archie was just attempt number two. He sat down on the stone altar as the truth sank in.

"They brought them together, and gave them the idea to make you," Hachi told him. "Maybe they even let the ancient book with the instructions fall into their hands. We saw the library they've got at Atlantis Station. They brought them together, gave them the idea, and the money to do it. If it didn't work, the murders were on somebody else—people they wanted to get rid of in the first place. But if it did . . . they would just bust up the group and swoop in and take you and raise you for their own. Which is exactly what they did."

They knew. The Septemberist Society knew how Archie had been created, because they were the ones behind it all. That's how Moffett had known. She wasn't the one to set it up—she'd come along too late for that—but she'd found the evidence, digging for proof of the Septemberists' involvement in her own creation. She and Archie really were alike. The Septemberists had made them both what they were, trying to create a brand new League. Only Archie had been the lucky one—if you called having a hundred men murdered so you could live "lucky."

Archie passed a hand over the maze of lines in the top of the altar where their blood had run. "They did the same thing to Moffett. Now she's marching across the country with the Dragon Lantern, turning people into Manglespawn as revenge. Everything that's happening now—Moffett, the Monster War, the Shadow League, the rise of the Mangleborn, the League of Seven—the Septemberist Society's secret plotting and scheming caused it all. They created the problem they made us to fix."

"We can't work for them anymore, Archie," Hachi said. "They're as bad as Edison and Blavatsky and all the others."

Archie nodded. "But we still have to stop Moffett," he told her. "We still have to be a League of Seven, even if we were created for all the wrong reasons. Just like I have to still be a hero. We stop Moffett, then we take care of the Septemberist Society."

Hachi nodded. It was agreed. She held out her hand, and Archie took it, letting her help him up off the altar. She squeezed his hand before letting it go. They were okay. As okay as either of them was ever going to get.

Archie looked down at the altar, and he felt the anger over it all build up inside him like steam in a boiler. He slammed his fist down on it with the strength of a hundred men— KraKOOM!—and smashed it to pieces.

They watched the dust and rubble settle, and Archie knocked the last of the pieces over with his foot. "The hundred men who live inside me," he asked. "Will you teach me their names?"

Hachi looked surprised. "Yes. If you want."

She took his arm as they walked back out of the clearing for the last time.

"So . . . we have a giant steam man now?" she asked, looking up at Buster.

"Yeah," Archie said.

"Brass."

13

Buster met *The Kraken* just south of the Chickasaw city of Memphis, at the border of Louisiana and Pawnee territory. Martine's sub had come up the Mississippi River while Buster marched west, and neither of them had seen Moffett or her Monster Army. She either had to be farther west still, or farther north.

"I think she'll hit Cahokia in the Clouds," Hachi said. "I would. It's a big city. She can do a lot of damage there."

"Cahokia's another couple days' march north up the river," Clyde said. "Me and Buster need a break. We'll stay in Memphis overnight."

Hachi frowned. "But Buster's a steam man. He can't get tired."

"Tell that to Buster," Clyde said.

The big steam man lay on his side like a big dog, head on the ground, arms and legs stretched out straight in front of him. Clyde had marched him hard to get this far this fast, and he was sound asleep.

"Overnight then, I guess," Hachi said. "Anybody ever been to Memphis before?"

The Chickasaw city stretched out on the bluffs beyond them. Like Standing Peachtree, Memphis had a few skyscrapers reaching up to ten stories tall, with a monorail snaking in and around them and across the wide Mississippi River. There was even a giant Ferris wheel, poking up among a scattering of long rectangular buildings in a park beside the river. But what dominated the skyline were the three pink marble pyramids the ancient Aegyptians had built long, long ago. They were step pyramids, a series of square terraces stacked on top of each other that got smaller and smaller as they went up, like a wedding cake, and they towered over everything else. Like the Houston Astral Dome and Cahokia in the Clouds, the Memphis pyramids were one of the Seven Wonders of the New World.

"*Memphis*," Señor X scoffed. "This isn't an old Aegyptian city. I've been to the *real* Memphis, in Aegypt, and the pyramids there don't look anything like these. Aegyptian pyramids are smooth. Triangular. Like the one the Septemberists use in their symbol."

Archie and Hachi shared a look. He still wore his Septemberist pin, with the pyramid eye inside a seven-pointed star, but when all this was over, he was done with the society for good.

"If it's not Aegyptian, what is it?" Gonzalo asked him.

"Atlan," Señor X said.

"Atlantis?" Archie asked.

"No. Atlan. Where the Azteks came from. The founding members of Lemuria. They buried a Mangleborn under those pyramids before moving south. Atlantis came later. "

Clyde shook his head. "I'm still not sure I believe any of this stuff about ancient civilizations."

Fergus nodded. "I felt the same way. Until I saw Atlantis Station."

"Even if it's not Aegyptian, it sounds brass," Gonzalo said.

"Want to see it?" Kitsune asked.

Gonzalo hesitated. "Yes," he said at last, and he took a deep breath and arranged himself like he was bracing to be run down by a mechanical bull. "Go."

Nothing happened—nothing the rest of them could see, at least. But a change came over Gonzalo. On the trip to Memphis he'd put on a white cowboy hat and tied a black blindfold over his eyes—it scared criminals to no end to be chased by a boy with a blindfold on, he told them—but he swept his head back and forth like he could see the city straight through it.

"Ain't that somethin'," he said.

"If you want, I could show you where we are all the time," Kitsune said.

"*Gracias, señorita.* But no. I'm used to the darkness. Unless you see fireflies. I would very much like to see a firefly."

Buster awoke with a start, startling them all.

"What is it, big guy?" Clyde asked. "You have a nightmare?"

"How can a steam man have a nightmare?" Hachi asked.

"The soul of a little dog got blasted into him," Archie told her.

Buster hopped to his feet, which in a ten-story-tall steam man was a scary thing. Everybody took a step back. Buster whistled once and looked around.

"He's got the scent of something," Clyde said. "He got this way when he smelled Archie in Houston. What is it, Buster?"

Buster whistle-barked again, and tore off toward the city.

"Whoa! Heel! Buster, heel!" Clyde yelled, but the big steam man with the soul of a dog kept chasing whatever it was he was after.

"I hope he's not after the monorail," Kitsune said, remembering their time in Don Francisco.

Gonzalo put his fingers in his mouth and whistled, and Alamo came galloping up. Gonzalo swung onto the steam-horse's back and pulled Clyde up with him. "Follow that steam man!" Gonzalo said. "*Ándale!*"

"Take *The Kraken!*" Clyde called back to the rest of them as they rode away. *The Kraken's* tentacles were already picking them up and pulling them back inside the submarine, and soon Martine had the submarine gliding up the Mississippi into town.

Clyde and Gonzalo found Buster bouncing around the outside of a warehouse on the outskirts of town, whistling and wagging his exhaust-pipe tail. Clyde still hadn't brought him to heel by the time the others caught up to them.

"Dang it, Buster! What's got into you?" Clyde called to the steam man. "He's usually much better behaved than this! Buster, sit. Sit!"

Buster finally thunked his big brass bottom down on the ground long enough for Clyde, Archie, and Hachi to climb inside. Clyde hurried up to the cockpit, followed by Archie and Hachi.

"Let's see what's got him all fired up," Clyde said. "Okay, Buster! Get to work!"

Buster hopped to his feet again, and Archie and Hachi held on to not fall over. Buster sniffed around the warehouse doors, then stood straight and leaned out over the roof of the one-story warehouse, peering inside through the cantilevered windows at the top. He spotted something and whistled happily, sticking one of his big brass hands straight through the glass to grab it. *Krissh!* His hand came out with a wiggling brass Tik Tok, and brought it up to his face to "lick" it.

He was an odd-looking Tik Tok, to be sure. He looked more like a human being made out of brass, and wore human clothes: brown leather pants, a white shirt, a long black jacket, and a brown cowboy hat.

"Okay, okay, Buster," the Tik Tok said, putting his hands up in surrender. "You got me." He petted Buster's head. "Hey, boy."

Archie recognized the Emartha Mark III Machine Man right away. "Jesse James!"

"Jesse James the outlaw?" Hachi asked.

"We met him back at Dodge City," Archie told her. "He's the one who made Mr. Rivets a FreeTok, and helped us pull Sings-In-The-Night from the blue amber where she was frozen."

"Blue amber?" Hachi asked.

"All right, Buster. Put him down already," Clyde told the steam man. "Buster, leave it!"

Buster put the Tik Tok outlaw down, and Clyde, Archie, and Hachi went outside to join the other Leaguers.

"Mr. Rivets," Jesse James said, greeting his fellow machine man. "Or have you ditched your factory name?"

"Mr. Rivets I was, and Mr. Rivets I shall ever be," the Dent family Tik Tok said. "But it is good to see you, Mr. James."

Gonzalo pulled Señor X from his holster and aimed him at the outlaw.

"Whoa, hold on," Archie told him. "Jesse James is a friend."

"Jesse James is wanted in five territories for Tik Tok rustling, train robbery—"

"Six," James said proudly. "We hit Sioux territory two weeks ago."

"—and *murder*," Gonzalo finished. Señor X hummed with aether. "Jesse James, by the authority of the Republic of Texas you are hereby under arrest."

Jesse James put up his hands. "Now hold on, lawman. The only meatbags we killed had it coming."

"Tell that to their families," Gonzalo said.

"Gonzalo, we have bigger problems to take care of," Clyde told him.

"Like that monster army that's headed this way?" Jesse James said.

"You've seen them? You know where they are?" Kitsune asked.

"I can tell you all about it—including where they're headed," Jesse James said. "But only for immunity from your Texas Ranger here."

"No deal," Gonzalo said.

"Gonzalo—"

"The law's the law, Archie," Gonzalo said. "He's probably got a warehouse full of stolen Tik Toks in there right now."

"As a matter of fact, I do," Jesse James said. "Want me to show 'em to you?"

Gonzalo waved Señor X at him, and Jesse James led them inside. The warehouse *was* full of Tik Toks. There were a few wind-up brass Emartha Machine Man Mark IIs like Mr. Rivets, and a few of the newer platinum, steam-driven Mark IVs like Archie, Fergus, and Hachi had fought in Atlantis Station. But the rest of the Tik Toks were a kind of machine man Archie had never seen before. They were big, industrial Tik Toks, with five thin caterpillar treads like tanks spaced every few feet, and rake-like scoops like pointy combs on their fronts. Their bodies were round brass tubs, and giant gears with interlocking chains stuck out their sides.

The only heads Archie could see on the things were small and flat, about midway up the front of their bodies, with long, wide eyes and small, thin mouths.

"Waquini cotton gin Tik Toks," Fergus said. "Saw one or two of these back on the farm in Carolina."

"*Slaves,*" said a small old black Afrikan woman who joined Jesse James. She wore a black wrap dress and shawl, and covered her short woolly gray hair with a red bandana with white flowers on it. She was joined by another Tik Tok, a Mark IV with his factory nameplate removed, just like Jesse James, marking him as one of James's FreeTok brethren. The Mark IV had remade his body some the way many of the FreeToks did, this one choosing to refit his face with a platinum guard that hung down from his chin like a metal beard. Like Jesse James, he too wore human clothing—a black suit, white shirt, and black bow tie.

"They're not slaves," Gonzalo said. "They're property."

The Mark IV pointed an oscillating rifle at Gonzalo. "Same thing," he said.

"You won't shoot me," Gonzalo said. "You're a Tik Tok. Your programming won't allow it."

"Uh, Gonzalo? That machine man'll shoot you dead, and that's a fact," Clyde told him. "He's a FreeTok. He's had all that stuff taken out of his programming. He can lie and cheat and steal and kill."

"Just like you," the FreeTok said.

"Ladies and gents, may I present my fellow compatriots and partners in crime," Jesse James said. "Ms. Harriet Tubman, meatbag, and Mr. John Brown, FreeTok. *Not* his factory name, of course."

"Young man, these Tik Toks *are* slaves," Tubman said. "They aren't free to choose their own path in life."

"Of course they're not," Gonzalo said. "They're machines. Machines don't choose anything."

"Mr. Picker, a word if you please," Jesse James said.

The nearest cotton gin Tik Tok's head spun around toward them on its round body and clicked into place.

"Yessir," Mr. Picker said.

"I told you, you don't have to call me sir," Jesse James told him.

"Yessir," Mr. Picker said.

"You see? He couldn't call me Jesse if he tried. He's been programmed to talk and act and think a certain way. But even so, this Tik Tok dreams. Don't you, Mr. Picker?"

"Yessir."

"What do you dream of doing, Mr. Picker?"

"Playing music, sir."

"Playing music?" Fergus asked.

"Yessir."

"Would you care to play for us now, Mr. Picker?"

"Oh, yessir," the big mobile cotton gin said.

Mr. Picker's machinery clanked and clicked and whirred, and he shuddered like he was about to mow down a row of cotton plants. Then, subtly, surprisingly, the machine's random clanking and bonking turned into . . . a symphony. A song emerged from the cacophony and rose above the din, a song Archie recognized: "Oh My Darling, Clementine," a popular vaudeville tune. It was magical—a machine that was designed to pick cotton playing music with its spiked cylinders and hooked bailers and comb teeth.

Mr. Picker played the entirety of the song, then shuddered still again. All around him, the other Waquini cotton gin Tik Toks rattled and bonked.

"What are they doing?" Gonzalo asked.

"They're clapping," John Brown said.

"Amazing," said Kitsune.

"Very colorful," Martine said. She was staring at the air above the cotton gin, as though she could still see the notes hanging there. *Maybe she can*, thought Archie.

The floor shuddered, and the warehouse was filled with a sound like a locomotive coming into a station. Pistons slowed, brakes squealed, and gray-black smoke poured from a hole in the middle of the warehouse's floor.

"All aboard!" Harriet Tubman cried, and the Tik Toks began to move.

"All aboard?" Clyde asked. "All aboard *what*?"

"The Underground Railroad," John Brown said.

Jesse James smiled. "Stole us some tunneling machines off some Paiute digger pirates last year, and we built ourselves a subterranean network for taking Tik Toks to freedom. Runs from Standing Peachtree clear all the way to Acadia, and as far west as Dodge City."

FreeTok porters swarmed up from the hole in the ground, welcoming the newly freed Tik Toks and helping load them onto the Underground Railroad.

"Hold it!" Gonzalo said. "Nobody's going anywhere!"

"Let 'em go, kid," Señor X said.

Gonzalo deflated. "What? But . . . Señor X, the law says they're property."

"The law's wrong, Gonzalo," Señor X told him. "Tik Toks may not look like you, but they're living, thinking beings like you. Six thousand years ago, the Lemurians almost destroyed their own civilization fighting each other over whether robots should be free. The same thing's going to happen here and now unless people start to think differently. People like you."

"But . . . I don't make the law, Señor. That's not my job. I just enforce it."

"Seems to me you gotta decide whether you *agree* with a law before you decide to enforce it," Señor X said.

The FreeTok porters went on loading the stolen Tik Toks onto the Underground Railroad, and Gonzalo lowered his raygun.

"Thank you, Brother Raygun," Harriet Tubman told Señor X, and she hurried off to help load the train.

"You're all right for a meatbag," Jesse James told Gonzalo. "Just like your friends. Mr. Rivets, care to join us?"

"Join you, sir?"

"We can always use another good machine man on the railroad."

Mr. Rivets was taken aback. "I'm . . . I'm flattered, sir. But my place is with Archie."

Archie felt pride swell up in him again at Mr. Rivets's loyalty, even when he had the choice to live a different life.

Jesse James shook his head. "Well, being free means being free to make the wrong choices too, I suppose." He grinned. "First our freedom—then the *vote*." Jesse James tipped his hat. "Now, if you'll excuse me, we've got to clear this lot out to make room for tonight."

"Why? What's tonight?" Archie asked.

"What's tonight? Just the opening of the Memphis Centennial Exposition!"

Archie looked around at the other Leaguers, confused.

"You'll recall your studies, Master Archie," Mr. Rivets said. "This is the hundred-year anniversary of the founding of the United Nations. The centennial is being celebrated in a number of cities across the country."

"Rides, games, entertainment, exhibit halls—and a million people and their Tik Toks," Jesse James said. "You know I do like an audience."

"You intend to rob the Centennial Exposition," Gonzalo said coldly.

"That I do, Ranger," Jesse James said. "*If* I can beat that monster army to it. It's headed this way."

14

Buster stepped over the low concrete wall around the Memphis Centennial Exposition onto a wide lawn filled with picnickers. They snatched up their blankets and baskets and food and scrambled out of the way as he churned across the yard toward one of the wide pedestrian pathways.

"We've got to find whoever's in charge of this thing and tell them to send everybody home," Clyde said. He sat in the pilot's seat, carefully steering Buster so he didn't step on anybody.

Archie stood to Clyde's side, and Martine examined maps at the navigator's station. Hachi was in the drummer's chair high above Clyde, scanning the fairgrounds through Buster's big glass window eyes.

"There," Hachi said. She pointed at a big statue of Hiawatha, the man who founded the Iroquois Confederacy and laid the foundation for the United Nations. It stood at the center of the exhibition above a wide, round bandstand.

"Buster, give me magnification," Clyde said.

Click-click-click. Magnifying lenses fell into place over Buster's right eye, and they could see the statue of Hiawatha closer and closer each time. With the final click it was like they were standing right over the bandstand, where Chickasaw men and women were busy setting up chairs and hanging blue bunting everywhere. Pacing around in between them was a gaunt Chickasaw man with dark, bushy hair practicing a speech he was reading from a piece of paper. He wore a black tuxedo with five silver armbands high up on his left sleeve and a red sash over his shoulder. A gray eagle feather stuck up from a red ribbon around his tall black top hat.

"Guess it's like Mrs. DeMarcus used to say," Clyde said. " 'You want to find the most important man in the room, you look for the tallest hat.' "

The Centennial Exposition was laid out in a spiral shape popular among the Chickasaw. A curling paved road spiraled out from the statue of Hiawatha at the center, passing square, pyramid-roofed Chickasaw buildings, Iroquois-style longhouses, and columned Yankee mansions. Along the outside edges of the spiral stood the three giant step pyramids that dominated the Memphis skyline.

"It's a Fibonacci sequence," Martine said. She traced a spiral in the air with her finger. "Like a fern."

"A what?" Hachi asked.

"The path is a golden spiral created by plotting points according to a mathematical sequence. Each distance is the sum of the previous two distances," Martine explained. "Someone laid out the Memphis Centennial Exhibition mathematically."

Archie and Hachi shrugged their shoulders. They didn't understand at all. Not that it mattered.

The spiral path didn't matter to Clyde either. He stepped right over it, working his way around the exhibit halls, food stalls, and carnival rides as he headed straight for the bandstand at the center. The passengers on a Ferris wheel as tall as Buster stood in their seats and pointed at him as the giant steam man passed, and people all along the paths and in line for the exhibitions stopped and marveled at him.

And there were so *many* people. Archie had never seen a million people together in one place before. There were Chickasaw and Cherokee, Muskogee and Seminoles, Pawnee and Shawnee and Illini. There were Yankees too, both black and white, and even a few Mestizos from Texas. Men, women, and children filled the walkways and the lawns, rowed along the park's man-made lakes in gondolas, soared above the fair in hot air balloons. There were lines of people waiting to get into the Arts Pavilion and the Horticultural Hall, the Steam Exhibition and the Penny Arcade, the Raycannon Stand and the Clockwork Midway. And each of the United Nations' ten tribes and territories had exhibit halls of their own, including one for the Yankees, who belonged to every territory, and to none.

"If Moffett attacks this place before we can get all these people out of here, we're in a heap of trouble," Clyde said. "And that's a fact."

Clyde ran Buster right up the bandstand and leaned him over. Everyone stopped working and gawked at him.

"You have to call off the exhibition and send everybody

home!" he told them through Buster's speaking trumpet, magnifying his voice outside. "They're all in danger!"

"What?" the man in the top hat said. "Who *are* you?"

"Outside," Hachi said.

Clyde lowered Buster's head so they could climb out the mouth, and Archie called down for the rest of the League to follow them. Mr. Rivets stayed inside, but Gonzalo had his steamhorse lowered down with them. Clyde told Buster to sit when they were all on the bandstand, and the giant steam man thunked down onto the circular lawn, his tailpipe wagging.

"What in the name of Hiawatha . . . ?" the man in the top hat said.

"We're official representatives of the United Nations," Clyde lied. Archie supposed it was easier to explain than telling them they were a league of superheroes, and Buster did, after all, still have all the markings of a United Nations Steam Man. "Who might you be?"

The Chickasaw man in the top hat stood straighter. "Winchester Colbert. Chief of the Chickasaw."

Clyde shook his hand. "Nice to meet you, Chief," he said, sliding so easily into the leader role he'd been born for. "I'm real sorry to tell you, but you have to close down the Centennial Exhibition and send everybody home."

Colbert was incredulous. "What? Send a million people home? Why should I?"

"There's an army marching this way," Clyde told him.

"An army? What army? Louisiana? Wichita? Pawnee? Not the Sioux—"

"An army of *monsters*," Clyde told him. "Led by a monster

woman named Philomena Moffett. If you don't send everybody home, she'll kill 'em all."

Colbert looked around at the workers on the bandstand. "An army of *monsters*?" He laughed. "All right, young man. You and your little friends have had your fun. I don't know where you got that steam man, but I suggest you get back in it and go back home to your parents right now."

Archie slumped. Of course no one was going to take them seriously. He and the others had fought so many Mangleborn and Manglespawn that there was no question it was all real, and the fact that they were kids had nothing to do with whether they were qualified to be Leaguers or not. But nobody else was going to see that. To everybody else they were just a bunch of kids talking nonsense.

"Let me at him," Hachi growled, but Archie held her back.

"Your Honor," Clyde tried again, but he never got to finish. A woman's scream split the air, and a mob of fairgoers streamed out the doors of the Penny Arcade, chased by Manglespawn.

"The League of Seven!" crowed an all-too-familiar voice, and they spun. Philomena Moffett stood atop the statue of Hiawatha, the octopus-like tentacles that writhed beneath her skirts wrapped around the Iroquois hero's face.

In her hands, she held the Dragon Lantern.

Moffett laughed. "The League of Seven, together again for the first time!" Moffett said, her voice booming. Archie knew what she could do with that voice. If she wanted to, Moffett could bring every one of the exhibition's buildings down with a scream.

Winchester Colbert staggered back. "Who—? What—?"

"Allow me to introduce the League of Seven to the league I created," Moffett said. "The *Shadow* League!"

There were more screams, and crowds streamed out of the Steam Exhibition, the Art Pavilion, the Clockwork Midway, the Raycannon Stand, and the Horticultural Hall, more Manglespawn at their heels. On the rooftops of the buildings appeared a succession of horrors: a walking junk pile; a hulking piece of living crystal; a man-sized locust; a thing that was more spider than man; a coiling, twisting mass of vines; and a blinding white blur of a man engulfed in purple flames.

"These would be the monsters Moffett made at Alcatraz, I take it?" Fergus asked, lektricity already crackling around his clenched fists.

Archie nodded. "She made them with the Dragon Lantern. They're all criminals."

"They are *infamous* criminals," Moffett told them. "The worst of the worst. Sakuruta, the Pawnee kidnapper, now a spider man. Honda Nobuharu, the Ametokai Strangler, now a suffocating kudzu vine that can't be killed. Naalnish, the Navajo bank robber, now a human locust. Hector Villarreal, the serial killer from New Spain, a magnet so powerful all metal becomes a part of him. Leaning Oak, the Shikaakwa gangster, now made of solid, indestructible crystal. And William Tecumseh Sherman, the Yankee arsonist, whose body burns with never-ending flames. And me, of course. But you know what I can do."

"Yeah," said Archie. "We know you, Philomena Moffett. And we're going to stop you."

"Now see here!" Winchester Colbert warned Moffett.

Moffett ignored him. "You cannot hope to stop us," she told Archie. "Thanks to the Dragon Lantern, we seven have known pain and suffering in ways no one else has. And now we intend to visit that pain and suffering on the United Nations."

She was wrong, Archie thought. Each member of the League of Seven had suffered in some way too: alienation, loss, abandonment, blindness, loneliness, physical injury. And every day, every minute, Archie dealt with the guilt of being the cause of so much death. They were all broken, in a way. But it was the broken parts of them that made them stronger. That made them superheroes.

"We've known plenty of pain and suffering," Hachi told her.

"Prepare to know more," Moffett said. "Shadow League—attack!"

Moffett's monsters leaped off their rooftops into the crowds below or disappeared inside the buildings they stood on, and the screams began again.

"We need a plan!" Clyde said. "Archie, you and Kitsune—" he began, but the other Leaguers were already running off in different directions. "Wait!" Clyde called. No one did. In moments, only he and Archie still stood on the bandstand.

"I'll take care of Moffett!" Archie told him. "You go after that big magnetic man!"

"We should be working together!" Clyde said.

Archie put his arms around the base of the Hiawatha statue and pulled. *Crack!* The stone pedestal broke off, and Archie stepped back with the giant statue—and Moffett on top of it—in his hands.

"I got this! Go!" Archie said.

Clyde climbed in Buster as Archie swung the statue like a hammer. *Wham!* Grass and dirt went flying as Hiawatha slammed into the ground.

"Great Chicksah!" Colbert said, falling back on the bandstand. "How did you—how did you do that?"

"Just stay back," Archie said. "I think I got her, but—"

WOMWOMWOMWOMWOM! Moffett's sonic scream knocked Archie head over heels into the broken pedestal, and he crashed through it in an explosion of dust and stone. When she ran out of breath he stood and hurled a chunk of debris at her before she could scream again. Moffett jumped behind the downed statue. Archie picked it up and held it over his head, meaning to smash her with it again.

WOMWOMWOMWOMWOM! Moffett hit Archie with her scream and he dropped the statue. THOOM! It landed on top of him, driving him through the wooden floor of the stage and destroying half the bandstand. He pushed the statue off him and stood, expecting another blast from Moffett, but she was gone.

"Where'd she go?" he asked Colbert.

The Chickasaw chief sat shaking in the wreckage of the stage, staring at Archie like he was a nightmare come to life. Perhaps he was.

"Where'd she go?" he asked again.

Colbert shook his head slowly. He didn't know. Archie looked around the fair and saw his friends battling Moffett's Shadow League. They looked like they were doing about as well as he was. Gonzalo rode in circles around the burning man, but his raygun didn't seem to be doing any damage to him. Hachi was caught up in the curling kudzu vines of the Ametokai Strangler. Clyde and Buster were trading body blows with Hector Villarreal, but the magnetic man kept getting bigger and bigger as they plowed through the exhibit halls.

Fergus was shooting lightning at the spider man, who skittered away up the side of the Horticultural Hall. Outside the Clockwork Midway, Kitsune had the locust man hopping in circles to some illusion, but he kept catching fairgoers. There were still too many people around, even with the stampede for the exit.

And no Moffett anywhere.

Archie picked up the statue of Hiawatha to take with him as a club. If he couldn't find Moffett, at least he could help one of the others. But the sun was going down. Soon they wouldn't be able to see any of the Shadow Leaguers to fight, except of course for the one who glowed white-hot like the sun.

"Gaslights!" Archie told the Chickasaw chief.

Colbert stared blankly at the horror show his Centennial Exposition had become. Archie groaned. He'd forgotten how paralyzing it was for most people when they first saw the primeval horrors that lived just beyond their normal lives. Archie tossed aside the statue of Hiawatha and helped Winchester Colbert to his feet.

"Listen to me," Archie said. "I need you to turn on the gaslights. Can you do that? If you don't we won't be able to see to stop them. Chief!"

Colbert shook himself. He wasn't all there—he might never be all there again—but he was back enough to focus hazily on Archie.

"Yes," he said. "Yes. The lights." He staggered through the remains of the bandstand, looking for something. "Yes. The lights."

He found a metal box with a big-handled switch on top and righted it. "The lights," he said.

Archie frowned. What kind of gaslights had a switch like that to turn them on? And why was it on the bandstand?

Colbert threw the switch—*ka-chung*—and lights flickered on across the park. Streetlights. Interior lights. Lights on strings hung between the buildings. Lines of lights outlining the edges of every exhibition hall and pyramid. Not gaslights, Archie realized with horror.

Lektric lights.

Archie threw himself at the box and flipped the switch back. Nothing happened. Archie flipped it again and again, trying to kill the lektric lights, but they wouldn't turn off.

"No no no no no!" Archie said.

"Ladies and gentlemen, the wonder of our age," Colbert said, giving the speech he'd been practicing to some imaginary crowd, "*the lektric light.*"

"This is so clinker," Archie said. He stood and backed away. "Do you have any idea what you've done?"

The ground shook. The lektric lights flickered. The pyramids crumbled.

Beneath their feet, a Mangleborn was stirring.

15

Fergus was the first one back.

"Shut it down!" he cried. "You've got to shut the blinking thing down!"

"I tried!" Archie told him. He flipped the switch back and forth to show him. "See? It's not working anymore!"

Fergus tried the switch himself as the others ran up.

"Moffett called her Shadow League away when the lights came on," Clyde said through Buster's speaking trumpet.

The ground shook again as the Mangleborn beneath them stirred, strengthened by the surge of lektricity.

"We have to get those lights turned off *now*," said Hachi.

Fergus cast the switchbox aside. "This dingus is just for the muckety-muck ceremony." He turned to Winchester Colbert. "Where's the generator?"

"Powered by a . . ." The chief paused, trying to remember his speech. "Powered by a self-exciting, lektromagnetic dynamo built by the Chickasaw tribe's very own inventor extraordinaire, Nashoba Farmer."

"Yes, that's all fine and good," Fergus said, "but where *is* it?"

"It doesn't matter," Señor X told them. "I was here the last time this one was put down. The lektricity might strengthen it, but it's not getting up again."

The ground rumbled, knocking a pillar loose from one of the exhibition halls.

"You sure about that?" Kitsune asked.

"Yeah," Señor X said. "Not unless somebody happened to arrange all these lektrified buildings mathematically using a Fibonacci sequence."

Hachi and Archie looked at each other, wide-eyed.

"We're in trouble," said Hachi.

The earth trembled again, and the Yankee Exhibition Hall exploded. *Boom!* When the dust cleared, they saw a giant webbed claw hooked on the ground. *Boom!* The Clockwork Midway exploded, and another webbed claw reached into the sky.

"The buildings *are* situated in a Fibonacci spiral," Martine said quietly. "I noted the arrangement as we arrived."

"Yeeeeeah," Señor X said. "Then we're in trouble."

"Crivens! This Nashoba Farmer guy who installed the lights must have been a madman!" Fergus said.

"Isn't *everybody* who messes with lektricity a madman?" Hachi shot back at him.

"Well, now that you mention it . . . ," Fergus said.

They all flinched as the step pyramids around the edges of the Centennial Exhibition crumbled. The ground beneath them began to rumble and rise, and Clyde scooped them all up in Buster's hands and stepped back.

The gigantic thing that pulled itself from under the earth had a greenish gray head like a crocodile, and was covered all over with bony spikes. Its teeth were jagged and sharp, and not confined to its mouth—every joint on its body had another mouth full of barbed teeth on it.

"Mr. Rivets says he's never seen this one before in any book," Clyde told them. "Señor X?"

"Its name is Cipactli," he told them. "The Lemurian League took him down more than six millennia ago, but not before it ate Tezcatlipoca's foot."

Archie remembered Tezcatlipoca from his vision—he was the Lemurian League's shadow. The other-Archie.

"Great," said Archie.

Clyde set them all on the ground. "So how do we beat him?" he asked.

"We have to stretch him out. Pull him apart at the mouths," Señor X said. "And *don't* let him get to the water!"

Cipactli had pulled itself up from the ground and was slithering off toward the Mississippi River, its scaly hind frog legs pushing it through the ruins of the Centennial Exhibition.

"Archie!" Clyde cried.

Archie grabbed the Mangleborn's spiked crocodile tail as it swung by them and dug in his feet. Cipactli dragged him along, carving out a swishing, Archie-sized trench, until Archie's feet caught the foundation of the wrecked Art Pavilion. Archie strained against the foundation, straightening his legs and digging his fingers into the Mangleborn's tail until he'd stopped the thing in its tracks.

"Hold on!" Clyde called. Buster picked up the fallen statue of Hiawatha and rammed it through Cipactli's tail. The Mangleborn roared and thrashed, but it was pinned to the spot.

Archie let go and ran for one of Cipactli's frog legs. "Clyde! Grab the other side!" he yelled.

The webbed, clawed frog leg was slimy and smelled like dead fish, but Archie found a place to hold on and pulled. So did Clyde. Cipactli *flumped* to the ground, but its front legs still clawed the ground and its main mouth bit into an empty concert hall. Most of the million or so fairgoers, thankfully, had long since run screaming into the night.

"We need help!" Clyde called.

"And where am I supposed to get a Mangleborn Stretcher-Outer?" Fergus asked.

Hachi sprinted away like she had a plan. Hachi always had a plan. "You're the maker," she called over her shoulder. "*Make one!*"

"'Make one,' she says," Fergus muttered. "Like I can just throw together a Mangleborn Stretcher-Outer out of . . ." His eyes fell on the Exhibition's giant Ferris wheel. "Well gag my hopper. Gonzalo, give a mate a lift?"

Archie played tug-of-war with Clyde as the other Leaguers scattered. He hoped they had some idea how to pull the rest of the Mangleborn apart, and soon. The Archie-sized mouth on Cipactli's ankle snapped at him hungrily, and the building-sized mouth on its head turned to join it. *Chomp!* Archie was just out of reach. Whoever got the front claws wouldn't be so lucky.

"Archie! Take one of the front claws!" Hachi said. She ran up behind him, her flying circus carrying a steel cable beside her. The end of the cable had a twisted piece of metal tied to it. Hachi's clockwork toys flew right for the mouth on the monster's ankle. It snapped up the metal anchor hungrily, swallowing the end of the steel cable with it.

"Hook, line, and sinker," Hachi said. "I've got this one!" she yelled as she ran off.

Archie had no idea what she'd tied the other end to, but he trusted Hachi to know what she was doing.

On the other side of Cipactli, Gonzalo rode up on Alamo and blasted a hole in the back of the mouth at the Mangleborn's other ankle with Señor X. Cipactli roared and thrashed, knocking Archie to the ground as he tried to grab hold of one of its front claws. Before Archie was even on his feet again, Gonzalo was off his horse and hog-tying the other back leg through the hole he'd shot in it. "Me and Fergus got this one, *amigo!*" he told Clyde, and he hopped back on Alamo and spurred him away.

"That's the legs and tail," Clyde called, taking up a position on the other front paw across from Archie. "But we still need the head! Where's Martine?"

POOM. A puff of smoke rose on the river, and Archie heard something whistling toward them in the night sky. *THUNK!* A giant harpoon buried itself in Cipactli's head and drew tight.

"Right on time," Archie muttered. Cipactli's claw was beating him into the ground like a steamhammer.

Hachi's steel cable went tight. Across the fairgrounds, Archie heard the music of the Ferris wheel start to play, and the steel cable Gonzalo had put in went tight.

"All right, everybody," Clyde boomed. "*PULL!*"

Archie punched the thrashing claw he held, and it went still for a moment. That was all he needed. He planted his heels in the Chickasaw dirt and pulled. Across from him, Buster's exhaust pipe wagged and smoked as Clyde pulled with every ounce of pressure in the steam man's boiler.

"Make a wish!" Clyde called to Archie.

CRACK! The front legs came off at the shoulders, breaking at the man-sized jaws there, and Archie and Clyde fell back into the grass. *CRACK!* The mouths at Cipactli's hips split, and its flopping frog legs zipped away on steel cables. *CRACK!* The Mangleborn's head and tail ripped off its body, tearing at the mouths on its neck and butt.

Archie waited for the Mangleborn to start fighting again, but it was dead. No—not dead. Just pulled apart. That's why the Lemurian League had buried it in different places under giant pyramids—so it couldn't come back together again.

"We did it," Clyde said. Buster stood over the drawn and quartered Mangleborn, staring down at their handiwork. "We actually did it!"

"Well of course we did," Fergus said. He rode up with Gonzalo on the back of Alamo.

Hachi came running from the other side. "Did it work?"

"I felt *The Kraken's* harpoon go slack," Martine said, joining them. "There was a 63.9 percent probability that the harpoon had dislodged before removing the Deep One's head." She tilted her head and stared at Cipactli's lifeless eyes. "This is improbable."

Fergus raised a finger. "But not impossible."

"How'd you do it?" Archie asked Fergus.

"He used the Ferris wheel," Gonzalo said. "It was genius."

"Had to tinker with it," Fergus bragged. "Reinforce it a wee bit, and up the pounds per square inch we were getting out of the engine. But then I just ran that steel cable around it like a winch. After the ranger here attached the other end for me. What I want to know is how you did yours," he asked Hachi.

"Streetcar," Hachi said. "They run right by the exhibition grounds."

"Since when do you know how to drive a streetcar?" Archie asked.

"I've had a little practice," Hachi said.

"We're gonna have to get some help burying this guy back in the ground," Clyde said through Buster's loudspeakers. "But everybody should be safe for now."

"Do you think so, steam man?" Philomena Moffett asked.

Moffett clung to the top of the upturned statue of Hiawatha still stuck in Cipactli's tail. Archie ran at her, but she was faster.

WOMWOMWOMWOMWOM!

Archie planted his feet and stood his ground against the sonic waves. Behind him, Clyde threw Buster's arms around the others to protect them from the blast.

"Ah ah ah," Moffett said when she'd stopped screaming. "I may not be able to hurt you, Archie, but I can shake that steam man to pieces and do worse to your little friends."

Buster's boiler growled at her.

"Then what now?" Archie asked.

"Now you leave me alone," Moffett told him.

Clyde laughed. "Yeah, right, lady."

"Oh, you will," Moffett purred. "You know the lektric dynamo that woke your playmate there? I have it."

They had been so busy dealing with the Mangleborn, none of them had realized the lektric lights had gone out all over the exhibition grounds. With that lektric dynamo, Moffett could do the only thing worse than turning half the continent into Manglespawn. She could raise Mangleborn.

"What have you done with it?" Archie demanded. "Where is it?"

Moffett smiled. "That's for you to find out. I've divided my Shadow League into pairs and sent them to the four winds. One pair has the dynamo. But which one?"

"Seven cannot be divided into four pairs," Martine pointed out. "Unless you have cut one of them in half."

Everyone looked back at her, but she didn't seem to notice.

"The Dragon Lantern and I make a good pair, don't you think?" Moffett asked, holding it up with one of her tentacles.

"You've got the dynamo," Hachi said. "You have to. You'd never give up a weapon like that."

"Do I?" Moffett asked. She shrugged. "Then follow me, and take the chance that one of the others won't release a Mangleborn on some unsuspecting city. The choice is yours."

Moffett had barely finished when she screamed again. Clyde threw Buster's arms around the others, and Archie closed his eyes against the sonic waves.

When the last of the reverberations died away and Archie opened his eyes, Moffett was gone.

Kitsune hopped up on Buster's arm. "It's a trick. It has to be. A good one too."

"Given what I know about Philomena Moffett," Martine said, "there is a 92.5 percent chance she will keep the dynamo and use it herself."

Clyde and Mr. Rivets climbed out of Buster's mouth. "Yeah, but what about that other seven and a half percent?" Clyde asked. "We can't afford to take that chance."

Hachi threw a dagger into the hide of Cipactli. "So what do we do?"

"We split up," Fergus said. "We have to."

"But we just formed up this posse," Gonzalo said.

"And we're so good together!" Archie said. "We just took down a Mangleborn in minutes!"

"I don't see any other way," Clyde said. "We split up. She said she's sent her League to the four winds. Hachi, you and Martine go south through the Gulf on Martine's submarine. Me and Fergus'll go west in Buster. Gonzalo and Kitsune, you go north."

"We won't cover near as much ground on Alamo as you two'll cover in *The Kraken* and Buster," Gonzalo pointed out.

"*The Kraken* has an airship," Martine told them. "A small one. But big enough for the two of us," she told Hachi. "We will take the airship south, and Gonzalo and Kitsune can ride *The Kraken* north."

"And who's going to pilot it?" Kitsune asked.

"*The Kraken* can pilot herself up the Mississippi River," Martine said.

That was news to everyone else, but Martine never seemed to lie or make jokes, so Archie figured it must be true.

"And what about me?" Archie asked, though he already knew the answer.

"You go after Moffett. Somebody has to," Clyde said, "and you're the only one of us who can stand up to her on your own. Heck, you're the only one who can stand up to *anything* on your own."

"How do you know she's the one going east?" Fergus asked.

"Because it's always been east for her," Hachi said. "Ever since she got the Dragon Lantern. She wants only one thing in this world: revenge. And she's not going to do anything that would slow her down. Trust me. I know."

"Then it's settled. Archie will head up east after Moffett and her monster army," Clyde said.

"I don't like it," Hachi said.

"What part?"

"The part about Archie being on his own," Hachi said.

Archie looked away in embarrassment.

"I'm sorry, Archie. But you know why it's not good for you to be alone. I think everybody here does."

"I do not understand," Martine said.

"When he gets mad, he loses control, and when he loses control, he hurts people," Hachi told her.

"Not all the time!" Archie said.

"Only, you know, when you knocked me into a rock wall and attacked me and Fergus with a big metal pole," Hachi said.

"I had just found out I wasn't human! That my parents weren't really my parents! I was dealing with a lot of stuff!"

"Or the time you went crazy and started punching the Moving City of Cheyenne?" Clyde asked.

"And zoned out inside the Hippocamp?" Señor X said.

"The Mangleborn got inside my head!"

"Or the time you destroyed half of Alcatraz and let Moffett kill Sings-In-The-Night," Kitsune said.

"That was—I had Moffett *and* a Mangleborn messing with me that time," Archie said quietly. Watching Moffett kill Sings-In-The-Night, not being able to stop it from happening, was his biggest regret in life, after how he'd been born. It was an image that would haunt him to his dying day—whenever that was.

"I'm not going to get mad and lose control again," Archie said, trying to sound calm. "I don't do that anymore."

"Right," said Señor X from Gonzalo's holster. "And I've given up shooting people."

"I want to go back to the part about you not being human," Gonzalo said.

"*I've got a handle on it!*" Archie yelled.

Kitsune took a step back, and Gonzalo put a hand to his raygun.

Archie closed his eyes. "I've got a handle on it," he said more calmly.

"This is exactly what I'm talking about," Hachi said. "You're an overheated boiler when you're *not* fighting monsters."

"I shall go with him," Mr. Rivets said. "Master Archie has been in my care since shortly after he was born. I'm sure I can manage him."

Archie burned inside. *Manage him? He was twelve years old! He didn't need a babysitter.*

"I still don't like it," Hachi said. She took a deep breath. "But I don't see as we have any other choice."

"Okay then," Clyde said. "Everybody knows what they have

to do. Find your pair of Shadow Leaguers and take 'em down, dynamo or no dynamo."

"Moffett's got that lektric dynamo, I just know it," Hachi muttered.

"How are we going to know when and where to meet back up?" Gonzalo asked.

"We can just talk to each other on the shells," Martine said.

Everyone looked at her again. "The shells?" Fergus asked.

"I told you about them when I gave them to you," Martine said. She tilted her head. "Unless I only imagined we had that conversation. I sometimes do that."

"I think this is one you only imagined," said Clyde.

"I wondered why nobody was using them but me," Martine said. She fished in her pouch and brought out a handful of tiny seashells.

Fergus's tattoos rearranged themselves as he cautiously stuck one in his ear.

"What do we do with these, put them to our ears and listen to the ocean?" Kitsune said.

"No. You touch your finger to it and talk, like this," Martine said, "and everyone else can hear you."

"Gah!" Fergus said, pulling his out quickly. "It sounded like you were inside my head!"

The others put the shells in their ears and tried it. Archie and Hachi shared a frightened look—it was very much like hearing a Mangleborn inside your head.

"How does it work? How do you even power something this small?" Fergus said. He pushed his around in his palm, examining it with a magnifying glass from his sporran.

"Aether," Martine said.

"Right," Fergus said. "Because you understand Mangleborn math."

"What's the range on these?" Clyde asked.

"There is no limit," Martine told them. "At least not that I have discovered."

"Okay then," Clyde said. "So now we can stay in touch. We'll let each other know when we're finished, and pick a place to meet up after that. Everybody good?"

There were nods all round.

"Then let's do it," Clyde said. "Like Mrs. DeMarcus says, 'There's no better time than the present.' We can't let another Mangleborn get free."

Hachi pulled Fergus aside before the tinker joined Clyde in the giant steam man. Archie thought it was so they could say good-bye in private, maybe even kiss, but whatever Hachi said to Fergus made him mad. He looked over his shoulder at Archie, and Archie quickly looked away. He didn't want them to know he'd been spying.

"Come, Master Archie," Mr. Rivets said. "I have an idea how we can pursue Mrs. Moffett sub rosa, as it were."

16

A nervous young Septemberist agent met Gonzalo and Kitsune at the docks by the Clark Street Bridge in Shikaakwa. Martine's submarine had brought them up the Mississippi River, across the ancient Shikaakwa Portage Canal, and up the Shikaakwa River in just a few days, but Moffett's Shadow Leaguers had apparently already beaten them to the city. Shikaakwans were piling into boats with whatever they could carry and pushing away downriver.

"Thank goodness you're here!" the Septemberist said. He was a young, athletic Yankee in a gray suit and tie. "They're running roughshod over the whole city. Two of them. Monsters. Er, Manglespawn. Half the buildings in downtown have up and left the Loop and run north across the river or south to Hide

Park, where they always go whenever there's trouble. Everybody who can't afford to pack up shop and move is panicking."

Gonzalo walked on, Alamo at his heels, but the Septemberist stood by the submarine, waiting for more people to come out.

"It's—it's just you? Where are the others? I thought the whole League was coming!" the young Septemberist said. He couldn't see Kitsune, though she walked along right beside Gonzalo. They had both agreed she should make herself invisible until they figured out what they were up against.

"One riot, one Ranger," Gonzalo told him. "Everything's going to be fine. First things first: Thirty days hath September."

"Oh. Oh yes!" the Septemberist said. "Um, seven heroes we remember!"

Gonzalo nodded. "What's your name?"

"Oh. Albert Spalding! I—I play lacrosse for the Shikaakwa Cubs."

Gonzalo turned his blindfolded eyes toward Spalding. "Sorry. I don't watch lacrosse."

"Right. No," Spalding said. "It's okay. I—I just took over for the Septemberist agent who'd been here before. Something about a bug? On the back of his neck?"

"Let's just focus on the here and now," Gonzalo told him. More Illini people ran past, trying to escape to the lake. "What's that rumbling?" Gonzalo asked. He could feel it beneath his feet, like a slow, steady earthquake.

"It's the buildings," Señor X told him. "Gonzalo, the buildings—*they're moving.*"

Señor X and Kitsune watched as a hardware store trundled across the Clark Street Bridge, heading north. The entire building was raised up off the ground by five or six feet, and rode upon heavy steel rails. Black smoke poured from its chimney as its thundering steam engine drove it away from downtown.

The hardware store was followed by a towering, seven-story hotel called the Palmer House, also making its way north. A hotel guest watched them out the window of her third-story window.

"*Yare yare,*" Kitsune muttered.

"Who—who said that?" Spalding said, looking around for the voices of Señor X and Kitsune.

"My horse," Gonzalo told him.

"Howdy," Alamo said.

Albert Spalding was speechless.

"Why are the buildings moving?" Gonzalo asked.

"They uh, they move all the time. Shikaakwa's just about the same level as Lake Michigan, so water doesn't drain away. The streets were always turning to muck, so they lifted all the buildings up with hydraulics to put in sewage pipes. Turns out everybody liked being able to raise and lower their buildings, so they left the hydraulics. Then people wanted to move their houses from neighborhood to neighborhood, so they built rails all over. The whole city's on a raised grid. Any building can move anywhere else in the city any time it wants to—as long as there's room, and they've got the money to move."

A Cathay restaurant chugged by, headed west. Diners sat at tables eating fried rice and watching the city roll by.

"Well, if that don't beat all," Alamo said.

A powerful gust of wind hit Gonzalo in the face, spinning him around. He tried to steady himself, but the wind changed direction and knocked him sideways, almost like it was deliberately messing with him. He held his hat and stood his ground. Beside him, the wind pushed Kitsune into Alamo.

"Strong wind," Gonzalo said. "That from all the buildings moving around?"

"Er, no. That's just regular old Shikaakwa," Spalding said. "They don't call us the Windy City for nothing. Plays havoc with long balls on the lacrosse field."

"It's more than that," Señor X said. "G-man, I've been here before. A long, long time ago. That wind? It's a remnant of an air elemental Mangleborn the Atlantean League defeated. Wuchowsen. The Wind Eagle. They couldn't kill it, of course, but they could disperse it. Scatter it. It's still here, still alive, still mean, but just . . . broken up."

"And who—who was that?" Spalding asked.

"My raygun," Gonzalo said.

Spalding looked more confused than ever.

"Gonzalo, if those Shadow Leaguers *did* bring the lektric dynamo here, they could put Wuchowsen together again," Señor X told him. "They do that, and all these buildings are going to be doing a lot more moving, just not in any direction they want to go."

"All right," Gonzalo said. "Where are they?"

Ka-*THOOM*. A boiler exploded somewhere just south of them, and over the moving rooftops Kitsune and Spalding saw the twenty-story Sears and Roe Buck Building rock and tilt sideways.

"There, I think," said Señor X.

Gonzalo mounted Alamo, and Kitsune hopped up behind him. "Tell people to stay out of the way!" he told Spalding. "Giddyup!"

- 153 -

Alamo dodged a fleeing grocery store, a flower shop, and a saloon, all of which were steaming as quickly as they could away from downtown. Drinkers hung off the saloon, laughing and singing, and more Shikaakwans hopped on board as it passed. The steamhorse pulled to a stop at the edge of Brant Park, across the street from the leaning Sears and Roe Buck Building. People crowded the lobby and leaned out the windows, looking for some way to escape. The skyscraper had been knocked off its tracks by a gleaming crystal man with a lamppost in his hands.

"Leaning Oak," Señor X said.

"Arrested in 1862 for gambling, graft, extortion, and murder," Gonzalo said.

"And turned into a crystalline monster in 1876 by Philomena Moffett," Kitsune said.

Leaning Oak still had a human-shaped body, but it was entirely clear crystal, like ice, or diamond. His shoulders were big and hunched, and out of his back grew spiky crystal shards, like the floor of a diamond mine. Señor X described him to Gonzalo.

"This city is mine, ya hear me? Mine!" Leaning Oak roared.

ZaPOW! Gonzalo shot the lamppost out of Leaning Oak's hands.

"Not if I have anything to say about it," Gonzalo told him.

Leaning Oak picked up a steambuggy. "You don't!" he yelled, hurling it at Gonzalo.

Alamo galloped out of the way.

"Keep him busy while I get the rest of the people out of that building!" Kitsune whispered, and she was gone.

"Not a problem," Gonzalo said. He took aim and shot the crystal man right in the chest.

Ka-POW! Señor X's yellow beam hit Leaning Oak and refracted, like light hitting a prism. *Shing! Shing-shing-shing-shing!* Yellow beams shot out from him in all directions, taking out trees, Sears and Roe Buck windows, and a pneumatic post office tube. *Ka-POW!* One of the beams shot back and hit Alamo, and the steamhorse reared back and fell.

"Alamo! Alamo, are you all right?" Gonzalo asked.

"I'll be okay, boss," Alamo said. The steamhorse tried one of his bent legs, but it wouldn't move. "I think I'm out of this rodeo though."

"My ray refracted, G-man," Señor X said. "You can't shoot him again—it's too dangerous."

Leaning Oak laughed and came lumbering after Gonzalo. "Not so hot when you can't shoot me with your raygun, are you, Ranger?" the crystal man said. He raised a big crystal paw to smash Gonzalo where he lay, but suddenly he took a step back and swung wildly at the empty air.

"Get away from me! Get away from me, you freaks!" he cried.

"What—?" Gonzalo asked.

"It's the fox-girl," Señor X said. "She's making him see something that isn't there."

Kitsune grabbed Gonzalo under the arms and pulled him out from under Alamo. He hadn't even heard her sneak back.

"Bat men," said Kitsune. "Want to see them?"

"Not really," Gonzalo told her. "You get those people out?"

"Pretended I was a Shikaakwa fireman. Got them to use the back door."

Gonzalo was trying to stand when something coiled around his arms and legs and lifted him off his feet.

"Vines!" Kitsune said. They were both caught up in thick

green vines that hadn't been there a moment before. "That plant man. He must be the other—*lerk!*"

Kitsune choked as a green vine sprouted from the ground and slithered around her neck.

A flower bud opened on one of the vines, and the green face of Honda Nobuharu, the Ametokai Strangler, grinned down at them. "*Konichiwa*," Honda said. "Very nice to make your acquaintance, even if it is only for a short time."

Gonzalo felt a vine curl around his neck and tighten. He lifted his raygun to shoot Honda, but the pain from the vine made it too hard to focus his other senses.

"Up, right, right, up," Señor X said, guiding Gonzalo, and the ranger struggled to follow his direction. *Ka-POW!* Señor X sliced through the vine right below Honda's face, deadheading him. The vines slackened, and Gonzalo and Kitsune hit the ground.

"So, there's two of you," Leaning Oak said. Kitsune's illusion was broken. He could see both of them now. "That's okay— there's two of us too!"

New kudzu vines sprouted beside Leaning Oak and took a vaguely human shape. A flower budded and opened, and Honda Nobuharu's face appeared again. "That wasn't very nice of you," he told Gonzalo.

Kitsune jumped up and ran away.

"Hahahaha!" Leaning Oak laughed. "Guess there's only *one* of you now!" He charged across the park at Gonzalo, his big heavy crystal legs leaving holes in the soft earth. *Thoom. Thoom. Thoom.* Gonzalo raised his raygun again.

"G-man—no! The refraction—" *Ka-POW!* Gonzalo fired Señor X, but not at the gangster. He shot the beam at the ground a few feet ahead of Leaning Oak's thundering feet, blasting a giant hole. The big crystal man couldn't slow his momentum in time and fell into it, sprawling in Shikaakwa's famous muck.

Gonzalo heard Honda Nobuharu slither back into the ground, but instead of growing up at Gonzalo's feet, the strangler grew back in the muck underneath Leaning Oak. It would be harder than lifting Gonzalo and Kitsune off the ground, but in time Honda would put Leaning Oak back on his feet. Gonzalo aimed his gun at the sound, waiting for Señor X to give him directions.

"Gonzalo, *run*," Señor X said.

Gonzalo felt a shadow cross his face, blocking out the warm sun. The shadow of something big.

"*Run, run, run!*" Señor X yelled.

Gonzalo ran. Something creaked and groaned, tinkling with the sound of bricks falling on bricks, and *KA-THOOM!* The earth bucked like a steambronco and Gonzalo went flying. He landed with a thud and lay dazed on the ground.

"Gonzalo? Are you all right?"

It was Kitsune.

"Y-yeah. What did you do?"

"I dropped the Sears and Roe Buck Building on them."

She showed him an image in his head: the once-tall twenty-story building lay sprawled across Brant Park and the nearby vacated city blocks like a dead snake in the middle of a road.

"How?" Gonzalo asked.

"I just turned on some of the hydraulic pumps on the back until they tipped it all the way over."

Gonzalo sat up, his ears still ringing from the crash. "Well, that ought to take care of them.

Kisssh! Broken bricks and glass flew as a big crystal arm

punched its way up through the rubble. Another pile of bricks tinkled and tumbled away as a green vine pushed its way out from under it.

"*Órale*, you gotta be kidding!" Gonzalo said. "That crystal man's as strong as diamond, and the plant keeps coming back like a weed! If dropping a skyscraper on them doesn't kill them, what will?"

"You're right—Honda is a weed!" Kitsune said. "And what do you use to kill weeds?"

"A really big hoe?"

"No—*weed killer!*" Kitsune said. "I think I saw a flower shop drive by before, if I can just catch up to it. I'll be back!"

Kitsune bounded away. Gonzalo heard more bricks shift out of the way and stood, wondering if he could keep the two monsters occupied long enough for Kitsune to return. Even if she did get back in time, how were they going to take down the crystal man?

Gonzalo stood very still, putting together an image of what was happening around him with his other senses. He felt the muck at his feet and the malevolent wind swirling around him. Smelled the brick dust in the air, the gardenias growing in Brant Park, the lingering grease and smoke odor of Shikaakwa's elevated train. He heard the tinkle of broken bricks and the vibration from a gas lamp as it rattled in the wind.

"Señor," Gonzalo said, an idea coming to him. "The crystal man. We gotta shatter him."

"We tried that," Señor X told him. "He refracted my beam like a prism."

"Not with an aether beam," Gonzalo said. "With *sound*. We vibrate him until he shatters! Can you do it aggregating aether?"

"Yeah, I think so," Señor X said. "But you're gonna have to manually override my aggregator settings. Cranking the aggregator up that high will overload me, and my programming won't allow me to kill myself."

"What? No!"

"Kid, shattering him with sound waves is brilliant. It's the only way we're gonna take this guy out. But to do it you gotta overload me."

"But if you overload you'll explode!"

"And I'll take that monster with me."

"No," said Gonzalo.

"Gonzalo, listen to me. Killing monsters is what I was *built* for. It's my whole reason for being. It's not programming—it's a choice. And I choose to go out fighting."

"You think dropping a building on me is gonna stop me?" Leaning Oak called. "You only slowed me down, Ranger!" Gonzalo heard the bricks shift again. Heard people in the street scream. Any moment, Leaning Oak would be free of the rubble and smashing up Shikaakwa again. Hurting people again.

Gonzalo took a deep breath. There was only one thing to do. Gonzalo set Xiuhcoatl's aether aggregator to overload and ran for the sound of the shifting bricks.

"You made the right choice, kid. The hero's choice. Just like I knew you would," Señor X told him. "Listen, before I go, I gotta tell you the truth. It wasn't an accident that you found me. I found *you*. I'm Xiuhcoatl. The turquoise fire serpent. I was built millennia ago to be wielded by each League of Seven's Lawbringer. Somebody who's totally fearless, and always knows right from wrong. Sometimes I find them; sometimes I don't. But as soon as I heard about the blind kid who was a Texas Ranger, I knew you were the one. It took me eleven years of moving from lowlife to lowlife until I finally found one who got in the way of your Texas Ranger family. That's how I found you. Passed from one criminal to the next until we were together at last. I was made by the finest tekno-mages of Lemuria to find the most fearless, righteous man in the world and turn him into a hero, but when I found you, Gonzalo, the joke was on me. You already were one."

Gonzalo stumbled to a stop. "Why—why didn't you tell me before?" he asked.

"Well, I didn't want you getting a big head now, did I?" Señor X said.

Gonzalo couldn't believe it. For as long as he'd wielded Señor X, he'd always thought it had been luck that had brought the two of them together. But if what Señor X said was true—

Leaning Oak shed bricks as he stood. "Here I come, little ranger!"

"Climb! Climb!" Señor X said.

Gonzalo stumbled into the pile of bricks and scrambled up them, scratching and tearing his skin in his hurry.

"Just lodge me in the mess of crystals growing out of his back, and then run for the hills!" Señor X said. But all Gonzalo could think about was what the raygun had told him. He leaped on Leaning Oak's back and clung to the giant crystals that grew there as the gangster stood. Leaning Oak twisted and turned, trying to swat Gonzalo off, but he couldn't reach him.

"Ah, forget it," the gangster said. "Come along for the ride if you want. It's not like you can stop me!"

VmmmmmmmMMMMMMMM. The turquoise raygun shook as it passed its safety limit.

"Gonzalo! Leave me and get out of here!" Señor X yelled.

"No!" Gonzalo yelled back. "You found me and I found you. We're *partners*! We were meant for each other! You said so! So I'm sticking it out, no matter what happens!"

VMMMMMMMMMMMMMMMMMM.

"I didn't tell you all that so you'd go and do something *stupid*! Run, you idiot!"

"No! You'd stay with me if it was the other way around!"

"That's because I don't have any legs, *estúpido*!"

"What are you yelling about up there?" Leaning Oak said. "Whoa—hey. What's going on?"

The gangster's crystal body was vibrating. The higher pitched Señor X got, the more he shook.

"Hey. Hey!" Leaning Oak spun, trying to knock Gonzalo off. "Hey, plant man! Where are you? I need some help here!"

But Honda Nobuharu was gone. It was just Leaning Oak, Gonzalo, and Señor X.

VMMMMMMMMMMMMMMMMMMM!

"I—can't—I—can't—" Leaning Oak said, his body quaking. He dropped to his knees. "I can't—"

Señor X made a whine so high-pitched Gonzalo pulled his blindfold down and tightened it over his ears. The raygun was vibrating so hard he could barely hold on to it.

"Thiiiiiiiis iiiiiiiiis iiiiiiiit," Señor X said. "Ssssssssix thhhh hhoussssssand yyyyyyears iiiiiiiis a gooooooood ruuuuuuun fooooooor aaaaaaaanyyyyyyyybbbbbbbbbooooooooodddddddd yyyyyyy. Nnnnnnnniiiiiiiiiiiiiice knnnnnnnnnnnoooooooooo ooooowing yooooooooooooooooou, kkkkkkkkkkkkkkkkid!"

Leaning Oak made a high, keening sound that started in

his throat and spread to every inch of his vibrating crystalline body. "EeeeeeeeeeEEEEEEEEEEEEEEEEEEEE! KISSSSSSSSSSSSSSH!

The crystal man shattered before the raygun did, exploding into billions of shards. Gonzalo hit the ground, and Señor X tumbled from his fingers. A hail of crystals sliced through Gonzalo's clothes and skin and a thousand cuts sprang up all over him, but all he could think about was finding the turquoise raygun. He had to find it before it overloaded and exploded.

"Señor X?" he cried. "Señor X?" Gonzalo's ears rang so loudly he couldn't even hear himself yell. He fumbled around in the dark for the raygun, never so lost in his blindness as he was now. The whine from the overloading raygun was over-loading all Gonzalo's senses too. Tears streamed from his blind eyes as he clawed through the razor-sharp shards for his friend. Not there. Not there. Not there! Where was he? Where was he?

Gonzalo's stomach twisted in on itself, like a black hole of despair. He had lost him. He had lost Señor X, and now they were both going to die, all because he was born blind and couldn't see.

Something nudged him. Pushed the ancient raygun into his hands. *What!? How!?* Gonzalo's fingers scrambled for the aggregator and switched it off. The raygun's awful scream stopped, and Gonzalo fell to the ground, pulling Señor X into a fierce hug.

Alamo nudged Gonzalo again to make sure he was still alive, then collapsed onto the ground beside him.

Alamo limped into the stadium, and Kitsune ran to help take Gonzalo off the steamhorse. The Texas Ranger was bloody and torn, and clutched his strange turquoise raygun to his chest like he was an infant and the gun was his beloved stuffed animal. "Gonzalo, you look terrible!" Kitsune told him. "What happened?"

Gonzalo didn't answer. He was as deaf as he was blind. She spoke to him through the shell in her ear, the way she had told him where to find her: Wigwam Field, the home of the Shikaakwa Cubs. "Gonzalo! What happened?"

Gonzalo put a finger to his ear. "We won." He lifted his raygun, his hand shaking. "Where's Honda?"

Kitsune put a hand to Señor X and gently lowered him. "I've got him. Relax."

Gonzalo slumped gratefully onto her shoulder, and she led him to the outfield wall. "I'm going to show you, all right? In your head," she said through the shell. "Can you handle it?"

Gonzalo nodded.

Kitsune pushed the image of the world around them into his mind, the way she'd been able to since she was old enough to talk. The green grass, the pennants flapping in the breeze, the ivy growing up the red brick wall of the field.

"Where is he?" Gonzalo asked.

"You're looking at him," Kitsune told him. She flicked one of the ivy leaves, and a small bud opened. Honda Nobuharu's pained face glared back at her.

"What do you want, *warugaki*?" he said.

"Where is the dynamo?" Kitsune asked.

"Drop dead," Honda told her.

Kitsune raised a metal can and threatened to pour its contents on Honda's head.

"We don't have it! We don't have it!" he told her. "Moffett sent it with someone else."

"Who?" Kitsune asked.

"I don't know."

Kitsune threatened him with the can again.

"I don't know! I swear!" Honda cried. "She sent us out before any of the others. She gave it to one of them."

"He's telling the truth," Gonzalo said.

"How do you know?" Kitsune asked.

"I know."

"Okay," Kitsune said, and she dumped the rest of the can's contents on Honda Nobuharu's head and all over the ground. The little face cried out and shriveled away.

"Weed killer?" Gonzalo asked.

Kitsune nodded. "Hope they weren't attached to this ivy. Probably just killed it all." She chucked the can away and put her shoulder under Gonzalo's arm again. "Come on. Let's get you back to *The Kraken*. Maybe it can fix you up, just like it can drive itself." She put her finger to her ear again. "Um, Clyde? Clyde, can you hear me?"

"Whoa! Hey! Yeah!" Clyde said in her head. He was half a continent away, but it sounded like he was right there with her. She wondered if this was how other people felt when she sent thoughts and images into their brains.

"Gonzalo and I took out the crystal guy and the plant guy in Shikaakwa," Kitsune told him. "The dynamo's not here."

"Roger that," Clyde told her. "Looks like we're up next!"

17

"The last time me and Buster were in Wichita territory, we got hounded by a Wichita Cavalry regiment with an aether battle tank. Which turned out to be okay, 'cause Buster thought they were just playing chase with him."

Clyde looked over at Fergus, who sat in the navigator's chair to his right. The tattooed boy was lost in his own thoughts. And unhappy ones at that. He'd worn that same frown half the time they'd been marching west from Memphis.

"Fergus? What's up?" Clyde asked.

"Huh? What?" Fergus said, shaking himself out of it.

"You been worryin' over something since the minute we left, and that's a fact. Want to talk about it?"

"I—nae," Fergus said.

"No, you ain't worryin' about something, or no, you don't want to talk about it?"

"I don't want to talk about it," Fergus said.

"All right," Clyde said. "But Mrs. DeMarcus used to say that if you swallowed what was eatin' you, it'd eat you up instead."

"Your Mrs. DeMarcus was a wise woman," Fergus said, but he still wouldn't tell Clyde what was bothering him.

Buster whistled, and Clyde looked back out the big round windows on the steam man's bridge. A thick line of smoke hovered on the horizon.

"We got something," Clyde said.

Fergus consulted the maps. "This should be Broken Arrow. Big oil town. And a good place for a couple of Shadow Leaguers to make trouble."

The city of Broken Arrow stretched out for a mile in either direction. The outskirts were ringed with round Wichita buildings and homes, but the center of the town was all oil fields. Tall metal oil rigs pumped the liquid from the ground that the entire continent used to heat their homes and light their lamps, and refineries burned beside them day and night, pumping black smoke into the air above the city. It was a rich business, but a dirty one.

Red raycannons lit up the dark, hazy sky, and Buster clicked down his magnifying windows. Five Wichita aether battle tanks were firing at a towering metal monster. He was a walking junkyard: broken windmills, bent train tracks, old steel gears, copper pipes, velocipede wheels, tin cans, nails and screws, busted airships, crushed monowheels. Anything magnetic stuck to him. Clyde and Fergus watched as a stack of empty oil barrels flew up and clanked to his body, making him bigger.

"That'll be Hector Villarreal then," Clyde said. "Now where's number two?"

A building alarm went off across town, and Buster turned. The front wall of a bank exploded out into the street, and a locust man hopped outside, a sack of money thrown over his shoulder.

"Naalnish," Fergus said. "Didn't he used to be a bank robber?"

"Still is, by the looks of it," Clyde said. "All right, so—"

"Um, Clyde? Clyde, can you hear me?"

Clyde put a finger to the shell in his ear. "Whoa! Hey! Yeah!"

It was Kitsune, calling to tell them they had taken care of the crystal man and the plant man in Shikaakwa.

"Roger that," Clyde told her. "Looks like we're up next!"

Fergus climbed the ladder that led to the hatch on top of Buster's head. "I'll take the grasshopper."

"And I'll take Buckethead," Clyde said. "Good luck!"

Gyrocopter blades popped up out of a backpack Fergus wore, and with a blue spark of lektricity they whirred and lifted him away.

"Okay, Buster. Playtime!" Clyde said, and Buster whistled happily.

The Wichita Cavalry had the magnetic monster surrounded just beyond the houses and shops on the east side of town, but Villarreal had already taken out one of their aether tanks and was pushing toward the heart of the city. Clyde flipped a switch, and Buster's left hand retracted, turning his entire arm into a giant raycannon. The air inside the bridge crackled as it charged up with aether, and he aimed the ray-cannon right at Villarreal's chest.

"Kaboom," Clyde said.

BWAAAAT!

The massive red beam from Buster's raycannon slammed into the magnetic man, blasting away tons of metal scrap and knocking him back. Clyde stepped over the Wichita aether tanks and punched Villarreal hard with Buster's other hand across what passed for the criminal's face. *KRANK!* More scrap metal went flying. Buster didn't stick to him because he was made of non-magnetic brass.

Villarreal hit him back—*KERCHANK*—and Buster spun. *BWAAAAT!* Two of the aether tanks blasted Buster with their twelve-inch raycannons, and he fell backward into Villarreal.

"Hey!" Clyde called through his speaking trumpet. "I'm on your side, dang it!"

Villarreal pushed Buster away, and the magnetic man re-absorbed all the metal scrap the steam man's raycannon had shot away, growing back to his original size.

"Okay," Clyde told Buster. "This might be a little harder than I thought."

Fergus flew through the hazy sky, wishing he'd thought to bring a bandana to cover his nose and mouth. The air right above the city was filthy, and he flew higher looking for clean sky.

How could the people of Broken Arrow live like this, right

in the middle of a poisonous cloud? The money had to be good—very good. But why build all the oil rigs in one place, right in the center of town? Why not spread them out across the plains?

The oil had to all be in one place. But why? Why here and nowhere else? Fergus studied the oil rigs as he flew toward the bank Naalnish had robbed when it hit him. He stopped and hovered, flying higher to get an even better view.

The oil rigs were all arranged in a recognizable shape.

"Clyde—Clyde, can you hear me?" Fergus said.

"Yeah. Little busy right now."

"Clyde, the oil rigs here—they're laid out in the shape of a giant lizard."

"*What?*"

"Hundreds of them, all filling the outline of a big lizard. And I mean *big*. I think it's a Mangleborn."

"Why would they drill for oil on top of a Mangleborn?" Clyde asked.

"Because maybe that's the only place the oil comes from," Fergus said.

"Are you saying—are you saying the heating oil everybody uses is, what, Mangleborn blood?"

"Yeah," said Fergus. "I think they're drilling down and sucking it out."

"That's all kinds of messed up, and that's a fact," said Clyde.

"Yeah," said Fergus. "But Clyde, what it means is, if these guys have the lektric dynamo, they could raise that thing and destroy the entire city."

"Roger that," said Clyde. "Gotta go. I've got a—" Clyde grunted. "I've got a scrap heap to send back to the junkyard."

Another alarm went off, and Fergus swooped down as fast as he could. Naalnish the locust man hopped out of the First Nations Bank of Wichita with another bag of money over his shoulder.

Fergus landed in the street ahead of him as people fled.

"Hold it, bug man," Fergus said. "I don't think that money belongs to you."

Naalnish studied Fergus with his big, compound eyes. He had the head, torso, and rear legs of a grasshopper, but his upper limbs were human arms. The hairy mandibles that sprouted from the bottom of his face moved in and out, and his antennae quivered.

"It does now," Naalnish said. His voice was scratchy like corn husks.

Fergus thrust his hands out, firing bolts of lektricity at the human locust—*Kssssssssh!*—but faster than lightning he jumped. He leaped over Fergus's head, ripping off his gyrocopter along the way.

"Hey! It took me a long time to build that!" Fergus said. He thrust his hands out again. *Kssssssssh!* Naalnish leaped away down an alley.

"I don't need a gyrocopter to catch you!" Fergus said. He chased the big grasshopper down the alley, his rebuilt knee brace actually making him faster, not slower. *Maybe I should build one for my good knee too*, Fergus thought.

Naalnish pounced on Fergus from the shadows, whacking him with the bag of money and knocking him to the ground. Fergus lektrified his whole body, and the locust-man leaped off him with an angry *kss-kss-kss-kss!*

"Yeah! How'd you like that, huh?" Fergus called. He got

up and came after Naalnish. The alley was a dead end. The locust-man was trapped. "Come here, you big ugly beastie," Fergus said. "You can't jump high enough to get out of this one. Time to—"

Naalnish spread his thin, membranous wings and flew away.

"Aw, crivens," said Fergus.

He'd forgotten that grasshoppers could fly.

Clyde wrenched on the controls to push Buster up off the ground, and the steam man climbed back to his feet. They were taking a pounding from Hector Villarreal, and that was a fact. Clyde watched as the magnetic man picked up one of the Wichita's aether tanks, ripped off its raycannon, and added the wrecked hulk to its chest.

"We gotta do something different to break this guy up," Clyde told Buster, "or he's gonna get so big we *can't* break him up."

Buster growled deep down in his boiler.

BWAAAAT. BWAAAAT. BWAAAAT. The Wichita aether tanks kept the magnetic man busy while Clyde converted Buster's raycannon back into a hand. KRANK! KRANK! KRANK! Clyde pounded on Hector Villarreal, knocking off as much scrap metal as he could, then grabbed the magnetic man's arm, twisted it over Buster's head, and hurled Villarreal over his shoulder. The walking junkyard flew through the air and landed with an earth-shaking crash in the middle of the oil fields, scattering scrap metal for acres.

"Ha! Take that!" Clyde crowed.

Buster had just started to pick his way through the houses and shops that surrounded the oil field when Hector Villarreal began to pull himself together. First the scrap metal that had fallen off him slid back, attracted by the magnetic man at the core. Then the busted oil rigs twisted and turned and rolled into him. He grew bigger, and bigger, yanking the rest of the steel rigs from the ground. Black oil spurted up all around him as he stood, three times as big as he had been before.

"Oh slag," Clyde said.

He was just rolling up his sleeves for what he thought would be his and Buster's last fight when the steam man bent his head to the street. Fergus was down there waving madly at them, and Buster opened his mouth to let him inside.

"Looks like you did better with yours than I did with mine," Clyde said as Fergus climbed onto the bridge.

"Nae, I didn't," Fergus said. "I can't catch the blinking bug. He's still out there robbing banks and scaring people."

"Well, I just made Hector Villarreal three times bigger," Clyde said. "I think we're beat."

"Not yet," Fergus said. "I've got an idea. I'll help you with yours if you help me with mine."

"No offense, Fergus, but how are you gonna help take down *that* thing? It's gotta be thirty stories tall! I can barely reach past his knees!"

"Well, I'm not going to be hitting him. That's your job," Fergus climbed down to the balloon deck. "Keep him busy for me while I get inside him!"

"*Inside him?*" Clyde called.

The giant scrap heap raised a foot to step on the steam man, and Buster leaped out of the way. The foot came down on an empty house, smashing it to pieces and picking up even more metal.

"We gotta get this guy outside of town," Clyde said. "Let's go, Buster! Play chase!"

Buster sprinted happily down the street, turning back every few blocks to whistle at Hector Villarreal and make sure he was still chasing them. Clyde's control panel told him that Fergus had launched one of the aeronaut suits, and soon he saw Fergus floating away, hanging from one of the one-man red, white, and blue balloons. Fergus steered around behind the big magnetic man and disappeared.

"I hope you know what you're doing," Clyde told him through the shell in his ear.

"Me too," said Fergus.

The big magnetic man wasn't paying any attention to Fergus. And why would he? Fergus was a fly compared to Hector Villarreal now. The farther this guy walked, the bigger he got. If they didn't stop him, he'd get as tall as Cahokia in the Clouds. Taller.

Fergus aimed his one-man balloon for the tangle of scrap metal on Hector Villarreal's back and grabbed hold of something thin and shiny.

"I say, hello?" the shiny thing said.

"Gah!" said Fergus. He let go and almost floated away before scrambling to grab hold of an old rusted bed frame. "Who's there?"

"Mr. Toggle, sir," said a musical voice. A shiny face swiveled to look at him through an old radiator coil. It was a titanium Mark IV Machine Man, sucked up by the magnetic man like so much junk!

"How'd you get in there?" Fergus asked.

"I was working as a porter for Apache Airlines in Albuquerque, when suddenly I was swept up by what I at first took to be a tornado," the machine man said.

"Yeah, it's not a tornado," Fergus said.

"Have you come to rescue me, sir?" Mr. Toggle asked.

"You and everybody else in this thing's path." Fergus hooked himself to the magnetic man with an anchor from the aeronaut equipment belt he wore and rubbed his hands together. "Let's see if this works."

The black lines on Fergus's skin rearranged themselves, and he took hold of the radiator coil. Fergus hummed with lektricity, and the radiator coil disengaged from Hector Villarreal with a *clink*.

"Yes!" Fergus cried. He slid the radiator coil up his arm, hummed again, and disengaged the bed frame. It tumbled down the scrap heap on Villarreal's back and fell all the way to the ground, where it stayed.

"What are you doing, sir?" Mr. Toggle asked.

"Demagnetizing the magnetic man, one piece at a time," Fergus said. Another piece of metal fell away. "By generating a reverse, decreasing lektromagnetic field, I can strip each piece of its magnetic properties!"

"I'm sure I don't understand," said Mr. Toggle.

"That's all right," Fergus said. "Just trust me—it works."

But slowly, he told himself. He couldn't take Villarreal apart one piece at a time. There was only one thing for it: he was going to have to demagnetize the magnetic man himself.

Fergus demagnetized another piece and chucked it away,

digging straight for the heart of the scrap heap and disappearing inside.

"I'll just wait here then, shall I, sir?" Mr. Toggle asked.

Buster turned and whistled, baiting the giant magnetic man. It batted at him with an arm as big as the Emartha Machine Man Building in Standing Peachtree, just missing Buster's brass head.

"Don't stop, you big bucket of bolts!" Clyde said, torquing the controls. "He's almost got us!"

Buster swung back, whistle-barking, and Hector Villarreal's big metal paw caught them. *KRANK!* Buster went spinning head over heels into the plains outside of town. At least they'd got the magnetic man outside of town before he'd caught them. Clyde was desperately trying to right the steam man when the magnetic man picked them up off the ground like a child.

This is it, Clyde thought. Brass wasn't magnetic, so Hector Villarreal couldn't add him to his increasing mass. But that's not what the magnetic serial killer had in mind for him.

Villarreal reared back to throw the squirming Buster across the city when a tiny red toy wagon came loose from his chest and clattered twenty stories down to the ground. Villarreal's giant scrap heap face looked down at it in confusion, and then every piece of metal on him let go and fell at the same time like an avalanche.

Kerrrrrrrr*WHOOM!*

Buster crashed to the ground with a jarring crunch and was quickly buried by a mountain of junk.

"Clyde! Clyde, you okay?" Fergus called.

Clyde felt like he'd gone ten rounds with the magnetic man

himself, but he was okay. He hung upside down from the pilot's chair, held in by his seat belt.

"Yeah. Give me a minute," he told Fergus.

Clyde tried the controls, and found that Buster was strong enough to lift the scrap heap piled on top of them. Buster pushed his head up through the pile of metal and shook himself from head to foot like he was shedding seeds and burrs from a tromp in the woods.

Fergus hung in the air on his balloon, holding the limp body of Hector Villarreal in his arms. Villarreal still wore his black-and-white-striped prison uniform.

"All right," said Fergus. "A deal's a deal. I helped you with yours, now you help me with mine."

Fergus chased Naalnish into another alley.

"I think we've been here before," the locust man told him, his hairy mandibles flexing.

"Aye, but I've got you this time," Fergus told him. Lektricity crackled from his fingertips.

Naalnish shook his head. "What's different this time?"

Kshoom. Kshoom. Kshoom. Buster the ten-story-tall steam man leaned down over the alley.

"This time, I brought a friend," Fergus told the thief.

Naalnish's compound eyes grew wider. He spread his wings and leaped into the air, but Buster was faster. The steam man with the soul of a dog sprang into the air and caught the grasshopper in his teeth. *Chomp!* Buster landed and shook the locust man like a rag bone, growling deep down in his boiler.

"Good dog!" Clyde said. "Good boy, Buster. Now leave it."

Buster dropped Naalnish's sagging body on the cobble-stones and whistled happily.

"That's two," Clyde told Fergus.

Fergus called Hachi on the shell in his ear as he climbed back inside Buster.

"What?" Hachi said. "I'm busy."

"So lovely to hear from you too," Fergus said. "We're done. The dynamo's not here."

"You're sure?"

"Aye. If she sent it here, it would have been in all the junk on the big magnetic man. It wasn't."

"Of course it wasn't," Hachi said. "Moffett has it. She's always had it."

"You beat yours then?" Fergus asked.

"No. We just got here. But I'm sure Moffett has it. Why would she give something like that to one of her minions when she could use it herself? But we'll take care of our two just to be sure."

"Yeah," Fergus said. "Okay. We'll head back, then."

"After you run that errand," Hachi told him.

"Nae. I don't like it."

"I don't care if you like it or not. Just do it. We're going to need it, and you know it. Hachi out."

Fergus growled as he climbed the last ladder to the bridge. Slag Hachi and her slagging sneaky plans.

"Time to regroup?" Clyde asked.

Fergus huffed. This was a bad idea, and he knew it.

"Nae," he told Clyde. "Hachi wants us to pick something up first."

"Pick something up? What? Where?" Clyde asked.

Fergus sighed. "I need you to take me to Dodge City."

18

Standing Peachtree was burning.

Buildings roasted like coals in a locomotive's firebox. Red-orange flames rippled from the rooftops, their thick smoke blacker than the night sky. A blazing foundry crumpled in on itself. A boiler exploded, hurling red-hot steel. Everywhere, on every street, people swarmed away from the scorching city on steamhorses and airships and by foot.

Standing Peachtree was burning, and Fergus was arguing ethics.

"I don't care if you like it or not," Hachi told Fergus. "Just do it. We're going to need it, and you know it. Hachi out."

Hachi threw a pile of maps to the floor of the little airship. Slag Fergus. He'd better do it. This wasn't the time to get all sentimental. The world was ending one way or another, and she wanted it to be her way.

"There," Hachi told Martine. She pointed to a burning building on the north end of town.

Martine tilted her head. "The source of the conflagration is clearly midtown," she said. She didn't have to point. William Tecumseh Sherman, the burning man, stood out like a bright lilac star in the center of town.

"We'll go there next. But first there. That white building with the columns."

Martine steered her little airship, *The Jellyfish*, away from Sherman and toward the burning building on the north end of town. Away from the water, she had changed into tall black boots and a weather-beaten old black coat. Tall, gray, tattooed Martine was a steamhorse of a different metal, that was for sure. She didn't understand emotions, or sarcasm, or humor, and rarely spoke. And when she did speak, it was usually to say something so blinking strange that it stopped you in your tracks. But none of that mattered to Hachi. What mattered was that when Hachi told her they had to go north to Buckhead before taking on Sherman, she didn't ask why. She just did it. She and Hachi were going to get along just fine.

Martine piloted *The Jellyfish* over a lacrosse field next to the square white building. Smoke clouded the airship's windows, and flames licked out of the square white building's windows and doors.

Lady Josephine's Academy for Spirited Girls was on fire.

"I need to see if anybody's still left inside," Hachi said.

Again, Martine didn't ask questions. Instead she steered *The Jellyfish* directly over the building, set the autopilot to hold station, and took control of the strange tendrils that hung from the underside of the airship. *Ptoom!* One of them rammed straight down into the roof like a grappling hook, burying itself in the wood and tiles. Another of the tendrils glowed with aether and carved a slow circle in the roof around the grappling hook. The round roof piece separated with a tug on the airship, but *The Jellyfish* righted itself and rose, lifting away the circular section of ceiling.

"Brass," said Hachi.

Martine handed Hachi a harness, helped her get strapped in, and clipped the harness to a winch in the ceiling. Martine stepped away and the floor irised open, leaving Hachi swinging in space over the hole in the burning building. Heat and smoke assaulted them.

"Fire is a child," Martine said. "He is not angry or malicious. He is merely a hungry child who gorges himself on everything in the pantry, and then starves when there is nothing left to eat." Martine put a hand to the winch controls. "Do not be eaten, Hachi Emartha."

"Good advice," said Hachi.

The winch released, and Hachi shot down into the burning building. The line slowed as she reached the blue-green marble floor, and she unhooked her harness and dropped the rest of the way. The bronze statue of the academy's founder, Lady Josephine, loomed over her, a book in one hand, a sword in the other. "If I cannot move heaven, I shall raise hell," said the Latin words on her pedestal. Surrounded as she was by walls of roiling flame, it looked as though she had done just that.

"Hello?" Hachi called. *"Hello? Is anyone still here?"*

A cough answered her, and Amelia Ambrose, the headmistress, staggered out from behind the statue's pedestal. In one hand she held a handkerchief to her face. In her other hand, she held an empty water bucket. Hachi got to her as she slumped against the pedestal.

"Miss Ambrose! What are you still doing here? Where's everybody else?"

"Gone," Miss Ambrose wheezed. "Sent them . . . through the tunnel."

"Why didn't you go with them?" Hachi asked.

"Couldn't leave . . . Lady Josephine."

Hachi understood. She loved the long-dead sword-wielding scholar as much as Miss Ambrose did, but Lady Josephine would have understood when to stand and fight, and when to make a tactical retreat.

"Let's get you out of here," Hachi said. She half dragged Miss Ambrose to the line hanging down through the ceiling, hooked herself back on, and gave it a tug. Miss Ambrose went limp in her arms.

"But what about . . . Lady Josephine?" she muttered.

Hachi watched the flames engulf the tall, proud lady as the winch hauled them up past her.

"We'll come back for her," Hachi promised. "We'll come back and rebuild everything—bigger and better than before."

Sherman staggered down one of the many streets named Peachtree, setting wooden sidewalks and storefronts on fire. He didn't have to touch any of them—his purple-hot fire was so intense anything wood or flesh within a ten-yard radius burst into flames. Sherman roared an inhuman howl of pain and rage, his face nothing more than a dark smear with a wailing mouth at its center.

"I think he is both angry and malicious," Hachi said.

Martine tilted her head, watching with Hachi from behind an overturned steamwagon. "Yes. I think you are right. He is displaying characteristics I have learned are associated with both of those emotions."

Hachi had dropped Miss Ambrose with an ambulance heading for Grady Hospital, and now she and Martine were trying to figure out how to stop Sherman's march here in Standing Peachtree. Hachi's flying circus was loose, and flew around her head chittering warnings and ideas.

"You two! What are you doing here?" a man yelled at them, running across the street. "You should be long gone! We gave the order to evacuate hours ago!"

The man was Cherokee or Muskogee, or maybe both, and wore a black uniform with a star on it and a holster with an ivory-handled aether pistol in it. Hachi recognized him from her last time in town.

"Sheriff Sikwai," she said.

"Yes, do I know you?" he said. His face cleared with recognition. "I've got it—the Battle of Lady Josephine's. You and those two boys—the one with the white hair, and the one with the tattoos who saved those people on the train. Fergus."

Hachi nodded. "Hachi and Martine. We came to help."

The look on Sheriff Sikwai's face said he didn't think two teenage girls were any help to him at all. "We've got to get you off the street," he told them.

"We are out of the burning man's range," Martine said, "and this brass vehicle should shield us from much of his heat."

"Yeah, but not the water. We're getting ready to drop a water tower on him."

Hachi and Martine ran across the street with the sheriff to an alley, where a number of Cherokee warriors were crouching. Tusker, Hachi's little flying clockwork elephant, shot away from the rest of her circus and trumpeted around the head of one of the Cherokee men—not a warrior, but an old medicine man from the looks of him.

"Haha! Yes! Yes, hello, my little friend," he said. "And where is Archie?"

"You know Archie?" Hachi asked.

"I do! And Tusker here too," the old man said. "I met them both when they fell from the sky."

"You're John Otter!" Hachi said. He was bent and wrinkled, but his eyes sparkled with cleverness. He wore a white shirt and black vest, with a bright red scarf to tie back his black hair.

"The same," John Otter said. "And you, I take it, are . . . the warrior?"

Hachi blushed. She still wasn't comfortable with being some prophesied member of a team of superheroes, no matter what she'd seen and done with them. "Hachi Emartha," she told John Otter. "And that's Martine," she said. "Our, um . . . scientist."

Martine certainly looked the part. She stood apart from them down the alley over a smoldering shard that must have been thrown off Sherman, passing her glowing green harpoon over it and reading the small symbols that appeared on the harpoon's handle.

"So, you have found more Leaguers then?" John Otter said, delighted.

"We've found all of them. But we had to split up to chase

these guys. There's seven of them too. Have you seen the other one?"

"Another Manglespawn? Here in Standing Peachtree? Great Hiawatha, no. One is enough. What does he look like?"

"I don't know," Hachi told him. "All I know is there's supposed to be a pair of them." She didn't even bother mentioning the lektric dynamo. Moffett had that somewhere else, she was sure.

"There it goes!" Sheriff Sikwai cried. "Everybody back!"

High above them, a water tower creaked and tilted.

"Water will not help," Martine said as they joined her farther back in the alley. "In fact, it will make things worse."

"Worse?" Hachi said. "How can it make things worse? It's water, he's fire. End of story."

The water tower's wooden legs snapped, and it crashed down on top of Sherman in the middle of the street. *Ker-sploosh!* *WHOMPH!*

Sherman's brilliant purple flame exploded out from him, blasting the buildings along the street to splinters. Hachi ducked with Sikwai and the Cherokee warriors, but the blast was too big. Too strong. They were all going to die. Hachi knew it in the horrible moment before the shockwave hit them.

FOOM!

The explosion leveled a city block, knocking down all the buildings around them. Hachi felt the heat, but not the flames. She wasn't dead! The blast hadn't killed her. Hadn't killed any of them! But how were they alive?

Hachi looked up and saw Martine standing calmly above her, holding out what looked like a tall, wide shield made entirely of green aether. Purple-hot flames coiled and spun around it, missing the group but knocking down the buildings behind them. She'd saved them all.

When the blast was done, Martine pushed a button on a bracelet hidden among the tattoos on her wrist, and the aether shield disappeared.

Still howling, Sherman the Yankee arsonist stumbled on down the street, glowing as hot and bright as ever.

"That was—How did you—?" Hachi stammered. She and the others stood, all of them marveling at Martine. If Sheriff Sikwai had doubted they could help, he surely didn't now.

"An analysis of one of his cast-off shards reveals that William Tecumseh Sherman has become pure potassium," Martine told them. "Once ignited, potassium burns so hot it is almost impossible to extinguish. When burning potassium comes into contact with water, it burns the oxygen and leaves the hydrogen to react again with atmospheric oxygen, forming more water, which burns and leaves more hydrogen, which reacts again with atmospheric oxygen, which forms more water, which—"

Hachi put up a hand. "We get it."

"I don't," said Sheriff Sikwai.

"It's no good pouring water on it," Hachi told him. "It just makes him burn hotter."

"Okay," Sheriff Sikwai said. "I got that."

"So what can we use to put him out?" John Otter asked.

Martine tilted her head. "A large amount of liquid ammonia."

"And if we don't just happen to have a large amount of liquid ammonia sitting around?" Hachi asked.

Martine thought for a moment. "Sand." She looked at Hachi. "Fire is hungry. To stop it from eating, we must take away its food."

John Otter understood. "We have to smother it. Him. In sand. We have to take away all the oxygen for him to burn."

"Yes," said Martine.

"Where can we find that much sand?" Sheriff Sikwai asked.

"I know where," Hachi said. "The Emartha Machine Man Foundry."

The Cherokee warriors whooped and hollered insults at the burning man, peppering Sherman with raygun blasts while staying just out of range on the backs of their steamhorses. Behind them, the Emartha Machine Man Foundry's huge blast furnaces roared, melting brass and titanium to mold into Tik Tok bodies. But the heat was nothing compared to the potassium man who chased them, burning purple. The foundry's big metal doors sagged and bent on their hinges as he passed.

"Now?" Hachi asked, her hands on the foundry's fire-suppression controls.

"No," Martine said.

The Cherokee warriors backed farther into the foundry, and Sherman followed.

"Now?" Hachi asked. The heat from the foundry, plus the heat from Sherman, was almost too much. Hachi wiped the pouring sweat from her eyes.

The Cherokee warriors backed as far as they could against the foundry's far wall, trapped between the coke furnaces and the burning man. They still whooped and hollered though, proving their fearlessness.

"Now?" Hachi asked.

Martine said nothing.

The air wobbled. Or was Hachi wobbling? *"Now?"*

". . . Now," Martine said.

Hachi pulled the lever on the fire-suppression system, and sixteen tons of sand poured from a reservoir in the ceiling, thundering down on William Tecumseh Sherman. He roared as the sand buried him, the raging potassium fire that consumed his body fighting for air. But there was too much sand. It poured and poured and poured, Sherman's bright-hot fire melting it into glass that cooled around him like a clear sarcophagus. The glass and sand cracked and shifted as it cooled, and then the heat and the howling were gone. William Tecumseh Sherman, the Yankee arsonist, had been extinguished.

Sheriff Sikwai and John Otter joined Hachi and Martine on the foundry floor, where they congratulated the brave Cherokee warriors who had lured Sherman into the factory.

"We'll have to dig him out of there, of course," John Otter said. "Who knows, he might even still be—"

The earth shook with the force of an earthquake, rattling the foundry's massive furnaces, and something roared with a sound like a tornado. The Cherokee warriors drew their oscillating rifles and aimed them at the pile of sand.

"No," said Hachi, trying to stay on her feet. "No—it's not him. It's something else. Something bigger."

The tornado-like roar became a piercing shriek, as though the city were being attacked by a giant bird of prey.

"Tlanuwa!" John Otter said. "No! It must not be!"

"Out! Out of the foundry!" Sheriff Sikwai told everyone.

"What? What's Tlanuwa?" Hachi said as they ran.

"A giant mythological bird with metal feathers that nests in the flames of volcanoes," Martine said. "A phoenix."

"It's not mythological," John Otter said. "Tlanuwa sleeps beneath Standing Peachtree, and is watched over by the Cherokee and the Muskogee."

"A Mangleborn," Hachi said. The ground still shook beneath their feet. "But how? The flames?"

"No," John Otter said. "That wouldn't be enough—"

"The lektric dynamo," Martine said. "The other Shadow Leaguer here must have it."

"No," Hachi said. "No. That's impossible." It didn't make sense: why wouldn't Philomena Moffett keep a weapon like that for herself?

But Martine was right. Artificial lightning crackled around the top of the tallest building in Standing Peachtree: the Emartha Machine Man headquarters. The second Shadow Leaguer must have taken the dynamo there.

"We have to get up there and shut that thing down before it raises Tlanuwa," Hachi said.

"I will call my airship," Martine said.

"There's no time," John Otter said. "You two, give them your steamhorses."

Two of the Cherokee warriors hopped off their mounts, and Hachi and Martine climbed on.

"We will do what we can to make sure people are moved to safety," John Otter told them as they rode away. "Fight well! And tell Archie he still owes me the rest of the story!"

"Miss Hachi! Welcome back to the Emartha Machine Man headquarters," said a shiny new Mark IV Machine Man in the lobby. There were three of them—one to open the door and two more behind a reception desk. The one at the door was named Mr. Bouncer.

"What are you still doing here?" Hachi asked them. "Why didn't you evacuate? Are there people still in the building?"

"All humans have left, Miss Hachi," said Mr. Spindle, one of the two Tik Toks behind the desk. "Ms. Sawni told us to remain and put out any fires, should they arise."

Of course she did, Hachi thought bitterly. *Save your own behind and leave the Tik Toks to die in the fire.* The room shook, and Hachi and Martine grabbed each other not to fall. A potted plant fell over and smashed, spilling dirt all over the floor. Mr. Spindle moved to clean it up.

"No—stop. I'm countermanding Sawni's orders," Hachi said. She was the only person who could. "I want every Tik Tok out of this building and on the streets, with orders to see any injured humans to Grady Hospital."

"Yes, Miss Hachi," Mr. Spindle said. He and Mr. Bouncer left immediately, and the third machine man disappeared behind a service door, presumably to relay the message to the other Tik Toks still in the building.

Hachi and Martine ran for the express elevator.

"Who is Sawni?" Martine asked.

"Sawni Emartha, chief executive officer of the Emartha Machine Man Company," Hachi said as the doors closed. "And my aunt."

A long minute's ride later the elevator stopped with a ding, and Hachi and Martine stepped out into the penthouse office of Sawni Emartha. The lights were off and it was dark, except for the lektric blue tendrils of lightning that arced from the dynamo, which sat in the center of the room. All over the walls and ceiling were swathes of white thread, like stretched cotton, or—

"Spiderweb," Martine said, pulling her hand away with the viscous stuff stuck to it.

"'Welcome to my parlor, said the spider to the fly,'" a gurgling voice said from above. A man-sized spider hung upside down from the ceiling on a thin piece of web, clinging to it with eight hairy legs. He looked down at them with four pairs of human eyes.

"Sakuruta," Hachi said. "The Pawnee kidnapper."

Martine's aether harpoon glowed green, and she aimed it at the dynamo.

"Ah ah ah—I wouldn't do that," Sakuruta said. "Not unless you want me to kill Ms. Emartha."

"You're not killing me," Hachi said.

"Oh, you're an Emartha too? No, I meant *this* Ms. Emartha." Sakuruta pulled himself up closer to a bundle of spiderwebs on the ceiling and bared his fangs. Hachi's aunt Sawni looked out from the web cocoon with wild eyes. So Hachi's aunt hadn't run away after all. Or if she had, she hadn't gotten very far.

Hachi and Martine shared a look, and neither of them needed Martine's shells to tell each other what they were thinking.

Martine hurled the harpoon. Sakuruta shot a stream of silk at it. Hachi hurled a throwing knife. The spiderweb hit the harpoon with a *splurch*, pinning it to the floor. The throwing knife sliced through the web connecting Sakuruta to the ceiling, and the spider man fell.

Martine ran behind the dynamo. Hachi ran for Sakuruta.

"Circus! Showtime!" she called, and her four clockwork animals burst from her bandolier. "Cut Sawni down!" she told them.

Sakuruta jumped for the wall, but Hachi grabbed one of his hairy legs. He turned and struck her with another. Hachi ducked and swept her foot at another of his legs, but he lifted it out of the way.

"I seem to have a leg up on you," Sakuruta said, his eight eyes flashing. He advanced on Hachi. "It's eight to two."

"You're forgetting about a couple more of mine," Hachi said.

Martine leaped on Sakuruta's back. He squirmed, but she held fast.

"Ha! What good are you without your harpoon, Karankawan?" Sakuruta crowed. "It's still stuck to the floor!"

Martine tapped the bracelet on her wrist. *Vommmm*. The aether shield spiraled out from it, slicing off Sakuruta's head. His body *slurch*ed to the ground, its eight hairy legs curling in on themselves, and his head bounced to Hachi's feet and looked up at her with eight stunned eyes.

"Nice," Hachi said.

Thunk! Hachi's aunt hit the carpet behind them and clambered to her feet, yanking spiderwebs from her arms and legs.

"Hachi!" she said. Hachi's flying circus flew around her head, chirping happily, but Sawni batted them away. "Ugh. My brother and his damned *toys*. What are you doing here? What do you have to do with this—this monster and this machine?"

"You're welcome," Hachi said. "I'm sure you wish he'd killed me, so you could have the company all to yourself."

Martine pulled her harpoon free at last and aimed it at the dynamo.

"No! Stop!" Aunt Sawni said. "It's some kind of—some kind of generator, isn't it? A lektrical generator! The energy it's putting out—if we could harness that energy, put it inside a machine man, we could make a fortune!"

"We already make a fortune," Hachi said. She nodded to Martine, and the science-pirate stabbed her glowing harpoon deep into the dynamo. The lektrical generator sparked and popped and wound down with a whine. Hachi waited for more earthquakes, listened for more screeching, but they didn't come. She let out a deep breath she didn't know she'd been holding.

"Worthless," Aunt Sawni said. "Worthless at business, just like your father! He never could see the profit from all his foolish tinkering. That was me. All *me*."

Hachi wanted to argue with her, wanted to tell her there were more important things than profit, like tracking down her brother's killers. But that was an argument for another time. Hachi had bigger problems right now.

She stared at the smoking dynamo. She was *sure* Moffett would have taken it with her, not sent it with one of the other pairs. But Moffett must not have cared about the lektric dynamo at all. Had she really just sent her minions out as decoys so she could get a head start on the League of Seven? With the dynamo in her hands, she could have unleashed half a dozen Mangleborn that would have kept the League busy far longer than that—maybe even defeated them once and for all. What was Moffett playing at? She had to have a plan. She had to know they would split into pairs to chase the Shadow League. Had to know they would separate.

"She separated us on purpose," Hachi told Martine. "Why would she separate us?"

Martine tilted her head. "To isolate all of us."

Hachi put her hands on Martine's shoulders. "No. No! To isolate *one* of us! Crivens, I should have seen it!"

Moffett knew they would split up and chase her Shadow League, but as Martine had pointed out, you couldn't split seven evenly. And Moffett *knew* who they'd send alone after her. The only one who'd ever fought her to a standstill. The only Leaguer she really had to worry about.

Hachi put a finger to her ear. "Archie! Archie, can you hear me? It's a trap! Archie, it's a trap!"

19

Archie ducked back behind the corner where Jesse James and Mr. Rivets hid. "She's here," he told them.

"'Bout time," said James. "You two come any farther on the Underground Railroad with us, you might as well be conductors."

Archie peeked around the corner again. Philomena Moffett stood on top of a giant statue of a snake in the middle of Sonnionto, telling the people of the Shawnee city how she was about to reveal their true natures with the Dragon Lantern. She really did love climbing on top of things.

"I don't see the lektric dynamo," Archie said, "but she's got to have it here somewhere. Jesse, you and I'll go after Moffett while Mr. Rivets gets as many people as he can to safety."

"Whoa, whoa, whoa," said James. "I gave you a ride on my railroad. That's it. I didn't sign on for fighting some octopus-woman with really bad breath. I'm here to free as many Tik Toks as I can."

Archie kicked away a snake that was crawling across his shoe. Slagging Jesse James. Having somebody else to worry Moffett would have helped, and Mr. Rivets wasn't much of a fighter, even with his Protector Card installed.

"The machine men of Sonnionto *are* in just as much danger from Mrs. Moffett as the humans of the city," Mr. Rivets pointed out.

Archie sagged. Ever since Mr. Rivets had become self-winding, he'd gotten a lot more vocal about Tik Tok rights.

"All right," Archie said. "Jesse James will round up the machine men, and Mr. Rivets, you'll get the people out of the way. Take them into the Underground Railroad. They'll be safe there."

Jesse James started to protest, but Archie cut him off. "Good public relations," he told him.

"In case you forgot, I'm an *outlaw*," Jesse James said.

"So do something good every now and then," Archie said. "It'll confuse the clinker out of them. And get you more press."

Jesse James seemed to like that idea. He tipped his cowboy hat with his raygun and slinked away.

A red light flashed around the corner, and a man screamed.

"Mr. Rivets! The people!" Archie cried. He turned the corner and ran for Moffett atop the Sonnionto Snake. The whole town was mad for snakes. The snake statue was old—as old as the city itself—and strangely shaped. The snake was upside down, with its head on the ground, its body irregularly wavy, and its tail curled at the end to form a big circle, like the eye of a huge needle. That's where Moffett stood, shining the Dragon Lantern down on anyone and everyone she could.

Archie lowered his shoulder and hit the statue at a run. *Ker-RACK!* The base of the snake cracked just below its head, and the statue lurched. Moffett caught herself with a tentacle before she could fall, the Dragon Lantern's beam skewing wildly. As Archie staggered back, he could see Mr. Rivets on the other side of the square chasing the crowds of Shawnee, Powhatan, and Iroquois people away from the circle.

"Archie Dent! I knew they'd send you after me alone," Moffett said, a smile on her face. "And you found me. At last."

It hadn't been that hard, really, Archie thought. Moffett had stopped in cities and towns across Shawnee territory to turn more people into monsters with the Dragon Lantern. It had taken him time to take care of the Manglespawn she'd left behind each time, but they had formed a kind of trail east that had been easy to follow. Now he could finish this once and for all.

Archie punched the bottom of the Sonnionto Snake. *Koom!* The place he hit exploded into dust, and the statue dropped and fell. Moffett jumped away right before it crashed into the street. *KaTHOOM.*

Moffett emerged from the dust. "You and I do know how to bring the house down, don't we?" she said. "And everything else with it."

Moffett filled her lungs, and Archie braced his feet and threw up his arms. *WOMWOMWOMWOMWOM!* Moffett's sonic scream ripped up the paved street and knocked down buildings behind him, but Archie stood his ground.

Archie waited for the sound waves to die away and ran for Moffett, but she was already on the move. People in the side streets were fighting and looting, feeling the side effects of the Dragon Lantern. It was like a portable Mangleborn, driving the weak-willed to insanity.

Moffett turned to scream again. No! Archie would survive, but she would kill all these people. Archie punched his hands down into the pavement at his feet and lifted, ripping the street up like he was peeling a giant banana. He raised the curled end of the pavement up over his head just as Moffett let loose. WOMWOMWOMWOMWOM! Moffett's sonic scream destroyed the wall of road he'd lifted, but the asphalt took the brunt of the blast. The people behind him were knocked to the ground, but not too injured.

Moffett smiled and ran away again. Where was she going?

Archie turned a corner and found Moffett clinging to the third-story window of a brick building.

"Do you want to know something interesting about Son-nionto?" Moffett called to him.

"No," Archie said. He punched the corner of the building and the wall crumbled. Moffett jumped into the street and hit him again with her sonic scream. WOMWOMWOMWOM-WOM!

"There's a puzzle trap here without a Mangleborn in it," she told him.

Archie ran headlong at her, and she ran around another corner.

"You learn such interesting things when you're the chief of the Septemberist Society," Moffett told Archie from atop a snake-shaped street lamp. Archie waited to attack as frightened

Sonniontans scurried for the protection of stairwells and shops. "An ancient League built it—we're not sure which one—" Moffett said, "for a Mangleborn called Uktena. The horned serpent."

The street was clear. Archie brought his hands together with all his strength. *THOOM!* The thunderclap tore up bricks, shattered glass, and ripped up street lamps. Philomena Moffett went flying. She tumbled along the pavement like a tentacled tumbleweed until she could at last right herself.

Moffett scowled at her torn dress and bloody arms. *WOM-WOMWOMWOMWOM!* She hit Archie with another blast without taunting him first. It knocked him head over heels, but Archie didn't mind. He was finally getting to her.

Moffett ran into a public park, and Archie followed. The thunderclap had surprised her, but she wasn't likely to fall for it again. He was going to have to think of something else to tip their stalemate.

JANDAL A HAAD.

Archie staggered to a halt, the voice in his head like a punch in the face. There was a Mangleborn close by, a Mangleborn talking to him. But Moffett had just said the puzzle trap here had no Mangleborn in it.

STONE COAT, the voice said. *WITH THE STRENGTH OF ONE HUNDRED MEN.*

Moffett climbed to the top of a grassy mound in the park. Archie shook off the Mangleborn's song and braced himself for another of Moffett's sonic screams.

"Whoever that ancient League was, they fought Uktena and defeated it," Moffett said, back to her history lesson instead.

"But they didn't have time to seal it inside their trap. Other Mangleborn to dispatch, I imagine."

JANDAL A HAAD, the Mangleborn said. MADE OF STONE.

"So the people of Sonnionto buried it themselves," Moffett went on. "Right here, in this very spot. Today they call it the Serpent Mound and think it only a giant earthwork monument built by their primitive ancestors. But we know the truth: Beneath this mound the Mangleborn Uktena has slept for thousands and thousands of years, waiting for someone to rediscover lektricity and wake it up again."

JANDAL A HAAD, Uktena said. ALWAYS DIFFERENT, ALWAYS THE SAME.

Archie put his hands to his head, willing himself to block out the voice. "And—and that's what you're going to do," Archie said, trying to focus on the problem at hand. "With the lektric dynamo." He scanned the park for the machine.

"Oh no," Moffett said. "I sent that to Standing Peachtree with Sakuruta and Sherman to destroy everything your warrior has left to care about. But maybe the Dragon Lantern will work on it. Let's find out!"

Archie barely had time to be surprised that Moffett had sent the lektric dynamo somewhere else. She slid open the shields on the Dragon Lantern, and aetherical red light streamed into the ground.

The earth shook as Uktena stirred beneath their feet.

THE HORNED SERPENT WAKES, Uktena thundered.

"No!" Archie cried. He ripped a tree out of the ground and swung it at Moffett. She jumped out of the way, but the Dragon

Lantern's light wasn't hitting the mound anymore. The ground stopped shaking. Archie swung at her again, driving her away.

STONE COAT, Uktena called. FREE ME, STONE COAT.

"Nothing's going to stop me from punishing the Septemberist Society for what they did to me. To both of us," Moffett said. Her voice turned cold. "And by Hiawatha, I'm going to do it."

Archie lashed out at her again with the tree.

"That's right," Moffett told Archie. "Hit me. Hurt me!" THOOM. Her tentacles carried her out of the way of Archie's club again. "You're the only one who can, Jandal a Haad. Because you're a monster, like me!"

MONSTER, Uktena echoed. MANGLESPAWN.

"No!" Archie cried. He wanted to put his hands over his ears. Fall to his knees and curl into a ball. But he couldn't. Wouldn't. He'd promised. He swung the tree again, chasing Moffett out of the park, away from the Mangleborn. "I won't," Archie said. "I won't get mad. You can't make me lose control."

He tried to repeat the mantra Hachi had begun to teach him on the way back from Florida. "Talisse Fixico, the potter. Chelokee Yoholo, father of Ficka. Hathlun Harjo—Hathlun Harjo, the . . . the surgeon!"

Moffett kept trying to turn and scream at him, but Archie chased her out of town with the tree like an old man chasing a dog with a broom. "Was that your plan, Moffett?" Archie yelled. He slammed the tree down again and again. THOOM. "Get me to lose control again?" THOOM. "It's not going to work!" THOOM. "I'm stronger now. More focused."

"Ah, well, I hoped it would work," Moffett told him. She circled a hill outside of town, and Archie stalked after her. "To tell the truth, I'm impressed. But I did make sure to have a backup plan, just in case."

Archie panted, still clinging to the tree. It was all he could do not to give in to the anger, the hatred, the *pain*, and let the monster inside him rage against Moffett.

"Backup plan? What backup plan?" Archie asked.

Moffett smiled. "You remember that empty puzzle trap I was telling you about? The one just *waiting* for a monster to be imprisoned in it?"

Archie's feet struck a low, circular wall, and he almost tripped.

"Archie! Archie, can you hear me?" Hachi yelled, her voice coming to him through the aetherical shell in his ear. "It's a trap! Archie, it's a trap!"

WOMWOMWOMWOMWOM! Moffett blasted Archie with a sonic scream louder and more powerful than any she'd ever hit him with, and he went tumbling over the low wall into a dark, deep hole that had no end.

20

Philomena Moffett was gone by the time the League of Seven regrouped in Sonnionto, but she had left them a present. A giant horned snake rose above the city, breathing a foul green gas from its fanged mouth. It was red with yellow spots, yellow gills that stood out from its neck like a salamander, and enormous antlers like a stag. In between the antlers was a diamond-shaped mark that glowed like the morning star.

"Uktena," Señor X said. "Aka Misikinepikwa to the Shawnee, Pita-skog to the Abenaki, Olobit to the Natchez, aka—"

"We get it," Hachi said. "This thing gets around."

Hachi and Martine had come by airship; Kitsune and Gonzalo on *The Kraken*, by way of the Ohio River, which ran through town. Fergus and Clyde had marched straight there from Dodge City. All around them, the people of Sonnionto were streaming away in steamwagons full of children and pets and valuables.

"Is that beastie what got Archie?" Fergus asked. Every one of them had tried to contact him via the shells, but for some reason Archie wasn't answering. "How did Moffett raise it without the dynamo?"

"I don't know," said Hachi. "We've got to find Mr. Rivets and find out. If he's still in one piece."

"We have to deal with that Mangleborn first," Clyde told them. "Mr. X, how did the League beat it before?"

"I don't know," Señor X said. "I never fought this one."

"All right," Clyde said. "Like Mrs. DeMarcus says, sometimes you gotta make it up as you go. Kitsune, you and Fergus are on crowd control. If this Mangleborn's anything like the rest, it's already got a bunch of cultists dancing around making more trouble. Me and Hachi will wade in with Buster and see if we can't do some snake wrangling. Gonzalo, Martine, get to a rooftop and shoot at it. See if you can—uh, Martine?"

All the other Leaguers were pairing off to follow Clyde's plan, but Martine had wandered off down the street on her own, toward the Mangleborn. Her head was tilted, like she was studying it from a new angle, and when the League caught up to her, they saw the diamond gem on her forehead was glowing bright white.

Just like the one on the head of the Mangleborn.

"Crivens," said Fergus. "I thought that was just for decoration."

"Martine?" Hachi said. "Martine? What's going on?"

Martine didn't answer. Instead she made a hard right turn and walked directly through the front door of a hotel. The rest of the League looked at each other in bewilderment. But whatever was going on, the Mangleborn was just as mesmerized as Martine was. It stood stock still in the middle of the street, its body held up like a cobra, the white diamond on its head still glowing bright white.

"Go go go!" Clyde told the other Leaguers. They ran for the door of the hotel to follow Martine, and Clyde ran to climb back inside Buster. In moments, Martine stepped out onto the hotel's flat roof, the rest of the League a few yards behind.

Uktena turned, and the Mangleborn and Martine were face to face.

"Yes," she said. There was a pause, and then she said, "No." Another pause. "Forty-two."

"What's she saying?" Gonzalo asked.

"She's talking with it," Kitsune said.

"Purple," Martine said, "like trees."

"She makes even less sense than usual," Fergus said.

"When the west wind blows," Martine said.

Uktena stayed frozen where it was, and the diamonds on both their heads glowed even brighter.

"It's like she's a snake charmer!" Gonzalo said.

"Or it's charming her," Kitsune said.

"Yeah. Does anybody else think we need to be shooting this thing while it's just standing there?" Hachi asked.

"No, wait a minute," Clyde said. "I got an idea."

It was hard to say Buster "sneaked" up behind the giant

horned snake, because Buster didn't much sneak at all. But if Uktena noticed, it didn't react. Clyde reached out with one of Buster's hands, took the Mangleborn by the neck, and lifted it up off the ground.

"Well, I got it!" Clyde cried. "Now what do I do with it?"

"Señor X has got something," Gonzalo said.

"A deep hole, two clicks from our present location," the raygun said.

"I don't know what a click is," Clyde said, "but you just point me in the right direction, and I'll stuff it down the hole."

"What about Martine? What if she needs to still be near the thing to mesmerize it?" Fergus asked.

Clyde reached out Buster's other hand and picked her up. The Mangleborn in his right hand swiveled to look at her, and their weird conversation continued.

Gonzalo pulled Kitsune up onto Alamo with him, and together they rode off toward Señor X's hole in the ground. Buster followed not far behind with Uktena in one hand and Martine in the other. Fergus and Hachi stayed behind to look for Archie and Mr. Rivets.

"Well, that's the easiest Mangleborn we've ever beaten," Fergus said.

"I don't like it," Hachi said.

"Of course you don't. You didn't get to stick your pointy knives into anything."

"No—something's wrong here, Fergus. Where's Archie? Where's Mr. Rivets?" She stared down at the smashed snake statue in the traffic circle below them. "It was a mistake sending him here all by himself."

"What, you worried Archie got eaten by that beastie?"

"No," Hachi said. "I'm worried Archie became a beastie of his own."

Señor X led the strange little parade just outside of town, where a crumbling old ring of stones just big enough to stuff Uktena into was set into a hilltop.

"Huh," said Clyde. "It's like it was made just for this snake guy."

Buster peered down inside, his headlights clicking on. The hole was lined with smooth, seamless stone all the way down as far as they could see. Beyond that was just darkness. Deep, deep darkness.

"How far down does it go?" Kitsune asked. "It has to be deep enough Uktena can't climb out."

"Señor X's scanner don't reach the bottom," Gonzalo said. "Which means it's more'n half a mile deep."

Uktena's tail twitched.

"Deep enough," Kitsune said. "Flush it."

"But what about Martine?" Gonzalo asked. "What'll happen when that jackalope falls down the well? Will she still be all googly-eyed for it?"

"There's only one way to find out," Clyde said. Buster lowered the Mangleborn so that its tail slid down into the hole. When there was nothing left aboveground but its head, Clyde let it go.

Uktena dropped away into the darkness, and suddenly the bright white light from the gem on Martine's forehead winked out. Beneath them, Uktena's howls echoed and echoed up from the deep, deep hole, until finally they disappeared.

"Martine?" Clyde asked. "You okay?"

She blinked and tilted her head. "Yes. My calculations were wrong. A Mangleborn did not mate with my ancestor eight generations ago. It was two hundred and two generations ago."

"Wait a minute," said Gonzalo. "Are you saying that thing— are you saying that thing is your great-great-something-or-other-*granddaddy*?"

"Great to the two hundred and first grand*mother*," Martine said. "I have finally found my Mangleborn ancestor."

"Señor X did say that thing got around," Kitsune said.

Fergus's voice came booming to them through the shells in their ears. "Clyde! Wait! Don't drop that beastie down that hole! We found Mr. Rivets! He says Moffett dropped Archie down that hole before she freed Uktena. He thinks it's one of those puzzle traps the ancients built!"

Kitsune turned to look at Gonzalo, who just shook his head.

"Um, oops," Clyde said.

They had just dropped Martine's very angry great-great-something-or-other Mangleborn grandmother on Archie's head.

21

Like all ancient puzzle traps created by former Leagues, the one they'd dropped Uktena into—on top of Archie—had a way inside. A way besides the long, dark hole to the center of the earth. Martine found it on a hill nearby. It was another low, round wall, but over its wide opening there was a tarnished brass plate with two holes in it. One hole was round, and about the size of a manhole cover on a sewer, with a ladder leading down. The other hole was a rectangle that stretched from the round side of the metal plate to almost the center, tall enough and wide enough for three or four of them to crawl inside at once.

To the side of the two holes, engraved in the greenish brown metal, was the image of a slithering snake.

"The ladder goes down about forty feet and hits a dead end," Fergus said, climbing out. "But I'm pretty sure the floor moves. It's a separate piece from the chamber with the ladder."

"I guess we take the big hole then?" Kitsune asked, peering down into the rectangular opening

"There's always a trick to these things," Hachi said. She and Fergus were the only two of them who'd dealt with League puzzle traps before, and they were wary. "You don't have anything on this one, Mr. Rivets?" she asked.

"I'm sorry, miss," Mr. Rivets said, watching the six remaining Leaguers examine the entrance. "As this puzzle trap was never used to trap a Mangleborn, no clues were ever written down to be passed along as nursery rhymes. Or at least, none survive."

"Nursery rhymes?" Clyde asked.

"Aye," said Fergus. "The ancient Leagues thought it'd be cute to write up the instructions on how to get inside these things as children's rhymes, so nobody'd ever forget them. People remember the rhymes, all right, but the trouble is, nobody remembers what they mean."

"How about, 'Humpty Dumpty sat on a wall. Humpty Dumpty had a great fall,'" Kitsune joked.

"But Uktena the horned serpent does not resemble the character in that rhyme," Martine said.

"Who said I was talking about the snake?" Kitsune said.

Fergus frowned. "Archie is not Humpty Dumpty."

"It's not about either of them," Hachi said testily. "There isn't a rhyme for the trap."

"Mr. X, you got nothing on this one?" Clyde asked.

"No. This one was before my time," Señor X said. Which was saying something, if his other stories were to be believed.

"Okay," Clyde said. "Archie's down there with Martine's great-grandmother, and if there's one thing we've learned, it's that you don't leave a man—or woman—behind," he said, glancing at Hachi. "So we go in for him." He nodded at the rectangle. "And this looks like our only way in."

"What about you?" Hachi asked. "You can't take Buster in with you."

The giant steam man sat in the grass beside the big round seal, his tailpipe wagging.

"Yeah," Clyde said. "But I'm still coming. I'm a UN Cavalry-man, don't forget."

"I shall remain with Buster," Mr. Rivets said. "The ancient Leaguers did not design their puzzle traps for machine men, either."

The League climbed inside the rectangular hole, Fergus's whole body glowing like a lektric lightbulb to light their way. Eerie flames flickered around Martine's aetherical harpoon too, casting a green pall over everything.

There was a narrow floor just below the top cover with barely enough room for them to all fit. Across a small gap in the floor was a six-foot-tall round brass cone on its side, pointed right at them.

"Uh, I don't like that," Fergus said. "That's gonna come shooting at us in a minute, mark my words."

Kitsune slipped down through the gap in the floor before any of them could say not to.

"Give me a light," she said from below.

Martine stuck the tip of her harpoon in the hole.

"It's the same thing here. Another ledge, another gap, another round brass cone pointing sideways."

Clyde told Kitsune to wait, and they all climbed down with her floor by floor. There were five ledges in all, each with its own sideways brass cone. Some of the brass cones were short, leaving them lots of room to stand on the ledge. Others were long, taking up almost the entire space.

There was no gap between the floor and the brass cone on the last ledge.

"Dead end," Fergus said. "We're not getting down there through this mess. Must be the other hole up there that leads through."

"But it dead-ends too. How do we open it?" Gonzalo asked.

"It's got to be with these," Hachi said, putting a hand to the brass cone pointed at them.

Martine played again with the little aetherical gizmo she carried and turned its glowing screen toward them. It showed them a layout of the five floors they'd just climbed down, as well as chambers they couldn't see beyond the brass cones.

"There are coils behind these cones," Martine told them. "Springs."

"Crivens," Fergus said. "I told you! Any second now they're going to come flying at us and smush us against these walls!"

"I do not think so," Martine said. She tapped the screen, and mathematical equations appeared beside the diagram. "The springs are at their tensile extremity."

Hachi, Gonzalo, Clyde, and Kitsune had no idea what she was talking about.

Fergus took the gizmo from her and studied it. "She means the springs in the wall are already stretched out as far as they go."

"Why put springs behind the walls if they can't stretch far enough to push the things?" Hachi asked.

Kitsune's eyes went wide. "So they can be pushed *back*," she said. "And I know why. I know what this is! It's a lock!"

It was her turn to be stared at.

"Look," she said, taking Martine's gizmo. "You slide a key straight down, from above, and the teeth on the key push the brass cones back into the wall. That lets you turn the entire round chamber—"

"Which means the tube with the ladder moves, not the floor," Fergus said. He showed them on the diagram. "See? The chamber turns, and so does the tube. I'll bet it lines up with another hole that lets us keep climbing down."

Kitsune nodded. "All we need is the key!"

"That's one *muy grande* key," Gonzalo said.

"One they knew only somebody with the superpowers of a Leaguer could turn," Clyde said.

"They wouldn't have built a huge lock without leaving a huge key behind for it," Hachi said.

"Aye, and I think I've seen it," Fergus said. "Or what's left of it. Martine, you don't by chance have a scan of that big snake statue from town, do you? The one with the wiggly body and the tail in the shape of a circle?"

Martine tapped at the screen of her gizmo, and an image of the statue appeared, to scale with the puzzle trap. She moved it around on the screen with her fingers and it slid inside, the bends in its body pushing all of the brass cones back perfectly. With a twist of her fingers she turned the looping tail that stuck out the top, and the lock turned.

"Brass," Hachi said. "So all we need to open the puzzle trap to get Archie out is the giant key that Archie smashed fighting Moffett."

"It's all right," Kitsune said. "I can pick the lock."

"Of course you can," Gonzalo said.

"You can pick a giant lock?" Clyde asked. "How?"

"Well, I know *how* to pick a lock. We just need to push each of these pins back at the same time so the room can turn."

Hachi pushed on the brass pin beside them. Only when Clyde pushed with her were they able to slide the pin back into the wall.

"So. It just takes two of us to push one pin back," Hachi said. "There are five pins, and six of us. How are we going to push them all back at the same time?"

"I bet I can push one of them back with Señor X," Gonzalo said.

"No raygun can sustain that kind of beam," Hachi said.

"I'm not your average raygun, kid," Señor X said.

"I can do the same with my harpoon," Martine said.

"If Buster doesn't mind me borrowing a few odd pieces here and there, I can pull something together for another one," Fergus said.

"And I think I can get one of Buster's fingers in the top hole," Clyde said.

"Which is how we can turn it too," Kitsune said. "That just leaves the last one for me and you," she said to Hachi.

"Let's do it," Clyde said. "Archie's already been down there for hours with that thing."

They all hurried to get into position, waiting only for Fergus to pull together something using a cargo winch and some brass rails from Buster's engine room.

"Ready," Fergus called at last.

"We all have to push our pins back until the row of pins

behind them are flush with the wall," Kitsune told them via shell, "and all at the same time. If just one pin is out of place, the room won't turn."

"All right," Clyde said. "Ready Leaguers? Full steam ahead!"

Buster's finger curled inside, pushing his pin back easily. The green flame around the shaft of Martine's harpoon pushed like water on the tip of her brass pin. Señor X fired a spreading repulsor beam that Gonzalo held steady. Fergus's contraption chugged and steamed, slowly ratcheting two poles in opposite directions: one backward, against the wall, the other forward, against his pin. And on the final ledge, Kitsune and Hachi put their backs into it, pushing with everything they had.

One by one the pins clicked into place, but Kitsune and Hachi weren't strong enough to push theirs. Not even with the added help of Hachi's flying circus.

"*Push*," Hachi grunted.

"*I'm pushing*," Kitsune told her.

Suddenly the rectangular section of wall in front of them rumbled and cracked, separating itself from the rest of the chamber. *Krrrrrrrr*. It pushed toward them, threatening to squash them if they didn't slide the pin into place in time.

"The wall! It's going to crush us!" Hachi yelled. She found an extra ounce of strength somewhere and pushed even harder, and their pin finally clicked into place. The room turned with the pressure from Buster's finger, and Hachi and Kitsune slid to the floor, their pin safely tucked behind the wall of the turning room.

Hachi frowned. The wall in front of them wasn't rumbling at them anymore. In fact, it looked as smooth as it had when they'd begun.

"But how—?" Hachi said. And then she understood. "*You,*" she said to Kitsune. "That wall was never moving. You just made me think it was."

Kitsune grinned. "It's funny how fear makes you do things you never thought you could do."

"No," Hachi said. "It's not funny at all."

Once the lock was in place, they all climbed back out to the top. The tube with the ladder, just as Fergus had guessed, had rotated so that it didn't dead-end any more. There was another ladder in another tube beneath it.

"Down we go," Fergus said.

THOOM. THOOM. THOOM. Something beat against the walls of the prison far below, shaking the earth for a mile above it.

"Sounds like somebody's really, really angry," Kitsune said.

"Martine mesmerized Uktena before. She can probably do it again," Clyde said.

Kitsune's whispered response made them all get quiet.

"Who said I was talking about the snake?"

22

THOOM. THOOM. THOOM. Whatever was pounding on the walls of the puzzle trap below, it was strong. And angry. It kept pounding, again and again and again. None of them had to say what they were all thinking: that Archie had been trapped in an ancient League prison like he was a monster, and then they had dropped a Mangleborn on top of him. He had every right to be mad. But how mad was he? If Archie had lost control down there they could all be working hard to free a monster as bad as a Mangleborn.

The rest of the League climbed down the ladder into a tall, round, smooth-walled chamber directly below the giant lock. Strange symbols, each about the size of a fist, were carved in rows of seven characters each all the way down the brass wall.

Hachi traced the patterns of the symbols with her fingers. "Atlantean?" she asked.

"No," Martine said. She was taking the steps on the ladder very slowly, scanning each line.

"Older," Señor X said. "Older than me. If it's words, I don't know what it says."

"There must be dozens of characters," Clyde said.

"There are forty-one unique pictographs," Martine said, still scanning the lines. "No. Forty-two."

The lines of symbols ended with the ladder at the floor of the chamber. The last row had only six characters. In place of the seventh was a small opening with part of a spinning dial showing through it, like the back end of a steamboat. As the dial was spun, each of the forty-two characters Martine had counted appeared one at a time.

Beside the little window with the dial was a button, almost like a period at the end of a very long sentence.

"That's just brass," said Fergus. "So we're supposed to turn that wee wheel to the right character, I suppose, and then push the button. Only we have no idea what any of this says."

"A nursery rhyme clue would have been a lot of help right now," Hachi said.

"Why don't we just try them all?" Kitsune said. She reached for the button.

Hachi caught her wrist.

"Ah ah ah ah," Fergus said. "We know better than that, Foxy. The minute you start guessing, bad things start happening."

Kitsune looked around the empty room. "What's going to happen?"

Hachi glared at her. "Oh, I don't know. Maybe the wall will start closing in on us."

THOOM. THOOM. THOOM. The room shook so hard from the beating the prison was getting that most of them staggered.

"All the king's horses and all his steam men couldn't put Humpty together again," Gonzalo said.

"*Archie is not Humpty Dumpty,*" Fergus said again. "He's not some nursery rhyme monster. He's a real boy, just like the rest of us."

THOOM. THOOM. THOOM.

"Okay. Maybe not just like the rest of us," Fergus allowed. "And maybe he's not a real boy either. But he's not a monster. He's my *friend*. And yours too. All of you."

Fergus's words hung in the air a moment, as though no one was quite willing to challenge him. Or agree with him.

THOOM. THOOM. THOOM.

"He's Archie Dent, and he's a Leaguer," Clyde said, ending the discussion. "Now, somebody figure out what character we're supposed to put in in the next five minutes, or I'm gonna start guessing."

"Martine?" Hachi asked. The tall Karankawan science-pirate was staring at the lines of text, her head tilted thoughtfully. But whatever she was thinking, she kept it to herself. Fergus and Kitsune tried puzzling out the symbols, thinking that perhaps like Aegyptian hieroglyphs each picture had some real-world corollary, but it didn't get them anywhere. For her part, Hachi had no idea what any of it meant.

THOOM. THOOM. THOOM. The room rocked again,

and dirt and rock shook loose from the wall. Whatever was beating on the walls was going to bring the whole puzzle trap down around them.

"Okay, we gotta do something," Clyde said at last. "Here goes nothing."

Everyone stepped back as Clyde spun the dial. It stopped randomly on a character that looked like a mountain with wavy lines over it. He looked around at them to make sure they were all ready, and pushed the button.

Shunk. The door in the ceiling closed and a panel about two feet wide by one foot tall slid open high on the round wall. Water cascaded from it, hitting the floor with a splash. Five of the six heroes stepped back out of the growing puddle's reach. Only Martine stood where she was, still studying the symbols.

"That's not good," Fergus said. In moments, the whole floor would be covered in water.

"Quick! Try another symbol!" Kitsune said.

Clyde spun the dial to a different character and pushed the button.

Shunk. An identical hole opened up below and to the side of the first, pouring twice as much water into the room as before—and twice as fast.

"Told you so!" Fergus said.

Kitsune spun the dial again and hit the button.

Shunk. Another panel opened, and more water gushed in. It swirled around their feet and swallowed their ankles.

"Don't!" Hachi told her.

"Well what else are we supposed to do now?" she threw back.

Gonzalo pulled Señor X from his holster and shot low at the wall. The raygun beam ricocheted harmlessly into the water at their feet.

"No, no," Clyde said. "I'll stay down here and keep trying symbols. Everybody else, on the ladder! Now!"

Gonzalo and Kitsune sloshed over to the ladder and climbed, and Fergus pulled Hachi along with them. Martine stayed where she was, staring at the words on the wall, while Clyde tried the other characters one by one. If there had only been three holes spilling water, he would have had time to try them all. But each time he pushed the button on a wrong symbol, another panel opened up and more water poured in. The water rose faster and faster, coming up to Clyde's chin and Martine's chest.

"Martine! Martine, get up the ladder! You'll drown!" Clyde gasped, treading water to keep his head above water.

"She can't drown," Gonzalo called down. "She can breathe underwater."

"*What?*" Clyde said. "Why didn't anybody say so? Martine, put in more symbols! Hurry! One of them has to work!"

But Martine just stood there, staring at the rows of characters.

Clyde didn't have time to get through to her. He held his breath and dove, trying another symbol. Another panel opened. The water swallowed Martine entirely and she floated off the surface, still staring at the rows of symbols as she rose. Clyde came up for air and tried to dive again, but it was already too far. He burst from the water gasping for air. They couldn't have put in a dozen of the forty-two possible characters yet.

"Martine!" Clyde yelled. "*Martine!*" She couldn't hear him underwater. Clyde put a finger to the shell in his ear. "Martine! You have to put in more symbols! Hurry! The water's more than halfway up!"

Martine didn't answer. She just stared at the rows of symbols on the wall like she was mesmerized.

Hachi helped pull Clyde onto the ladder.

"What's she doing?" Hachi asked over the roar of the waterfalls.

"I don't know!" Clyde said. "Maybe that Mangleborn's got her mesmerized again. She's not listening!"

"Gonzalo!" Hachi called. "Get her attention!"

"What?" he said. "How?"

"She means shoot her," Kitsune told him.

"I'm not going to shoot her!" Gonzalo told her.

The water rose so high Hachi and Clyde had to let go of the ladder and float, or they wouldn't be able to breathe. Martine still hung in the water below them, motionless.

"Just enough to get her attention!" Hachi said, fighting to keep her head above water. "An arm or a leg or something!"

The ceiling was just a few inches above their heads now. Fergus and Kitsune let go of the ladder so they wouldn't drown, and Hachi swam over and helped the struggling Fergus keep his face above the water.

"Gonzalo!" Clyde burbled. "Do it!"

Gonzalo drew his raygun and fought to aim it in the swirling water.

KaPOM. The raygun made a strange sound underwater, but it shot out straight at Martine.

"We missed!" Señor X said.

"What do you mean, you missed?" Kitsune said. "You never miss!"

"She moved!" Gonzalo told them.

Hachi ducked back underwater. He was right! Martine was swimming down to the dial! The tattooed Karankawan girl turned the dial until she found the symbol she was looking for, and pushed the button.

Shunk! The panels on the sides of the walls closed all at once, and the water drained quickly from the chamber. They rode the water down most of the way until it became a whirl-pool slurping down at the center of the room, and they grabbed hold of the ladder again not to be sucked down. The water emptied down the sewer-sized hole that had opened up in the floor with a *slurrrrrrrrrrch*, leaving Martine standing alone on the floor.

"You did it!" Gonzalo said as everyone climbed down to join her.

"And took your time about it," Hachi grumbled.

"Did you translate it?" Fergus asked. "What did it say?"

"I do not know what it says," Martine told them.

"Then . . . how'd you know what symbol to put in?" Clyde asked. "Did your great-grandmother tell you?"

"No," Martine said. "We are no longer in contact. And this room was built by humans, not by Mangleborn."

"But we saw you. You waited until the last second and just put in the one."

"The right one," Kitsune said, shaking out her fox tail.

"The friendliest one," Martine said.

"The . . . the friendliest one?" Hachi said.

Martine pointed to a symbol. "This one is remorseful. She's done something bad. This one is vigilant. I almost picked him, but he was orange, and orange is not a reliable color. This one," she said, "is bored. I was certainly not going to pick her."

"You picked a symbol because of the way it made you feel?" Gonzalo asked.

"No," Martine told him. "I picked a symbol because of the way *it* was feeling. And because it was blue. I like blue."

Hachi scanned the tall column of letters. Not one of them was any color but black. Hachi shook her head. Martine couldn't tell one human emotion from another, but she saw emotions in meaningless symbols. And they had almost drowned while she was off in la-la land doing it. But she had come back with the right answer. Just how she did it, none of them understood.

"Martine, it was right clever of you to figure all that out," Clyde told her. "But next time, we need you to talk to us, all right? You don't need to tell us *everything* you're thinking. Most of us wouldn't understand it if you *did*, and that's a fact. But you need to tell us if you're thinking things that can help, so we know what's going on. Got it?"

"I understand," Martine said. "I apologize for not being more communicative."

THOOM. THOOM. THOOM.

"Archie?" Clyde called on the shell again. "Archie? Can you hear me?"

Still nothing. Did no response mean there was something wrong with his shell, or something wrong with Archie?

THOOM. THOOM. THOOM.

Clyde motioned everyone down through the hole that had opened in the floor, where another ladder was visible.

"If you can hear me, Archie, hang tight," Clyde said. "We're coming for you."

23

The ladder from the water tank went down, down, down, for more thousands of feet than any of them besides Martine cared to count, finally ending in a tall, broad cavern carved from the bedrock far beneath Sonnionto. Curved metal braces in the shape of snakes ran up the rock wall to hold up the roof, and on the floor was engraved the enormous image of a snake eating its own tail. Martine bent to run a hand along the carving.

"The Ouroboros," Señor X whispered, sounding awed for the first time since any of them had met him.

"The what?" Clyde asked.

"The Ouroboros," Señor X said. "That symbol on the floor. That's what the Greeks called it. But the symbol was older than they were, far older. Older than Atlantis, or Lemuria, or Mu. The Greeks believed the symbol originated with the First Men, whom they called the Ouroboros—Greek for 'the tail-devouring snake.' The First Men were the first to understand that everything that happens has happened before, and will happen again and again and again, like a snake eating its own tail."

"That's cheery," Fergus said.

"No," said Martine. "It is not."

All around the room stood brass statues of Ouroboros warriors, their faces hidden behind broad helmets with long, pointed chins, slits for eyes, and U-shaped snakes on top like horns. On their short, squat bodies they wore scaled armor that hung like dresses down to their booted feet, and their long, muscular arms would have hung down almost as far if their hands weren't resting on the hilts of long, snake-shaped swords that were planted upside down in the ground in front of them.

"What I wouldn't give to have a look under one of those helmets," Señor X said.

"Aye. Be careful," Fergus said, "or you'll get your wish when one of those things comes after us swinging his big snaky sword."

"*Fergus*," Hachi said.

"What? You know I'm right!" Fergus said.

The Ouroboros warriors stood sentinel over a series of U-shaped snake statues throughout the hall. Beyond them on the far wall, ringed by another snake eating its tail, was an enormous door.

THOOM. THOOM. THOOM.

The door shook with the force of the blows from the thing behind it, rock and dust tinkling down from the ceiling each time. They stood and watched for a moment, none of them sure they really wanted to open that door and face what was behind it.

"Do you hear that?" Gonzalo asked.

"The big booming sounds? Aye, I think everyone in Sonnionto can hear that," Fergus said.

"No. The hum. Something around a high C," Gonzalo said.

"He's right," Señor X said. "I've got it. It's barely audible, but it's an E all right, somewhere around 510 hertz. Good ears, kid."

"There are more notes too," Gonzalo said. "E, B, A—"

THOOM. THOOM. THOOM. Everything in the room shook and vibrated.

"They're tuning forks," Fergus said. "The snake statues. That's why they're in U shapes. They're great metal tuning forks. The pounding's making them vibrate."

"They have to have something to do with opening the door," Hachi said. "That's the way these things work."

"Well, if we hit them harder, they'll ring louder," Gonzalo said. "But do we want to do that?"

"Nae, we don't," Fergus said.

"Yes, we do," said Clyde. "But which one?"

THOOM. THOOM. THOOM. The thing behind the door pounded away.

"There's nothing to do but try one," Hachi said.

Gonzalo took out Señor X and spun the raygun on his finger. "Just say which one."

The rest of the League looked at each other warily.

"Everybody get ready," Clyde said.

Hachi pulled out her knives and summoned her flying circus. Fergus tried to get a new spark after being shorted out in the pool. Martine's aether harpoon glowed. Kitsune disappeared.

"Go, Gonzalo," Clyde said.

Gonzalo shot across his body without moving, picking out one of the low humming tuning forks. *KaPOW!* Señor X's yellow beam hit the statue and glanced off into the rock wall beyond.

The tuning fork rang deep and long over the sound of pounding beyond the big set of doors. The low G that echoed in the chamber was matched by a second sound—another low G from the little U-shaped snake atop one of the Ouroboros warriors' helmets.

KA-shunk. Something mechanical activated inside the warrior, and the statue stirred. It moved haltingly at first, as though it was an old man getting up on a cold morning, but the dust quickly cleared from its ancient clockworks. The Ouroboros warrior pulled its sword from the ground and advanced on them, its enormous boots thundering in the tall, round cavern.

"What did I tell you?" Fergus cried. "What did I tell you?"

The Ouroboros warrior raised his giant snake sword.

"Leaguers—full steam ahead!" Clyde said.

Everyone ducked or ran or charged. The clockwork warrior's sword swooshed down, missing everyone but striking another of the U-shaped snake tuning forks.

Triiiiiiiiiiing. Another note rang out, and another Ouroboros warrior came to life.

KaPOW! KaPOW! KaPOW! Gonzalo shot the clockwork giants, knocking them back but not penetrating their brass bodies. Fergus tried shocking one with what little lektric charge he could muster, but to no effect. Martine buried her aether harpoon in the chest of one of the warriors, but the giant kept coming.

Triiiiiiiiiiiing. One of the warriors hit another of the tuning forks, and a third clockwork giant came to life.

"This is clinker!" Clyde cried.

"The U shapes on their helmets are matching the resonant frequencies of the larger tuning forks," Martine explained.

"Aye," said Fergus. "And they're using that vibration as an energy source. These clockworks don't wind, they run off vibrations! Brilliant!"

"You think we can marvel at the ingenuity of the ancients *after* we destroy it?" Hachi asked, jumping out of the way of a warrior's sword.

"Would stopping the big forks from vibrating stop the big guys from running?" Clyde asked.

"Nae, I don't think so," Fergus said. "Now that those thingies on their heads are vibrating, I'd say they'll run on their own for a long while. But they are helping, I suppose."

Triiiiiiiiiiiing. The warriors hit another tuning fork. Now there were four of the giants stomping around the cavern swinging swords at them. And so far, none of the Leaguers had found any way to stop them.

"There are three more tuning forks than there are clockwork warriors," Martine observed.

"The other three must be the ones that open the door!" Hachi said.

"Aye, but which three?" Fergus asked.

KaPOW! Gonzalo shot one of the still tuning forks. And another. And another. More Ouroboros warriors came to life.

"Gonzalo, what are you doing?" Clyde yelled. He jumped out of the way as one of the new warriors almost stomped him.

Gonzalo kept shooting tuning forks until every last one of them was ringing. All the clockwork warriors were awake and thundering around the room, chasing the Leaguers with their swords.

Gonzalo stood very still, listening. "Just keep 'em busy," he told the others.

"Keep 'em busy, he says!" Fergus cried.

Hachi climbed one of the snake-like supports on the wall and leaped onto a warrior's back. She tried grabbing onto the vibrating U on its helmet, but it quivered too much for her to hold on. Kitsune leaped from clockwork giant to clockwork giant, trying to get them to swing at her and hit each other instead. Martine hurled her aether harpoon. Clyde distracted one while Fergus tried to climb up under its armor.

"If you're gonna do something, Gonzalo, now would be a good time to do it!" Clyde said. *Thoom*. A giant sword smashed into the ground where he'd just been standing.

Gonzalo turned his head this way and that. "D. F. B . . . A," he said.

"Yeah," Señor X said. "That's what I get too."

Gonzalo ran across the cavern with Señor X and lined up a shot. *KaPOW!* A yellow beam shot out from his turquoise raygun, ricocheting from tuning fork to tuning fork. *Tring-tring-tring-tring!*

Nothing happened.

"Must have to hit them in order," Gonzalo said.

"There are twenty-four possible combinations in a four-note sequence," Martine called from across the room.

"Twenty-four? We're not going to make it through twenty-four tries!" Clyde cried. He and Fergus were hiding behind a rock that had shaken loose from the ceiling.

"Gonzalo—the Ouroboros," Señor X said. "There's a snake eating its tail on the floor."

"Where? Take me."

Señor X guided Gonzalo to the center of the room, dodging the giant battling warriors. Gonzalo spun slowly, listening to the vibrations from the tuning forks all around the room.

"Gonzalo! Look out!" Hachi cried. An Ouroboros warrior had found him, and was raising its sword high over its head to smash down on the ranger.

"No, I got it. I got it—" Gonzalo said. The clockwork giant swung. Gonzalo raised Señor X and fired. *Tring-tring-tring-tring!*

Whhhht. The Ouroboros warrior's sword stopped inches from Gonzalo's head, and the clockwork giant straightened and returned to his place. So did the rest.

Gonzalo spun Señor X on his finger and slid him back into his holster.

"You did it!" Clyde said, and they all rushed to congratulate him. "How'd you know which ones to hit?"

"Well, I just shot them all, then listened for the ones that didn't have matching resonant frequencies on the warriors. The ones without a match had to be the ones that opened the door."

"And you struck those notes in order by color, in order of decreasing wavelengths," Martine said.

"Um, no," Gonzalo said. "I stood in the circle the Ouroboros made on the floor, and there was only one way to hit all of them from there with one shot."

Martine tilted her head. "But you *did* strike the colors in order of decreasing wavelength."

Gonzalo shrugged. "Okay."

The last of the giant clockwork warriors returned to its place, and the only sound left was the echo of the chord Gonzalo had played.

KA-CHUNK. A mechanism inside the wall activated, and the half-circle doors inside the Ouroboros on the wall began to part.

"Oh, crivens," Hachi said.

"Everybody behind Gonzalo!" Clyde said. "Gonzalo, you know what to do!"

Gonzalo made an adjustment on his raygun and aimed it at the dark slit that appeared between the opening doors. If Uktena came at them through that door they had another big battle ahead of them. Unless Martine could snake-charm it again.

If an angry Archie came through that door, none of them was quite sure *what* they would do.

Skritch. Skritch. Skritch. Something moved in the darkness, and even Gonzalo, fearless as he was, took a step backward as the thing came out of the shadows into the light.

24

It was Archie.

His face was smudged, his clothes were torn, and everyone could see the crack in his arm—the crack that showed he was stone inside. He was dragging something behind him with both hands, which made him hunch forward like an ape.

From where they stood, none of them could tell if he'd gone berserk again. Hachi tensed. Gonzalo aimed his raygun. Martine activated her shield.

"Archie?" Fergus said.

Archie straightened. "Hey," he said. He smiled. "Took you guys long enough."

Nobody rushed to hug him. Not yet.

"You're not—you didn't—" Hachi tried.

"Lose control?" Archie said. "No." He raised his eyebrows at Gonzalo, who still had Señor X pointed at him. "What good was that going to do if I had?"

"It's okay, Gonzalo," Clyde said, and the ranger lowered his raygun.

Kitsune looked sheepish. "When we didn't hear from you on the shells, we thought—"

"Oh. Yeah. Sorry. Lost my shell thingy in the fall. Moffett *did* try to make me lose control," Archie told them. "And that fall didn't help. Neither did having a Mangleborn dropped on me."

Archie tossed the enormous pair of antlers he'd been dragging behind him into the cavern.

"You killed Martine's great-grandmother," Fergus said.

"I did *what*?" Archie asked.

"Never mind," Gonzalo said. "And Señor X says it's not dead, just sleeping."

"I snapped off its horns," Archie said. "That put it down."

The League stared at the giant things, each of them thinking how difficult it would have been for them to defeat Uktena without Archie, and how much harder it would be if they ever had to take on their friend themselves.

"I'm . . . impressed," Hachi said, still skeptical.

"See?" Fergus told her, as though he'd just won some argument.

"I practiced my mantra. The one you taught me," Archie told Hachi. "I kept saying the names and pounded on the walls, trying to bust my way out in case you couldn't come get me. But you did. Thank you."

Everyone came forward then to congratulate Archie and

shake his hand or hug him. Hachi kept watching him like she expected him to lose control any moment, but he seemed like regular old Archie.

Fergus pushed aside Archie's torn sleeve and ran his fingers down the crack in Archie's arm. "You know, I had me an idea about this crack, Archie," Fergus said. "I could put a metal brace over it, bolt it right into your arm, like they do with stone walls. Keep it from splitting open any wider."

Everyone stared at Fergus like he'd just pulled the pin on an aether grenade.

"What?" he said to them. "Archie gets it. Don't you?"

"Sure," Archie said. He pulled his torn sleeve back over the crack. "Yeah. Of course. Maybe later," he said. He looked away, and Hachi punched Fergus in the arm. Hard.

Ow, he mouthed silently.

"Want to say good-bye to granny?" Gonzalo asked Martine.

"No," she told him. "I know where she is and how to reach her again if I wish to study her in the future."

Gonzalo shot the tuning forks again, and the huge seal closed, trapping Uktena in the prison that had been designed for her so long ago.

"Now what?" Kitsune asked.

"Now I'm done fooling around," Archie said. "I want to take down Moffett and end this."

"We don't know where she went," Clyde told him. "She released Uktena and split."

"New Rome," Archie said. "That's where she's going. I'm sure of it. New Rome, to get her revenge on the Septemberist Society. That's where the headquarters is. But I'm going to catch her before she gets there, and I'm going to kill her."

A little of the dangerous fire they had all seen in Archie's eyes at one point or another flashed, and the League was scared all over again. Part of Archie hated those looks, but a growing part of him liked that he could make people afraid.

"Let's go," Archie said. He turned and stalked off toward the ladder up.

"All the king's horses and all his steam men couldn't put Humpty together again," Kitsune whispered when he was out of earshot.

Martine nodded. "The entropy of an isolated system never decreases," she said. Everyone looked at her. "Humpty Dumpty. The Second Law of Thermodynamics." She took their silent confusion as an invitation to elaborate. "The higher the entropy, the higher the disorder, thus it is increasingly improbable that Humpty Dumpty can be returned to his earlier state of lower entropy."

"Does anybody understand what she's talking about?" Hachi said.

"I do," said Fergus. He watched Archie, who walked away muttering to himself. "Every new thing that happens to Archie makes it more likely he'll crack—and less and less likely we'll be able to put him back together again when he does."

25

Buster was growling deep down in his boiler room long before any of the rest of them heard the booming in the distance.

"Raycannons," Gonzalo said. He drew Señor X. "Aether rifles too. Somebody's fighting. Lots of somebodies."

They were thirteen hours into a quick march north and east from Sonnionto up through the Appalachian Mountains, past the Powhatan city of Totopotomoi and north of the Yankee town of Baltimore. By Clyde's estimate, they were still half a day away from Philadelphia, but the explosions were close enough and loud enough to warrant a detour.

Buster crested a ridge, and the League of Seven crowded the bridge windows and gunwales to see. Stretched out before them along a broad, rolling, tree-dotted plain was the biggest battle any of them had ever seen. Thousands of soldiers wearing dark blue United Nations Army uniforms charged forward with oscillating rifles and aether pistols, filling the air with blue raygun beams. On ridges above them, three mobile raycannons rained down hot death.

"Who are they fighting? Manglespawn?" Hachi asked.

Buster's telescopic lenses clicked into place. No—it wasn't monsters the UN Army was fighting. It was First Nations tribesmen!

"Piscataway, maybe?" Clyde said. It was difficult to see from this far out. "Susquehannock? According to the map, we're just south of Peshtank."

"But why would UN soldiers be fighting against either of those tribes?" Archie asked. "They're all members of the United Nations!"

"Let's find out," Clyde said. "All hands, prepare for battle!" he called into his speaking trumpet. Clyde flipped a switch, and the steam man rumbled as its left arm transformed into a raycannon.

Buster ran up to the fight, and Clyde stepped over the UN's battle lines. The UN soldiers gave a cheer—to them, Buster was *Colossus*, a United Nations steam man cavalry unit, come to join the battle.

BWAAAAAAT! Clyde fired Buster's big raycannon, carving out a deep trench between the UN forces and whatever tribe that was fighting them. "You guys cut it out now!" Clyde called through his external speaker. "I ain't kidding!"

The ragged bunch of rebels turned their raygun fire on Buster, but it didn't even slow him down. Clyde fired into the sky, trying to scare them. *BWAAAAAAT!* Men and women dropped their oscillating rifles and ran away screaming.

"Wow. That was effective," said Hachi.

"I think we may have had a little help," Archie said.

Kitsune had snuck up onto the bridge and was perched in the drummer's chair behind Clyde.

"What'd you make them see?" Hachi asked.

Kitsune grinned. "Just Buster as himself," she said. "A ten-story-tall dog. Who also breathes fire."

Clyde fired the raycannon one more time just to scare off the stragglers. Men and women in the UN line cheered, and Clyde steered toward the flag that marked the location of the commander in charge: General Robert E. Lee. General Lee was a white-haired, bearded man in his fifties, wearing a smart blue UN uniform with the knee-length coat buttoned all the way to the top and tied tight at the waist with a belt of gold braid. From one side of his belt hung a sheathed saber; from the other hung a raygun holster. Archie knew Lee from the Septemberist headquarters—he was the current head of the Society's Warrior Guild, as well as being the war chief of the United Nations of America. If he was here, things were doubly bad.

"Private Clyde Magoro of the United Nations Seventh Steam Man Regiment, sir!" Clyde said, snapping to attention and saluting as soon as he and the other Leaguers were outside Buster. The steam man plopped his big brass bottom on the ground and wagged his tail.

General Lee frowned. "The UNSM *Colossus?*" he said. "The *Colossus* was reported lost with all hands under Captain Custer in Pawnee territory a month ago."

"Ah, yes sir," Clyde said. "Not exactly."

General Lee looked over the odd collection of kids, and then up at Buster, who was thumping his back leg against his brass body like he was scratching at a flea.

"Who's piloting *Colossus*?" General Lee asked.

Clyde rubbed the back of his head. "Well, nobody at present. It's a long story, sir, and that's a fact. But Archie here, he says all I really need to tell you is that we're the League of Seven."

"Thirty days hath September," Archie said.

"Seven heroes we remember," General Lee answered. But he still looked incredulous until Archie lifted an overturned cannon and set it back on its wheels. Recognition dawned on his face.

"You—you're—" General Lee said.

"Archie Dent. The strongman the Septemberist Council was getting reports on," Archie said darkly. *The strongman the Society created.* He breathed deeply, trying not to get angry, but he could feel the rage building like a coming storm. "I'm what you always wanted. And you got the rest of your League too."

General Lee ushered the seven of them and Mr. Rivets into his tent, and Clyde gave him the best summary he could of everything that had happened.

"First things first: I think you're due for a promotion, Mr. Magoro," General Lee said. He called to an attendant. "Bring me some captain's stripes for this young man."

"Captain! Dang. Wait'll I tell Mrs. DeMarcus."

"Can't have the leader of the League of Seven be a lowly private," General Lee said. He pinned the silver bars on Clyde's collar, and Clyde stood ten inches taller. "As for the rest of you,

you're just in time. That Monster Army Moffett created'll be here any time now, with her and three Mangleborn at the head of it."

The League looked around at each other. *Three* Mangleborn? At once?

"I've decided to make our stand here," General Lee said.

"Where's 'here,' sir?" Clyde asked.

"We're just outside a tiny Yankee village called Gettysburg," Lee told them, gesturing at a map on his table. "There's not a lot of civilians, and it's got good, defensible hills and a wide-open battlefield. And we're going to need it. I have fifty regiments, a hundred raycannon, and three more steam men are on the way. It's going to be a bloody thing, but I mean to do it before those monsters reach Philadelphia, or wherever it is they're headed."

Clyde whistled. "That's the biggest fighting force the United Nations has ever had in one place at one time."

"It will be if they don't all run off first," Lee said. "I'll be lucky if half those seventy thousand warriors show up. Just this morning I had a third of my troops go AWOL, running home to fight for their own tribes."

"Fight who?" Fergus asked.

"Each other. The Cherokee and the Muskogee are at it again. So are the Choctaw, Pawnee, and Illini. The Council of Three Fires has declared war on the Cree, and the Iroquois are invading Acadia. The United Nations is falling apart: it's civil war. It's that Dragon Lantern. Moffett's stirring up Manglespawn, and they're stirring up Mangleborn. And you know what happens to people when Mangleborn get inside their heads."

Archie felt like everyone was trying very hard not to look at him right then.

"We need UN forces in a dozen places right now," General Lee said, "and I have to pull them all back here to Nowheresville in Powhatan territory to take on twenty-five thousand Manglespawn we probably can't beat to begin with."

Twenty-five thousand Manglespawn? Archie'd had no idea. He'd wasted so much time, done so much moping. It was time to stop being Achilles sulking in his tent and take care of Moffett once and for all.

"We're here to help, sir," Clyde said.

"We need to take out Moffett first," Archie said.

"And what about the three wee Mangleborn she's bringing with her? Or the twenty-five thousand Manglespawn?" Fergus asked.

"If we don't take her out, she could make forty thousand *more* Manglespawn, and raise half a dozen more Mangleborn."

"Archie's got a point," Hachi said. "Any other heads we cut off will just keep growing back unless we cut her head off first. So to speak."

"Cutting off her head sounds like a good plan to me," Archie said, and they all gave him that look again.

"I think I have a lot simpler idea," said Clyde.

26

The Monster Army massed just beyond the Gettysburg plain, a snarling, writhing horde of grotesque shadows. Behind them, in a cloud of green mist, the League of Seven could see the vague shape of mountains moving behind them.

Mangleborn.

"He's right. There's three of 'em," Clyde told the other Leaguers by shell. "Two big ones and one small one. And by small I mean Buster-sized." He watched the great lumbering shapes through Buster's magnified eyes, high above the line of nervous soldiers.

"Crivens! Where'd they come from? How'd they get free?" Fergus asked. He waited with the rest of the Leaguers on the ground.

"It doesn't matter," Hachi said. She activated the aggregator on the personal wave cannon she held.

"She's right," Clyde said. "All that matters is we stop 'em."

One of the Mangleborn roared in the distance, a thundering sound like a drowning panther, and the line of UN soldiers started to back away. General Lee rode out into the empty plain on a steamhorse and wheeled to face his warriors.

"Men! Women! Listen to me! Five score years ago, our elders brought forth on this continent a new nation, conceived in liberty, and dedicated to the proposition that all tribes are created equal," Lee said. "Now we are engaged in a great war—a *monster* war—testing whether that nation, or any nation so conceived and dedicated, can long endure." Tendrils of steam rose off Lee's horse in the cool morning air. "The world will little note, nor long remember, what we say here. But it will never forget what we *do* here. It is for us, the living, to be dedicated here to the unfinished work our elders so nobly advanced—that these United Nations shall have a new birth of freedom, and that government of the tribes, by the tribes, *for* the tribes, shall not perish from the earth!"

The soldiers cheered. Chippewa, Mohawk, Shawnee, Choctaw, Yankees, Seminole, Cherokee, Muskogee, Illini, Algonquin, and more. They stood beside each other, *with* each other, ready to fight to preserve the Union, no matter what came howling over the ridge.

"Warriors," Lee bellowed. "Oscillators at the ready! Aggregate aether!"

The massive line clicked and hummed as fifty thousand oscillators, pistols, and raycannons drew energy from the aether.

Lee rode his steamhorse over to where the League stood. "You ready to do your part?"

"We'll take down Moffett," Archie said.

"And then we'll handle those Mangleborn," Hachi told him.

"I sure as Hades hope you can. Good luck," General Lee told them, then rode off to lead his troops.

"You find her yet?" Hachi asked Clyde via shell.

"Got her," Clyde told them. "You ain't gonna like it."

"Where is she?"

"Right in the middle of all them Manglespawn."

"Can you hide me?" Archie asked Kitsune.

"I think so," she said. "But that's a lot of brains to fool. And some of them aren't very human anymore."

"I just need you to hide me long enough to get close."

"Lemme just shoot her," Gonzalo said.

Hachi shook her head. "We've talked about this. You get close enough to shoot her, she's close enough to use that sonic scream of hers on you. Or worse, the Dragon Lantern. Hopefully Kitsune can keep Archie hidden until he's on top of her. If she figures it out somehow, he'll be all right. But you'd be dead. We all would be. There's no sense sending in anybody but Archie."

"I can do it," Archie said.

"You just focus on what you need to focus on," Hachi told him. "Don't go thinking bad thoughts. And don't listen to those Mangleborn."

Archie could already feel the giant monsters tugging at his consciousness. Probing his brain. They knew him. They knew he was here. The Jandal a Haad. And soon they would call to him.

He couldn't lose control. He wouldn't. Not here. Not now. Not ever. He closed his eyes and whispered the beginning of Hachi's mantra. *Talisse Fixico, the potter. Chelokee Yoholo, father of Ficka. Hathlun Harjo, the surgeon.* He had to be better. For them.

"We better get to it," Clyde told them. "It looks like she's whipping them into a frenzy. Battle's gonna start any minute now, and that's a fact."

"We'll be right behind you," Hachi told Archie.

"I won't be long," he promised them, and he walked off toward the Monster Army.

A thing covered in porcupine needles quivered past Archie on his left side. A monster with the head of a lizard, the beak of a bird, and the body of a horse stamped past on the right. A man with jagged rocks growing out through his skin staggered right toward him, a low moan coming from his rock-filled mouth, and Archie quickly sidestepped him. Archie was deep inside the Monster Army now, but Kitsune's illusion still held. Mangle-spawn slithered and wriggled and marched past him, oblivious to his existence, moving like mindless automatons toward the fields where General Lee's United Nations Army waited for them. Archie went in the opposite direction, slipping between them and around them and sometimes, frighteningly, *underneath* them, toward the center of the army. Toward Philomena Moffett.

Archie held his breath as he narrowly slid between an orange, flaming dog and a gasping fish-woman. He didn't need to breathe anyway, he thought.

Jandal a Haad, one of the Mangleborn whispered inside his head. *Made of stone.*

Mountainheart. Enemy to Both Sides, said the second.

Always different, but always the same, said the third.

No. No! Archie was closer to the Mangleborn now, those dark shapes hovering in the green mist beyond the Monster Army. He had to ignore their voices. Remember who he was. What he was doing. He was Archie Dent. He was a Leaguer. A hero.

And he was going to stop Philomena Moffett.

She stood on a low hill about fifty yards away, crowing something at the Manglespawn that swarmed past her. Archie stood still as an elephant-like man lumbered past him, then pushed on.

Something that looked like a cross between a bee and a bear stood on its hind legs off to his side, its nose high in the air. Archie froze. It sniffed in all directions, finally pointing itself at Archie. It might not be able to see through Kitsune's illusion, but whatever it was, it could *smell* through it. The Manglespawn stopped walking forward with the rest of the mob and pushed its way toward him, and Archie hurried forward. He still had to be careful not to brush any of the other monsters. Kitsune couldn't hide him knocking one of them over. And the things didn't move in straight lines. They stomped and fought and shook and swayed. It was like trying to slip across a dance floor without touching any of the dancers. Only in this case the dancers were super-ugly monsters.

The bee-bear's wings buzzed in excitement as it got closer and Archie's scent got stronger. No! Archie was almost to Moffett! He could even hear what she was saying now—

"My fellow monsters, this is our moment! This is our world!" Moffett cried. "And it is time to take back what's ours!"

Archie wasn't going to make it—the bee-bear was going to catch up to him before he got to Moffett. Worse, the bee-bear was making a beeline for him, plowing against the current of the other Manglespawn. If Moffett looked in their direction, she would see what amounted to an arrow pointing straight at him. She still might not see *him*, but she wasn't stupid. She would know something, some*one*, was there, and she would kill as many Manglespawn as it took to find him with her sonic scream.

The bee-bear snuffled and grunted through the Manglespawn. The stinger on its snout poked between a rolling ball of cats and a gelatinous blob, coming within inches of Archie. Still ranting, Moffett turned toward them on her tentacles. She was going to see the bee-bear. Find Archie, unless—

Archie thumped the bee-bear on the head. It dropped dead on the ground like a sack of potatoes. Archie froze. Moffett turned. Ranted. Her eyes swept past.

She hadn't seen them!

Archie let out the breath he hadn't realized he'd been holding, and turned. An oozing thing covered with eyeballs walked into him, blinded by Kitsune's illusion. Archie cried out, stumbled backwards, and tripped over the fallen bee-bear. He knocked three more Manglespawn over, and monsters began to pile up and fight with each other in the chaos.

Moffett quickly looked back. "What was that? What's going on?"

Slag it! Archie was such a klutz! He kicked and punched at the Manglespawn, trying to get them off of him, but they wriggled and writhed and oozed all over him. Then something was lifting the monsters off him and hurling them away, and there was Philomena Moffett, standing right over him. She frowned at the empty space Kitsune was making her see, until one of her tentacles snaked out and poked Archie in the stomach.

Suddenly the spell was broken. Moffett's eyes went wide with surprise. She could see him! She took a deep breath and opened her mouth to scream, but Archie was faster. He lunged forward and punched her in the stomach.

Philomena Moffett went flying. She slammed into the hill, bounced over it, and tumbled down the other side in a swirl of tentacles and bustle skirt. Archie chased her, knocking Manglespawn out of the way like bowling pins. Behind him, he heard Buster thundering toward them. Clyde and the others had seen what happened. *BWAAAAT!* Buster's raycannon carved a path through the Manglespawn, and in moments Archie and Buster stood together over the limp body of Mrs. Moffett. Archie raised a fist to hit her again, but she didn't move.

Philomena Moffett was down for the count.

Clyde used Buster's raycannon again to blast a deep trench around them that kept out most of the swarming Monster Army. Behind them, General Lee's aether pistol shot a blue beam into the sky, and they heard the UN Army roar and charge the Manglespawn, rayguns streaming. The Monster War had begun.

"Is she dead?" Clyde asked as Buster lowered the other Leaguers, Alamo, and Mr. Rivets to the ground.

"No," said Señor X. "Tough broad. You didn't even hurt her that badly."

Martine passed her harpoon over Moffett and read the

markings on the handle. "The raygun is correct. She is alive, but unconscious."

Kitsune collected the Dragon Lantern and made sure the slats in it were fully closed.

"So, we did it," Fergus said, amazed. "Moffett's down, and we've got the Dragon Lantern back. It's party time!"

Hachi punched him in the shoulder. "Except for the twenty-five thousand Manglespawn and three Mangleborn still to fight."

"Yeah, I don't want them at the party," Kitsune said.

"So what do we do about Moffett in the meantime?" Clyde asked. He swatted a leaping frog-woman away with Buster's hand. "We can't just leave her here. She's gonna wake up sometime, and then she's gonna start in all over again."

"Can we tie her up?" Kitsune asked.

"Maybe with my lasso," Gonzalo said. "But I sure don't have enough handcuffs for all those tentacles."

"Is there any kind of prison that could hold her with that sonic scream?" Hachi asked.

"Maybe something that canceled out her sound waves? A kind of sonic echo chamber," Fergus said to Martine.

"Or, you know, we could just kill her," said Señor X.

27

Señor X's suggestion that they just kill Moffett got everybody quiet. Archie'd been thinking it, but he hadn't wanted to say it. Maybe they all had. But could they really kill her? Here? Now? In cold blood?

"No," Gonzalo said. "I know—the amber!" He turned a knob on his raygun and aimed it at Moffett.

"No, wait," Hachi said. She reached out a hand to stop him, but it was too late. *Kishoooooom.* A blue stream from the raygun hit Philomena Moffett, and transparent blue resin splooshed onto her. Gonzalo kept shooting until the resin swallowed Moffett whole, encapsulating her from head to tentacles in a big blue block.

Blue amber, Archie realized. The stuff Sings-In-The-Night had been frozen in at Dodge City.

Gonzalo twirled his raygun and reholstered it. "Boom. Problem solved," he said.

Archie walked up to the big block of blue amber and put his hand to it. Philomena Moffett lay entombed inside, her eyes closed like she was sleeping.

Martine passed her harpoon over Moffett again. "The blue amber has created a perfect hibernation effect, as anticipated."

"'As anticipated?'" Archie said. He looked around at all the other Leaguers. Not one of them seemed as surprised as he was by what Gonzalo had just done. "I don't understand," Archie said. "Since when can your raygun shoot blue amber?"

The group grew still again the way they had when Señor X suggested they just kill Moffett. Gonzalo opened his mouth to say something, then closed it. Archie looked from Leaguer to Leaguer, but none of them would meet his eyes. None of them except Hachi.

A cold pit opened up in Archie's stomach, and an explanation began to form in the back of his brain, an idea that grew and spread like the crack in his arm.

Jandal a Haad, the Mangleborn whispered. *Mountainheart. Stone Coat.*

Enemy to Both Sides.

Archie tried to shake off the voices. "You said—you said your raygun didn't have a freeze ray. I asked you in Houston, Gonzalo, and you said no. So does someone want to tell me why his raygun can shoot the *blue amber* from Dodge City all of a sudden?" He punctuated the words 'blue amber' by slamming a fist into the block of the stuff that held Philomena Moffett. The block bounced a foot in the air before thudding back down.

Gonzalo put his hands out like he was trying to settle a shying horse. "Whoa now, Archie. Fergus and Martine just made some improvements to Señor X is all," he said.

Down in the valley, the United Nations raycannons *thoom*ed. Dirt exploded. Men screamed.

"Archie, we don't have time for this right now," Clyde told him. He turned Buster toward the fight. "Leaguers, full steam—"

Archie grabbed Buster's huge brass foot and wrenched him back.

"No," Archie said. "*Make* time."

"Archie, twenty-five thousand monsters are pouring over that hill," Fergus told him, "and there's three Mangleborn besides!"

Monsters. The Mangleborn whispered. *Like you.*

You know why Xiuhcoatl wields the amber now.

You know the monster it was meant for.

The voices. The voices! Archie grabbed a clump of his white hair, like he wanted to rip it out. "So—so the only place we ever saw blue amber before was Dodge City," he stammered. "But we didn't take it with us. So that means—that means Clyde and Fergus went back and got it when they went out west after those Shadow Leaguers, didn't they?"

Fergus frowned and glared at Hachi, but nobody said yes or no.

"But then, when did you modify Señor X?" Archie asked. "Because I never saw you do it."

"It's not a big deal, Archie!" Fergus said. "We did it in no time, didn't we?" he said to Martine.

"If by 'no time' you mean all the time we were together after you returned from Dodge City with the technology until recovering Archie in Sonnionto," Martine said.

Fergus put a hand to his tattooed forehead. "Oh, crivens," he muttered.

Monster, the Mangleborn whispered. *Beast. Abomination.*

"So—" Archie said, trying to focus, trying to put all the pieces together. "So, Fergus and Clyde went back to Dodge City while they were out west. Only nobody told me. Then Fergus and Martine worked on Señor X together in Buster on the way to Sonnionto. So you all knew. You all knew and nobody told me."

The fox-girl looked at the ground, and he knew he was right.

"And who's idea was it to begin with, I wonder?" Archie said, looking right at Hachi. "You didn't go back for it, or modify it, or agree to keep the secret from me. You're the one who came up with the idea in the first place, aren't you, Hachi?"

Screams and explosions and howls came from the battle raging a few hundred yards from where they stood.

"We'll talk about this later, Archie," Hachi told him.

"*No!*" Archie yelled. "We'll talk about it now!" He slammed a fist down on the blue amber again, harder this time. It flipped over and slammed into the ground.

Gonzalo drew Señor X and pointed it at him.

Archie laughed. He laughed so hard he had to put his hands on his knees to keep standing. "That's right—I should have remembered. When I came strolling out of that puzzle trap in

Sonnionto, you all thought I'd gone crazy, didn't you? My shell was broken, and when you couldn't reach me, you thought I'd gone crazy down in that deep, dark hole. Gone berserk. When I came out, you were all standing behind the ranger here, and he was pointing his little raygun at me like it could actually do something to me. But you thought it *could*, because you'd fixed it. You'd fixed it to shoot blue amber. All of you. Together."

They fear you, the Mangleborn whispered.

Hate you.

They always have.

And they always will.

Archie put his head in his hands. "You were all in on it. Every last one of you. You didn't modify Señor X to take down Moffett, did you? *You modified him to take down me.*"

Boom. Ka-thoom. Raaaaawr. Yeaaaaaaa! The battle tore on behind them.

"Archie—" Fergus began.

"No!" Archie yelled. "You don't trust me! You never did! None of you!" He pointed to Moffett, frozen in the amber, eyes closed like she was asleep. "How long were you going to keep me on ice?" he asked them. "Huh? If you froze me in amber, when were you going to let me out? You couldn't unfreeze me, because I would still be mad when I came out. *Madder.*" He spun. "How long, then? A day? A week? *Forever?*"

Archie slammed his fist into the block of blue amber again— *Kooom!*—and a crack opened across Moffett's face.

"Archie, don't!" Clyde said.

"*Or what?*" Archie cried. *Kooom.* He hit the amber again, knocking away a piece of the corner. "Gonzalo will trap me in blue amber like Moffett?" *Kooom*. He hit it again and more cracks opened.

Cracks like the one in my arm, Archie thought.

Nunyanuwi. Necoc Yoatl. Jandal a Haad.

Made of Stone.

The Mangleborn on the horizon sang to him. Called Archie. And he longed to join them. They were his brothers and sisters. His family.

Buster's giant raycannon charged. "Stop it, or I'll shoot you," Clyde said.

Archie laughed maniacally and raised his fist to hit the block of amber again.

BWAAAAT.

A thundering blue beam erupted from Buster's arm and destroyed the whole area where Archie stood. *Ka-THOOM!* The blast blew the League back off their feet and showered them with dirt and rock and bits of blue amber.

When the dust cleared, Archie and Philomena Moffett lay stunned in a huge crater in the earth. The blue amber that had encased her was completely gone.

Buster bent down and whimpered, and Clyde reached one of the giant steam man's hands out to nudge his friend.

"Archie—?" Clyde said.

Archie's eyes shot open, and he grabbed Buster's hand. *KEE-RANK!* He yanked the huge brass arm from its socket and used it like a club, smashing it into the side of the steam man's head. *KRANG*. Buster careened and fell, tearing out another huge crater.

"Master Archie—no!" Mr. Rivets cried.

Archie wasn't listening. He was too far gone. He tossed away

Buster's arm, punched a gaping hole in the steam man's head, and pulled Clyde from the pilot's chair. Before any of the other Leaguers could do anything to stop him, Archie tossed Clyde over his shoulder into the heart of the battle.

Buster growled and bit Archie, bending his brass mouth on Archie's stone body. *Crunk.* The giant steam man whistled angrily at Archie and ran off onto the battlefield after Clyde.

Archie stood and panted, glaring at the five remaining Leaguers. They looked at him like he was a, like he was a—

Monster, the creatures on the horizon sang. *Mangleborn.*

Yes. That's what the League thought. What they had *always* thought. That's why they had betrayed him. Worked against him in secret.

And now Archie was going to make them pay.

Kazaaaaaaak!

Archie staggered back as lektricity blasted him. It burned for a hot second, and then the sensation was gone. Lektricity still shot from Fergus's fingers, but Archie couldn't feel it anymore. He took a step forward, pushing against the force of the kicking, streaming lightning, and Fergus cut the current. Archie's singed clothes and white hair smoldered.

"Sorry, Archie," Fergus told him.

"Don't apologize," Hachi said, drawing her knives. "Just kill him."

28

Kishoooooom. A powerful blue beam from Gonzalo's raygun hit him in the chest, and he felt liquid resin begin to gel around him. The blue amber! Before Archie could think how to fight it, the stuff had swallowed his body, his arms, his legs, his head. *Krick-krick-krack.* Blue amber filled Archie's mouth and ears and eyes, consuming him inside and out.

And then it was over. Archie was frozen in blue amber.

"*Òrale,*" Gonzalo whispered. "It worked."

Through a blue haze, Archie watched them all walk up cautiously to see and touch the stuff.

"He's alive in there," Señor X said. "Best I can tell. He doesn't scan like a human being."

Archie pushed with his frozen arms. Pulled with his frozen legs.

"This is wrong," Fergus said. "I told you so from the start."

"Tell that to Clyde," Hachi said.

"We'd better go look for him," Gonzalo said. "He could be really hurt."

Archie strained against the amber, his muscles burning. *No. Not muscles. Living stone.*

"What about Archie?" Kitsune asked.

"I don't know," Hachi said. "But we've got bigger problems right now. Where did Moffett go?"

They looked around. Philomena Moffett was gone.

Krick. Krick-krack.

"What's that sound?" Gonzalo asked.

Martine consulted the symbols on the side of her aetherical harpoon. "The structural integrity of the amber is degrading," she said.

"It's what now?" Kitsune asked.

"The amber's cracking!" Fergus cried.

Krick-krick—KRACKOOM! Chunks of amber went flying as Archie broke free. Before Gonzalo could freeze him again, Archie grabbed the turquoise raygun and crushed it in his fist. *Bzzzzzz-tish!*

Señor X died in a shower of yellow sparks.

"Señor X—*no!*" Gonzalo cried. He went down on all fours, feeling for pieces of the shattered raygun. "Señor X!"

Martine swept Archie off his feet with her aetherical harpoon, and a giant two-legged green dinosaur stomped on him.

Thoom-thoom-thoom-thoom. Archie grabbed for the creature's foot, punched at it, but his hands went right through it.

Kitsune. Kitsune the deceiver.

The lizard wasn't real. But whatever was beating him into the ground *was. Hachi.* Hachi and her wave cannon.

Archie grabbed the tip of Martine's glowing green harpoon and yanked it out of her hands. *Whack!* He batted Hachi's wave cannon away even though he couldn't see it, and hurled the harpoon at the last place Kitsune had been standing.

Shunk.

The big green lizard disappeared and Kitsune appeared, staring down at the aetherical harpoon stuck straight through her left thigh. The Dragon Lantern clanked to the ground beside her, and she collapsed.

Fergus hit Archie with lektricity again. *Kazaaaaaaak!* Archie grabbed Fergus and hurled him, still sparking, at Martine. They tumbled away in a jumble of arms and legs and lektricity.

"Mr. Rivets! Your Surgeon card! Quick!" Hachi cried. She knelt on the ground with Kitsune's head in her lap, the wave cannon tossed aside. Dark red blood soaked Kitsune's white kimono around the glowing green harpoon. "Oh, Archie, what have you done?" Hachi whispered.

"What have I done?" Archie said. "What have *I* done? The same thing you have! You betrayed me!"

"*And what would you have done?*" Hachi yelled. "What would you have done if somebody you knew became a mindless monster any time he got mad and you had no way to stop him?"

"I would have trusted my friend!" Archie screamed.

"Really?" Hachi said. "Take a look around you, Archie, and tell me how that worked out for all your friends!"

Archie closed his eyes. "No," he said. "No, you did this to me. I only did this because you didn't trust me! Because you went behind my back!"

"No," Hachi told him. "You did this because you were always going to. Because of Moffett and the Mangleborn and the puzzle trap and everything else. *Because of how you were born*. You did this because you wanted to forget who you are—*what you are*—and just be a monster. Because being a monster is easier. I know." She got quiet. "I was just the idiot who gave you the push."

Archie opened his eyes. Hachi still sat on the ground with Kitsune's head in her lap while Mr. Rivets tended to her wound.

"All of them, they all did this to me," Archie said dully. He dragged Buster's severed arm to him and held it like a club. "Clyde and Fergus went to Dodge City to get the amber tech. Martine adapted it to Gonzalo's gun. Kitsune lied to me. But it was all your idea, Hachi. I know it was." Archie said. "Right from the start. Wasn't it. *Wasn't it?*" he roared, threatening her with his club.

Hachi raised her head and looked Archie straight in the eyes. "Yes," she said.

Archie lifted the club and slammed it down on her.

29

Hachi ducked, bending protectively over Kitsune.

Krunk.

She flinched, but the big arm didn't hit her. She looked up. Buster! Buster had caught it!

"That belongs to me," Clyde said through Buster's speakers. The big steam man yanked the brass arm out of Archie's hands and swung it at him like a golf club. *Thwank!* Archie went flying, landing somewhere in the middle of the battlefield half a mile away.

Mr. Rivets picked Kitsune up in his powerful brass arms. "My Surgeon card is inside Buster," he told Hachi.

Hachi caught movement out of the corner of her eye and turned. It was Moffett! Philomena Moffett had picked up the

Dragon Lantern and was running away. Away from them, and away from the Monster War. *Twisted pistons.* Hachi's first instinct was to chase her, but Archie was the bigger problem now.

"Clyde! Clyde, we need Buster's medical bay!" Hachi called.

Buster knelt and opened his mouth, and Clyde scrambled down to help Mr. Rivets bring Kitsune inside. Mr. Rivets took her directly to the steam man's surgery.

"Freckles! I need you," Hachi said, and the little brass giraffe her father had made her burst from its pouch on her bandolier and fluttered in front of her. "Follow Moffett. Find out where she's going. Then come back here and tell me. Got it?"

Freckles chittered at her and buzzed away.

Clyde gave Hachi a hand up into Buster's mouth. "Archie did that to Kitsune?" he asked.

"Yes," Hachi said. "And he's going to do worse if we don't stop him."

"Did Gonzalo use the blue amber?" Clyde asked.

"Yes," Martine said. She and Fergus led the crestfallen Gonzalo between them. In Gonzalo's hands, he held the smashed pieces of Señor X.

"Archie's strength exceeded the blue amber's stress tolerance," Martine told Clyde.

Clyde looked to Fergus.

"He broke out," Fergus translated. "And then he broke Señor X."

"*Está muerto,*" Gonzalo muttered, tears streaking his face below his black blindfold. "*Mi mejor amigo está muerto.*"

"*No está muerto,*" Martine told him. "*Está simplemente soñando.*"

"*¿Como?*" Gonzalo said.

"I will take care of Gonzalo and Señor X," Martine said, taking them both on board Buster.

"I'll do for Buster's broken arm," said Fergus.

"But what about Kitsune?" Clyde asked. He and Hachi followed Mr. Rivets to the medical bay, where he already had Kitsune strapped to a bed. She didn't look good.

"I will see to Miss Kitsune's wound as best I can," he said. "But please—you must help Archie. If you can."

"If the blue amber didn't work on him, how do we stop him?" Clyde asked Hachi.

"'All the king's horses and all the king's men,'" Kitsune muttered.

"Lie still now, miss," Mr. Rivets told Kitsune.

"No," Hachi said, suddenly hopeful again. "No—Edison's rhyme: 'Sticks and stones can't break his bones, but words can surely hurt him!' Archie's weakness is his human brain. It's what makes him lose control, and what makes him regain it. And I know just the words to tell him!"

Kitsune grabbed Hachi's arm. "No," she whispered. "*Show* him."

Archie picked up a squirming leech-like thing and ripped it in half. A UN soldier snapped off his bayonet on Archie's chest, and Archie hurled him aside. An airship's raycannon blasted the ground beneath his feet, and Archie went flying again. He landed with an *oomph* on a walrus-like creature with the head of an eagle, and punched a hole in the thing's chest before using it to club another UN warrior.

Tezcatlipoca, the voices sang. *Mountainheart.*

Enemy to Both Sides.

Rayguns hit him. Manglespawn bit him. Archie raged on, his anger blotting everything else out. The monsters and the men, the clanker tanks and giant steam men—who they fought for and what they fought for meant nothing to him. They were nothing but objects to vent his fury on.

And then they were gone. All of them. The warriors, the monsters, the airships, the clanker tanks. There were no searing rayguns, no explosions, no cries of pain. Day became night, and Archie spun on a dark, quiet glade in the middle of a tree-filled swamp, looking desperately for something to hit, something to destroy.

"Where—*where are you?*" Archie said, panting. "I'll kill you! I'll kill you all!"

Slowly, thickly, Archie's brain told him he wasn't in Gettysburg anymore. Wasn't even in Powhatan territory. He knew this place. Yes—he had been here before. He was sure of it. If he could just think—but all he wanted to do was rip a tree from the ground, use it to smash the other trees. Pound the tree to splinters. Rip up the stone altar and hurl it into the swamp.

The stone altar. Archie's thunderstorm brain cleared for the briefest of moments, and he remembered. Knew where he was.

Chuluota. Where it had all begun. Where Archie had been born.

Where the Jandal a Haad was reborn, the Mangleborn sang.

Archie pounded on the sides of his head, trying to unhear the voices.

When he looked up, there were people in the glade. Seven of them, all standing around the stone altar. Men and women, Yankees and First Nations, old and young. Archie knew one of them. Had fought one of them. Beaten on his cackling, metal body when the man was just a brain in a jar. Archie's fists clenched, longing to pound on him again.

Edison. That was the dead man's name. Edison.

Edison raised a pair of lektrical gauntlets, and the air crackled. The other people in the circle chanted words he didn't understand, and *whoosh*—swirling green flames erupted around something small and gray hidden underneath the stone altar.

Something small and gray and made of stone.

Something in the shape of a baby boy.

Archie staggered back like he'd been punched by a steam man. This was Chuluota, twelve years ago, and the lifeless stone homunculus under the altar was him, before he'd been brought to life.

"No!" Archie cried. "It's a trick! A trick!" He pulled a tree from the ground and hurled it at the circle of people, but it swept right through them.

A man in a black hood dragged a bound, struggling man into the circle of seven and threw him on the altar. One of the conspirators stepped forward with a knife, and with a flash of silver and red, the bound man's body went limp.

"Talisse Fixico, the potter," Hachi said.

Archie jumped. Hachi stood right beside him. Anger flared in him. "You're doing this!" he cried. Archie swung at her, but she disappeared, replaced by the gray, ghostly image of a Seminole man with clay-caked fingers. Archie drew back, afraid.

Another kicking, fighting Seminole man was dragged to the altar, and the gray ghost of a bent and bearded old man appeared beside Archie. He jumped away.

"Chelokee Yoholo, father of Ficka," Hachi said behind him.

He turned to hit her, but she was replaced by the ghost of a young Seminole man in a suit and neckerchief.

"Hathlun Harjo, the surgeon."

Everywhere Archie turned, there was a new ghost. A new victim. And every time, Hachi said the dead man's name.

"Odis Harjo, the poet."

"Iskote Te, the gray-haired."

"Oak Mulgee, the machinist."

"John Wise, the politician."

"Emartha Hadka, the hero of Hickory Ground."

Archie twisted away from each one, trying to get free, but they surrounded him. Penned him in. Archie put his hands over his ears and dropped to his knees, but he still heard Hachi's voice saying the names in his head.

Ficka Likee. Petolke Likee. Ockchan Harjo. Micco Chee. Sower Sullivan. Cosa Yoholo. Artus Harjo.

Name after name. The ghosts crowded out his rage as they filled his brain. They watched him. Stared at him. Not angry or hurt, but expectant. Like they were waiting for him to do something. As Hachi said the names, Archie found himself saying them with her, repeating the mantra she'd taught him. *Konip Fixico. Chular Fixico. Tallassee Tustunnugee. Long John Gibson. Talkis Yoholo.*

One hundred ghosts. One hundred men. By mantra's end, it was just Archie's voice calling their names. Including the last:

"Hololkee Emartha, father of Hachi."

Archie looked up. The ghosts were still there, waiting. Watching.

"What do you want from me?" Archie asked.

"You carry our blood," said Thomas Stidham, the horse breeder.

"You live for us," said Pompey Yoholo, the seventh son of a seventh son.

"I killed you!" Archie said.

"You weren't even born when we died," said Nehar Larne, the cogswright.

"But it's my fault you died!" Archie told the ghosts. "I'm a monster!"

"No," said Harmer Thlah, the wicked. "A monster wouldn't cry over the dead. Your remorse is what makes you human."

"You died so I could live!" Archie told them.

"Yes," said Abraham Emathlau, singer of songs. "And what do you do to honor our memory?"

Archie put his head in his hands.

"You carry our blood," Thomas Stidham said again.

"You know our names," said Hahyah Yechee, the sheriff.

"You have the strength of a hundred men," said Petolke Likee, the orange grower.

"What will you do with it?" asked Hololkee Emartha, father of Hachi.

"I'll—I'll be good," Archie said, sobbing. "I'll fight the monsters. All the monsters. I'll be the one monster who's good. I'll be the man you want me to be. I promise."

The ghosts had what they had come for. They nodded and disappeared, one by one, until only Hololkee Emartha, father of Hachi, was left. He gave Archie a small smile, and he was gone.

Hachi appeared in his place, tears running down her cheeks.

Still on his knees, Archie put his arms around her legs and lay the side of his face against her stomach.

"I'm sorry, Hachi," he said. "I'm so sorry. I didn't mean any of it. I just—I just forgot myself. I forgot everything."

Hachi put her hands on Archie's white hair. "I know," she told him.

Archie wept. "I'm not as strong as you," he told her.

"No," Hachi said. "You're stronger. If I had your power, there wouldn't be a world left to save."

30

Chuluota faded away with Archie's anger, and he could finally see what they'd done to get through to him. There was a metal hat on his head, like the ones Tesla had given them at Atlantis Station to keep out the voices of the Mangleborn, put there by Hachi's flying circus when no one else could get near him. Gonzalo, Martine, and Clyde fought to keep the monsters and soldiers out of the little circle they'd cleared around Archie on the battlefield, and Fergus hovered overhead on his rebuilt lektric gyrocopter, carrying a pale and sagging Kitsune in his arms.

Archie stood. "Oh gods. *Kitsune.*"

Fergus landed beside them, and Archie hurried to Kitsune's side.

"I'm so sorry, Kitsune. I didn't know what I was doing." He looked down at the red-stained bandage on her leg. "I could have hit you anywhere. I could have put that harpoon through your heart."

"I should have . . . hidden better," Kitsune said. "You're the only person . . . who's ever caught me twice."

"She's not good," Fergus said. "But she insisted on doing this."

"Never . . . stolen somebody else's memories before . . . and showed them to somebody else," she said.

"Stolen somebody's memories?" Archie said. "But you were only a baby when it happened," he said to Hachi. "You couldn't possibly remember all that."

"I don't remember it," Hachi said. "Not like that. But I've seen it. Every night when I close my eyes and sleep. Thanks to Malacar Ahasherat."

"They're breaking through!" Clyde cried, and suddenly Manglespawn were throwing themselves at them. Archie punched a snarling lion-like thing away before it could pounce on Hachi. Hachi ducked between the legs of a skinless man and came up behind him, knives flashing. Gonzalo used a raycannon to blast a metallic blob back into the trees. Fergus lit up a cross between a woman and a fish with lektricity. Martine hopped on the back of a short, squat thing that was all fingers and ears and drove her harpoon into it. Buster snatched up a ten-foot-tall tree man in his mouth like a stick.

But there were more of them—too many more. Just as the Manglespawn threatened to overrun them, there were fourteen Leaguers. Twenty-one. Twenty-eight. More. Twenty-eight Archies and Hachis and Gonzalos and Ferguses and Martines and Kitsunes, and twenty-eight Clydes riding twenty-eight Busters. The monsters jumped and gnashed and bit and slimed at them all while the Leaguers who were real moved among them, hitting and shooting and stomping and slicing, until it was just the seven of them, all standing in a circle with their backs to each other, their weapons raised to take on the world. Together. The League of Seven, reborn.

Raycannons and aether rifles still crackled as what was left of General Lee's army fought the thousands more Manglespawn that poured over the hill, but for the briefest of moments, the League found themselves in a lull in the storm.

A lull that ended when the three Mangleborn loomed up over the battlefield. One looked like a huge black mountain lion with fish fins on its back and backward deer horns on its head. That was the Buster-sized one. The second was a towering ice-man with broken pine trees and boulders buried in his frozen skin. The third looked like a giant skunk.

"What have we got, Mr. X?" Clyde asked.

"Mishipeshu, the Underwater Panther. The Wendigo, an ice giant with a human cannibal where its heart should be. And Aniwye—pretty much a giant skunk."

"Xiuhcoatl!" Archie said. "I thought I destroyed you!"

Gonzalo hefted the raycannon he carried. "Martine said he was only sleeping, and she was right! She couldn't rebuild his old body, so she woke him up and put him in this raycannon."

"I wasn't sleeping, I was in cyber-limbo. Nano-dormancy," Señor X said. "It's like existing in a great black space where the only thing you can see, hear, smell, feel, or taste is a flashing white cursor that just types whatever I think. Luckily *somebody* here knows how to migrate biocognitive lektroneurons into a fresh ecosystem."

"I have nae idea what any of that means," said Fergus.

"I do," said Martine.

"I may have more firepower now, but that don't mean I forgive you, kid," Señor X told Archie. "I liked my old body. It had style."

"Later," Hachi said. "Moffett's gone. I saw her take the Dragon Lantern."

Archie could feel the excitement the Leaguers had just been feeling ebb away.

"Confirmed," Martine said, consulting her harpoon.

"As Mrs. DeMarcus used to say, we got bigger chicken to fry. Fergus, Martine, Gonzalo, take down that big skunk," Clyde said. "Me, Hachi, and Kitsune will take care of the water panther. Mr. Rivets can see to Kitsune inside Buster. Archie, keep that Wendigo busy until we can all gang up on it together."

"You think that's a good idea?" Archie asked.

"I do," Clyde said. "You all got your assignments. League of Seven—full steam ahead!"

31

Gonzalo whistled for Alamo, and he, Fergus, and Martine rode off after Aniwye. The others ran for Buster.

"Give me a lift?" Archie asked.

Buster lowered his head to sniff Archie and wagged his tailpipe slowly and hopefully. Archie put a hand to the big steam man's face.

"I'm so sorry, boy," Archie said. "I didn't mean to hurt you."

Buster whistle-barked and licked him with the pneumatic loading ramp inside his mouth. *Clang! Clang! Clang!*

"Okay," Archie said, laughing. "Okay." Like a real dog, Buster was forgiving of his friends to a fault. Archie swore he would never betray that loyalty again.

Archie helped Hachi take Kitsune to the medical bay while Clyde got them moving toward the Mangleborn.

"I can't believe Buster forgives me," Archie said.

"You're part of our pack," Hachi said. "We all forgive you."

Hachi left for the bridge, and Archie stayed with Kitsune. She looked even paler than before. Mr. Rivets had barely bandaged her wound when she'd left to help pull Archie out of his madness, and holding the illusion had taken its toll on her.

"Is she going to be all right, Mr. Rivets?" Archie asked.

"Luckily the harpoon missed the femoral artery," Mr. Rivets told him. "But Miss Kitsune has suffered quite a shock to her system. We all have."

"I'm so sorry, Kitsune," Archie said again. "I'm the one who made you come along, and then I did this to you."

"I'm glad you did," she said. "Made me come along, that is. Not harpoon me." She coughed, and her fox ears drooped.

"You should save your strength, miss," Mr. Rivets said. "Master Archie, perhaps you should leave us now while I do what I can to repair Miss Kitsune."

"No," Kitsune said. She put a weak hand on Archie's arm. "I never did—I never did tell you where I came from. The truth."

"Not now," Archie told her. "Let Mr. Rivets help you."

She shook her head. "I may not get another chance. I promised. And I always . . . I always keep my promises."

Archie looked at Mr. Rivets, and the machine man lowered his medical instruments.

"I'm . . . I'm from a little village called Takayama, outside Ametokai in Beikoku Prefecture," Kitsune said. "My mother and father were rice farmers, regular people with a little house and three perfect children. Until they had me. They never meant to have me. Four is an unlucky number. The Japanese word for 'four' sounds just like the word for 'death.'"

Kitsune coughed again, and Mr. Rivets gave her water to drink.

"My fox ears and fox tail were a terrible omen, my mother said. My father called me a monster, and went to the kitchen for a knife. He was going to kill me on the spot, before the neighbors could see. But my grandmother stopped him. She told my parents she would take me out to the woods and leave me to die."

Kitsune had told Archie so many stories about who she was and where she'd come from, he'd gotten used to thinking everything she said was a lie. Maybe it was how weak she was, how much effort it took her to tell this story, but this felt like the truth at last.

"My grandmother did take me out to the woods, but instead of leaving me to die she hid me away in a tiny cabin and raised me in secret. She was the one who named me. Cared for me. But it was a lonely existence. My *sobo*'s face was the only one I knew growing up. She was the only person I ever spoke to, ever played with, ever touched. She was my only friend, but she couldn't always be with me.

"I fought my loneliness by creating worlds full of people in my head, and soon discovered I could share them with my *sobo*—could make her see anything I wanted her to see. She told me stories of the real world, and I brought them to life. Our little one-room cabin became the deck of an airship over Mt. Tacoma, the bridge of a submarine at the bottom of the Great Western Sea, a flower-filled valley on the moon. If I couldn't be taken out into the world, I could at least bring the world to our cabin.

"When I was old enough, my *sobo* told me how I came to be what I am. Long ago, a fox disguised herself as a woman and married a man of my clan. She was a good and faithful wife, but the man discovered what she was, and she was forced to flee. But before she ran away, she bore my ancestor a daughter. That baby didn't have fox ears or a fox tail, but her daughter did, as did her daughter's daughter's daughter. Fox blood runs through the women of my family, and every few generations, a monster like me is born."

"You're not a monster," Archie told her.

Kitsune closed her eyes. "One morning in my eighth year I awoke, but *Sobo* didn't. She was dead. There was nothing left for me then in that cabin. It was time for me to leave. I put on a white kimono—the color of death, for the rest of the world thought me dead—and took nothing else besides my grand-mother's pearl necklace."

"The one I grabbed from you," Archie said. "The one you wanted so badly you joined the League to get it back."

Kitsune nodded as well as she could. "I went back to Takayama, where I had been born, and hid myself from the villagers until I discovered which of them were my parents. Then I ruined them."

Archie could only imagine what she'd done to punish her family. Kitsune didn't say.

"I've been on my own ever since," Kitsune said.

"I'm . . . I'm sorry," Archie said.

"No. You don't understand," Kitsune said. "Except for *Sobo*, I've never had a family. Until now."

"Archie!" Clyde called. "This is your stop! You're up!"

"Don't die," Archie told Kitsune.

She gave a single, weak laugh. "I promise," she said. "And I always—I always—"

Kitsune faded away, and Mr. Rivets stepped in. "Go, Master Archie," he said.

KRI-CHANG! Archie felt Buster lurch as the Wendigo hit them.

"Buster! Open up!" Archie called, hurrying up inside the steam man's head. "I want to get a flying start!"

Buster's mouth opened, and the frozen shape of the giant ice cannibal filled the view. Archie felt something coursing through him, but it wasn't rage, and it wasn't adrenaline. It was love. Love for this new tribe of his. His new pack. His new family.

For the people he loved, he could be a hero.

"Raaaaaaaaaaaaaa!" Archie yelled, and he launched himself at the Mangleborn, punching it in the chest. Ka-THOOM!

Behind him, Clyde swung Buster for Mishipeshu, the Underwater Panther.

"All right," Clyde told Hachi. "Let's see if there's more than one way to skin a cat."

32

Mishipeshu swatted at soldiers with its big black cat paws, batting them around like cat toys. A Muskogee woman froze in front of it, the horror of what she was seeing paralyzing her, and the Underwater Panther leaped at her.

BWAAAAT!

Buster's raycannon knocked the Mangleborn to the ground, and the female soldier woke from her trance. She ran away screaming, but at least she was running away.

Buster hunkered down and whistled at the monster. Mishipeshu flattened its antlers against its head and stood up straight, ruffling its silky fur.

"Buster doesn't like cats," Clyde told Hachi.

"Yeah. I don't think it likes us much either. Is the arm Fergus reattached working all right?"

Clyde moved a lever with his right arm, and Buster's big brass right arm flexed. "It was a rush job, but so far so good," Clyde said. "I could beat this cat with one hand tied behind my back anyway. This one time at the orphanage I broke my arm climbing a tree. Well, falling out of a tree, really. Had my arm in a cast for a month."

"Clyde—" Hachi tried to break in.

"I had to learn how to write with my left hand, 'cause of course Mrs. DeMarcus wouldn't let me skip my schoolwork."

"*Clyde—*"

"Had to learn to eat left-handed too. What a mess! And boy, did that cast itch something awful! I had to take one of Mrs. DeMarcus's crochet hooks and wiggle it down in there."

"Clyde!"

The Underwater Panther leaped at them, knocking Buster backward to the ground. *KaSHUNK.* Clyde's seat belt held him in place, but Hachi had to grab on to a railing. She hung by her arms, her skirt swishing as her legs swung free. Buster's boiler growled, and the big cat and dog wrestled and tumbled on the ground, biting and scratching and kicking at each other.

"Mr. Rivets, you okay down there?" Hachi called.

"Miss Kitsune is strapped securely to her table," Mr. Rivets told her. "I, however, would appreciate a little warning before being thrown across the room."

"Mr. Rivets, you're about to be thrown across the room!" Clyde yelled.

BWAAAAT! Buster's raycannon blasted Mishipeshu into

the ground and launched the steam man backward onto his butt again. *KerKLANK.* The Underwater Panther flipped onto its feet and tried to run away, but Buster lurched forward and caught its tail. Mishipeshu screeched and pulled, but Clyde held tight.

"Okay, we got the tiger by the tail, as Mrs. DeMarcus used to say. Now what?"

"We can't kill this thing, so we've got to trap it somewhere," Hachi told him. "That's what the ancients did."

Clyde grunted, fighting to keep hold of the Underwater Panther. "How about a big hole in the ground?"

"That would work," Hachi said. "But where?"

"Right here!" Clyde said. He let go of Mishipeshu's tail. "Buster, dig!"

Buster whistled happily and attacked the ground, furiously scratching and clawing at it. Dirt and rock flew out behind him as the earth beneath the giant steam man disappeared.

Clyde held his hands away from Buster's controls, letting them swing and flail without him.

"Buster loves to dig," he told Hachi.

"We're going to have to lure Mishipeshu back," Hachi said. "And trick it into thinking there's not a hole there."

"One person for that job," Clyde said.

Hachi nodded and slid down the ladder to the floors inside Buster's chest. She hurried to the medical bay, where Mr. Rivets stood beside a sleeping Kitsune.

"How is she?" Hachi asked.

"Recovering," Mr. Rivets said. "The aetherical nature of the weapon helped the cauterization process."

"You can wake her, then?" Hachi asked.

"I wouldn't advise it, miss," Mr. Rivets said. "Miss Kitsune will still require a great deal of time to convalesce properly."

"We don't have a great a deal of time," Hachi said. "Kitsune, can you hear me? Kitsune?"

Kitsune stirred and looked at Hachi through half-lidded eyes.

"I'm sorry, Kitsune," Hachi said. "But we need your help. Buster's digging a hole, and we need you to make a Mangleborn think it isn't there."

"I can do that," Kitsune said. She tried to get up, but Mr. Rivets's restraints held her back.

"You can do it just as well from your bed," Mr. Rivets said, and Hachi took that to be as much as he would allow.

Hachi threw open a gun port. Buster had already dug out an enormous hole. "Use me," Hachi said. "Just like before. I'll be your eyes. Read my thoughts, and then project them to Mishipeshu."

Kitsune nodded.

"Okay, Clyde," Hachi told him via shell. "It looks deep enough. Back Buster away and we'll lure Mishipeshu over."

Buster pulled his head out of the hole and stood behind the huge pile of dirt he'd created. Hachi found Mishipeshu on the horizon, and imagined Buster was a very large mouse standing in the middle of a field that did *not* have a huge hole dug into it.

"Okay," Hachi told Kitsune. Hachi felt a tickle in her brain like before, and then got that odd sensation that someone else was inside her brain, the way you could tell when there was someone else in the room with you even when your eyes were closed. Hachi's instinct was to fight it, to push the other person out of her brain, but she let down all her barriers and invited Kitsune in.

"I see it," Kitsune said from the bed, her eyes closed. "I'm going to push the vision to Mishipeshu."

Hachi felt her own consciousness extend with Kitsune's and reach out to the mind of the Mangleborn in the distance. It was like stretching her hand out and touching the green flames of her nightmares, the aetherical fire that had engulfed her at Chuluota when she was a baby. The mystical inferno that had swallowed the soul of her father and brought Archie to life. Hachi's hand reached the flames, and all at once a flood of images assaulted her, making her scream. Mishipeshu devouring a canoe full of warriors. A raging storm. A circle of cultists making a sacrifice. A hero cutting off one of the panther's whiskers. Mishipeshu destroying a raycannon with its tail. The Underwater Panther stalking a steamboat. Ripping a battalion of soldiers apart with its claws.

There were other things too—images and sounds and ideas she couldn't understand. Things that were impossible. Math equations that added up wrong but were right. Floors that were also walls. A man who was his own grandfather. A staircase that twisted in on itself, so you would climb up and down it forever. The images came at Hachi so fast, so strong, they knocked her to her knees. She threw up every barrier she could, tried to push the thoughts away, but they gushed in on her like the water in the Sonnionto puzzle trap. They pushed at her and pulled at her and she choked on them, drowning. . . .

And then, as suddenly as the vision had swallowed her, she was spit back out on the floor of the medical bay, her mind clear but still vision-logged. Mr. Rivets helped her to her feet, and Hachi saw Kitsune was passed out on the sickbed, a metal, wire-covered hat on her head.

"Both of you started screaming, and I was unable to get through to you verbally," Mr. Rivets told Hachi. "I assumed something had gone wrong with your attempt to communicate telepathically with Mishipeshu, and one of Mr. Tesla's hats was all I could think to do to sever the link."

Hachi kept a hand on Mr. Rivets's shoulder. "You did good," she told the Tik Tok. "Saved us. I don't know exactly what happened, but I think connecting to somebody else's mind must be a two-way street for Kitsune. But she's usually the only one able to push thoughts through. That Mangleborn flooded us with visions. Memories. Stuff I didn't understand. Now I see why people with weak minds go insane around Mangleborn."

And maybe why Martine was so alien, if she was able to think the same way the Mangleborn did.

"Miss Kitsune suffered much worse than you did," Mr. Rivets said. "I cannot say how long she will be unconscious. She's had quite a shock."

Hachi nodded and climbed back up to the bridge. The images she'd seen still haunted her.

"Kitsune's out," she told Clyde. "We're going to have to do this the old-fashioned way. Can you cover the hole with trees?"

"Sure," Clyde said. "But how are we gonna lure Mishipeshu on it?"

"I'll take care of it. Just get that hole covered," Hachi said.

Hachi hurried back down through the steam man's interior and jumped outside. Mishipeshu loomed tall on the other side of the battlefield, swatting and snapping at United Nations soldiers and Manglespawn alike.

"Circus, showtime!" Hachi called, and three little wind-up animals burst out of her bandolier. They buzzed around her head, happy to be out and about. "See that big cat-thing?" she asked them. "I need to get its attention. Can you help me do that?"

"Roar-roar-roar!" Mr. Lion chirped.

"But don't get hurt!" Hachi called as they flittered away.

Hachi ran after them, dodging soldiers and Manglespawn as she ran. She knew she could be fighting the monsters, taking some of them out, but the soldiers could handle Manglespawn with their rayguns and cannons and clanker tanks. What they couldn't do was take out a Mangleborn. That was her job.

Mishipeshu looked much, much bigger from the ground, and Hachi caught herself wishing she was still inside the protective brass hull of Clyde's steam man. The Mangleborn's pelt was dark and wet, like an otter's, and its head was sinewy and round. Its eyes flashed bright like a cat's in the night, and it looked down at Hachi like a cat spying a mouse.

"Oh crivens," Hachi said.

Hachi leaped out of the way as Mishipeshu pounced. She'd escaped, but the Mangleborn was fast—too fast. It pounced again, pinning her to the ground under its massive paws. Hachi felt the wind blow out of her, and for the second time that day she felt like she was suffocating. Mishipeshu's mouth widened, baring its teeth in something like a gruesome smile, and it twisted its long snake-like neck down to eat her as she gasped for breath.

"Roar-roar-roar!" Mr. Lion growled.

"Ooh-ooh-ooh!" Jo-Jo the Gorilla grunted, thumping his chest.

Tusker the Elephant trumpeted, and together the Tik Tok toys fluttered in Mishipeshu's face. The Mangleborn snapped at them and batted at them like a cat chasing a silver bell on a string, and Hachi was free. She dragged herself away, gulping for air while her flying circus bought her time. She'd been foolish to rush in, thinking she could do everything herself. If Fergus had been there he would have scolded her. But he wasn't here, and neither were any of the other Leaguers. She was going to have to do this herself.

"Hey, furball!" Hachi called up at the Mangleborn. "Hey! You're not finished with me yet!"

Mishipeshu stopped snapping at the flying circus and bent its sleek round head down at her again. "*Merowrrr!*" it roared.

Hachi took off at a run toward Buster, the Mangleborn on her heels. She ran back and forth like a mouse across a kitchen floor, zigzagging through Manglespawn and raycannon craters and UN warriors, Mishipeshu's claws swiping at the air behind her. Clyde had just finished laying the last of the trees when Hachi ran out along a log to the middle of the trap. She turned and watched as the Mangleborn barreled across the battlefield toward her, knocking steam men and clanker tanks aside like they were toys.

Wait, she told herself. Wait . . .

"Hachi, jump!" Clyde called.

Mishipeshu leaped. Hachi turned and ran. The Mangle-born hit the covering of trees and the roof collapsed. Hachi jumped. Mishipeshu roared and thrashed. The tree beneath Hachi's feet fell away, and she was falling, but then Buster's big brass hand was there to catch her. Buster popped Hachi in his mouth and pounded on the Mangleborn—*KRANG! KRANG!*

KRANG!—before quickly pushing heaps of earth and rock back into the hole. Hachi scrambled up to the bridge as Clyde hammered on Mishipeshu again, keeping it in the hole while Buster kicked more dirt in on top of it.

"You're crazy!" Clyde told her.

"You're not the first person to say that," Hachi told him. Her flying circus fluttered in through the hole Archie had punched in the steam man's head, and Hachi was relieved to see that none of them were hurt. She let them buzz around the room while Clyde finished pushing dirt on top of Mishipeshu. When he'd piled on the last of it, he made Buster jump up and down on it. *CHOONG. CHOONG. CHOONG.*

When it was good and flat, Clyde told Buster to stay and waited to see if the Underwater Panther was going to dig its way out. When the ground didn't move beneath them, he looked at Hachi and smiled.

"Dogs rule, and cats drool!" Clyde said.

Buster whistled happily.

"Good work," Hachi said. "I just hope Fergus and the others are having as good a luck with that giant skunk."

33

Fergus, Martine, and Gonzalo weren't having any luck with the giant skunk.

Fergus couldn't lektrocute it, because Mangleborn fed on lektricity. Gonzalo couldn't shoot it, because Aniwye's thick black fur was too matted and monstrous for a raygun to cut through it. Señor X had only heard of it by legend, never fought it. And all Martine did was stare at the slagging thing.

The Mangleborn, meanwhile, would burrow down into the ground, pop up randomly somewhere on the battlefield, and lay waste to dozens of soldiers at a time with its toxic farts.

"Take cover!" Fergus yelled. "He's gonna blow!"

Brrrrrrrrrt! The Mangleborn filled the air with another cloud of the noxious green gas.

"I am getting seriously tired of this stinker," Fergus told the others through his gas mask. He'd whipped up masks for each of them using parts he'd found on the battlefield, and now they were the only ones who could get close to the Mangleborn without dying from his stench. Not that it had done them any good.

"I've shot it in the eyes, in the mouth, in the chest, and in the feet," Gonzalo said, "and none of it does any good."

"Martine? You got anything?" Fergus asked.

Martine tilted her head. "I need elevation," she said.

"That I *can* do," Fergus said. A rod shot up out of the backpack he wore and sprouted rotors. With a lektric blue spark they started spinning, and Fergus swooped over to pick up the science-pirate.

Aniwye burrowed down into the ground and disappeared.

Fergus sighed. At least that would give them a few moments where the Mangleborn wasn't killing swathes of UN soldiers. Gonzalo waited atop Alamo for Aniwye to reappear while Fergus lifted Martine high above the battlefield. From here, Fergus could see the ground all around dotted with massive holes where Aniwye had come and gone, each one surrounded by dead bodies in a fog of green haze. Fergus watched as Buster wrestled with the Underwater Panther and Archie hammered on the Wendigo with the barrel of a busted clanker tank, but Martine was focused on the holes.

"There," Martine said, pointing to part of the battlefield where UN soldiers still fought Manglespawn.

"What there?" Fergus asked.

The ground where Martine pointed ripped and split, and Aniwye burst up into the battle, squeezing off deadly green farts.

"Whoa!" Fergus said. "How did you know that's where the beastie'd come up?"

"I formulated a logistic regression model using the creature's previous occurrences to determine its future location," Martine said.

"You did what now?" Fergus asked.

"I did the math," Martine said.

"But it looks totally random!"

"Aniwye may not even be aware of it," Martine said. "But even Mangleborn operate within predictable parameters."

Aniwye burrowed underground again.

"All right then, where's he going to pop up next?"

Martine pointed to another spot on the battlefield, and Fergus swooped down quickly. "Gonzalo! Help us get these soldiers out of here!"

Gonzalo followed along at a gallop without asking questions.

"Oy, you lot!" Fergus called, amplifying his voice lektronically. "Clear out! That skunk thing's coming!"

Gonzalo helped hurry the warriors out of the way just as the ground began to shake and split open. Aniwye burst aboveground again, ripping a powerful green fart. *Brrrrrrrrrt!*

"Ha!" Fergus cried. "He who dealt it is the only one who smelt it!"

Aniwye growled and burrowed underground again.

"There," Martine said, predicting where he'd come up again. Fergus and Gonzalo hurried to clear away the UN soldiers from the area, and the Mangleborn erupted into another empty field.

Brrrrrrrrrt! Aniwye sprayed more toxic gas, but there was no one there to breathe it.

"Looks like you're making a stink over nothing, big guy," Fergus said.

Aniwye snapped at him, but Fergus easily took to the air to get away. The black-and-white Mangleborn had sharp teeth and powerful claws, but its real weapon was its stink bombs.

The giant skunk burrowed underground again, and Fergus landed beside Gonzalo and Martine.

"Okay," Fergus told them. "Thanks to Martine, we know where he's going to pop up. Now we need to find a way to put a cork in him."

"Yeah," Gonzalo said, "Um, I'm not doing that."

"I also would prefer not to get near its anus," Martine said.

"Well I'm not eager to go on butt patrol either," Fergus said. "But we gotta stop farting around. So to speak."

Together they cleared the next area Aniwye was due to appear. While they waited for the Mangleborn, Martine swept her aetherical harpoon through the air and studied the strange symbols that appeared on its handle.

"The gas the Deep One emits," Martine said. "It is flammable in high concentrations."

"Okay. Good to know," Fergus said. "Nobody light a candle around that thing's butt."

"No, that's *exactly* what we do," Gonzalo said.

"You mean, light one of its farts on fire?" Fergus asked.

"The *Mephitis mephitis*'s spray is not technically flatulence," said Martine. "Their defensive spray is produced by a pair of scent glands around the anus. To produce enough spray in a high enough concentration to ignite it, we would have to rupture one of the scent glands."

"Eh?" Fergus said.

"If we shoot it in the butt, we can light its farts on fire," Señor X translated.

"But what do we use to ignite it?" Fergus asked.

"A lektrical spark of sufficient strength should be enough to ignite the gas," Martine said.

"Oh, I see," said Fergus. "Meaning you want me to get close to that thing's butt and let it fart on me."

Martine frowned. "As I said, technically, the gas is not flatulence but—"

"Yeah, basically," said Señor X.

"I like this plan," said Gonzalo.

"Because you're not the one who has to get farted on," Fergus said.

The ground began to rumble.

"Let's do it," Gonzalo said, charging Señor X.

"Now wait a minute—" Fergus said.

Martine slipped a bracelet off her wrist and gave it to Fergus. "Before you spark the gas, push this button," she told him.

"Hold on a second—" Fergus said.

Croom. Aniwye burst from the ground. Fergus took off into the air just to get away, and Gonzalo spurred Alamo around behind the Mangleborn.

Aniwye laid down another toxic cloud. *Brrrrrrrrrt!* Green gas oozed across the field, but again there was no one around to breathe it.

Gonzalo reined Alamo to a stop. "Fire in the hole!" he cried.

BWAAAAT! The portable wave cannon Martine had put Señor X into erupted in a bright yellow beam, hitting Aniwye right in the anal scent gland. *POOM.* The gas sac exploded, and Fergus swooped in on his gyrocopter, his head turned away.

"Gross gross gross gross gross!" he said.

Fergus's fingers sparked, and—

KA-THOOM!

Trees flattened and the ground heaved like a meteor had struck the Earth, knocking most of the UN Army and the Manglespawn who were left on their butts. Martine and Gonzalo and Alamo went flying. When they picked themselves up, they found Aniwye a quarter of a mile away, upside down and unconscious. But there was no sign of Fergus.

"Do you think . . . Do you think he got blown up?" Gonzalo asked.

Martine tilted her head. "If he did not press the button on the bracelet in time, there is a 99.999998 percent probability that we are breathing in his atoms as I speak."

Gonzalo looked a little green.

Choom. Choom. Choom. Buster the steam man strode up to them. "Hey, you guys lose something?" Clyde asked through his speaking trumpet.

In Buster's hand was a very weary, very blackened Fergus MacFerguson. Martine's bracelet shield *fzzt*ed and crackled, winking on and off again with glowing green aetherical energy.

"Fergus!" Gonzalo cried.

"Silent but deadly," Fergus said. "That's me."

"Two down," said Hachi.

"Need help digging a hole for it?" Clyde asked. "Buster likes digging holes."

Buster whistled and wagged his tail pipe.

"This one's a digger," Gonzalo said. "It'd just dig its way out again."

"We'll get the UN Army to tie him down Gulliver-style until we can deal with him," Hachi said. "They've just about taken care of Moffett's Monster Army anyway. We need to get to Archie and help him with the Wendigo. He's been fighting that thing all by himself for a long time now. We just have to hope—"

She didn't have to say it. They were all thinking the same thing.

We just have to hope Archie hasn't blown a gasket again.

34

Wham! Wham! Wham! Archie pounded away at the Wendigo
with the shattered remains of an oak tree, knocking him away.
Thoom. Thoom Thoom. The mindless ice giant staggered back
toward Archie as he stopped to catch his breath. *Wham! Wham!*
Wham! Thoom. Thoom. Thoom. Wham! Wham! Wham!
Thoom. Thoom. Thoom. With each whack, the giant ice monster reeled back, and with each pause it marched forward again.
Three steps forward, three steps back. Three steps forward,
three steps back. Archie felt like the mythical Sisyphus, doomed
to roll a giant boulder up a hill only to watch it roll back down
again, over and over and over again for eternity. *Wham! Wham*
Wham! Thoom. Thoom. Thoom. Wham! Wham Wham! Thoom.
Thoom. Thoom.

Archie's mind wandered as he beat on the Wendigo. Was Sisyphus some Mangleborn instead? A giant dung beetle rolling around a world-crushing ball of manure, maybe? Or maybe Sisyphus was a hero, an ancient Leaguer who'd performed some incredible feat of strength like rolling a massive rock or a giant gear.

There didn't seem to be a great deal of difference sometimes between the Mangleborn and the heroes who fought them, Archie thought.

Wham! Wham Wham! Thoom. Thoom. Thoom.

Wham! Wham Wham! Thoom. Thoom. Thoom.

"Archie. Archie!" someone was yelling. It was Clyde, inside Buster. The rest of the League besides Kitsune stood on the ground at his feet. They looked at him hopefully, but Archie could sense the fear in them too. How long had Clyde been calling his name?

Wham! Wham Wham! Archie beat the Wendigo back again.

"Archie!" Clyde called again.

"Hey," Archie said, breathing heavily. "Sorry. I'm okay. Just . . . lost in my own thoughts . . . you know?"

Thoom. Thoom. Thoom. The Wendigo marched back toward them.

"Little help this time?" Archie asked.

Buster's arm became a raycannon. Gonzalo charged Señor X. Martine's aetherical harpoon glowed. Fergus's fists crackled with lektricity.

KA-THWAM!

The League unleashed the fury of its strength all at once,

and the ice giant went flying. *KOOM*. It landed on its back with an earth-shaking thud.

"Thanks," Archie said. He tossed the broken tree he'd been using on the pile of a dozen other shattered trunks he'd used to hold off the Wendigo while they were away.

The Wendigo stirred, trying to get up, but Buster sat on him and held him down. The others climbed up the icy crags and stood on the Mangleborn's chest.

"Now what?" Gonzalo asked.

"The Wendigo is a giant ice monster with a human heart," Señor X said. "By which I mean there's a human being inside him, where the thing's heart should be. A human cannibal. The ice is just an extension of him. It grows thicker every time he eats somebody."

"He must have eaten a lot of people," Fergus said.

"So what do we do, trap it like the others?" Hachi asked.

"The Wendigo never sleeps," Señor X said. "Not like other Mangleborn. It just keeps walking, keeps wandering, keeps eating. The only way to stop it is to kill the man at its heart."

"Whoa, whoa, whoa," said Fergus. "I thought you all said you can't kill a Mangleborn."

"You can't," Señor X said. "We can kill the man inside, but never the monster. This Wendigo will be gone, but the next time some frozen, starving wretch eats another human being to survive, his heart will turn to ice and he'll become a new Wendigo. He'll crave more human flesh, and the ice in his heart will grow. Surround him. Consume him. The more people he eats, the colder his heart will get, and the thicker the ice will become. Same monster, different person."

"Like me," Archie said quietly. He was the same shadow that had always plagued the League of Seven, just with a different name.

Archie slammed his fist into the Wendigo's chest—*KOOM*— and everyone jumped back.

"Archie, what are you—?" Clyde started to ask, but Archie hit the Wendigo again and again.

KOOM. KOOM. KOOM.

Huge chunks of ice went flying as Archie dug deeper, chipping away at the frozen cannibal. *KOOM. KOOM. KOOM.* The other Leaguers stood back and watched in silence, letting Archie lose himself in the work. *KOOM. KOOM. KOOM.*

At last Archie smashed all the way through the ice, revealing the head and shoulders and chest of the man trapped inside. He looked like he'd once been an Inuit, one of the tribes of the far, far north, but his skin was bluish-white now, his face shrunken and shriveled. Blood still stained his lips.

"Is he dead?" Fergus asked.

"My sensors indicate he is alive, in a way," Martine said, reading the symbols on the shaft of her harpoon. "Perhaps he is sleeping."

The cannibal's eyes shot open, and everyone took a frightened step back.

"K-k-k-kill . . . m-m-m-me," the man whispered. "K-kill m-me. Please. I'm s-s-sorry. I've s-suffered enough."

The Leaguers looked around at each other. Señor X had told them killing the cannibal at its heart was the only way to stop the Wendigo, but until now none of them had realized one of them was actually going to have to do it.

Archie nodded. It was his job. He was his League's Shadow,

after all. He already had the blood of a hundred men on his hands. What was one more?

Archie raised his fist, but Hachi put a hand to his arm to stop him. *Schnik*. She drew her dagger.

"No," Gonzalo said, pushing them both away. "I'm the Lawbringer." Gonzalo aimed Señor X at the frozen man's head. "What's your name?"

The blue Inuit looked inward in panic. He couldn't remember his own name.

"Taktuq!" he said at last with relief. "Taktuq. Taktuq. My name is Taktuq."

"Taktuq of the Inuit, it is against the laws of Texas and every other civilized tribe and nation to eat the flesh of another human being," Gonzalo said. "Moreover, it's against the laws of nature itself."

Taktuq sobbed once, and ice crystals formed in the corners of his eyes. "I'm s-sorry," he said.

"The sentence for cannibalism is death," Gonzalo told him.

Taktuq closed his eyes, and Señor X hummed.

"Make it as quick and painless as you can," Gonzalo told Señor X.

"Thank you," Taktuq whispered.

Señor X flashed yellow, and—*ka-POW*—Taktuq the cannibal was dead.

Krik. Krack. The ice beneath their feet began to break apart, and Clyde scooped everyone up into Buster's arms. They watched from above as the Mangleborn crumbled to pieces, burying the body of Taktuq in the ice his sins had collected.

"The fighting," Clyde told them. "It's just about over."

He was right. But for a few random raygun blasts as the last of the Manglespawn were put down, the Battle of Gettysburg was over. The Monster Army was destroyed, and the Mangleborn were defeated once more. For General Lee and the UN Army, there was still the work of keeping the Union together. But for Archie, Hachi, Fergus, Clyde, Kitsune, Gonzalo, and Martine, there was only one job left to do.

It was time for the League of Seven to stop Philomena Moffett. Together, and for good.

35

Buster stood at the edge of the Palisades Airship Park, over-looking the city of New Rome. The sky over the biggest city in the United Nations was still filled with airships of all sizes, and the skyline was still dominated by the seven-story-tall Emartha Machine Man building. Submarines still churned just beneath the choppy waters of the New Rome Harbor, and loco-motives still chugged crisscross patterns across the city. Archie felt the wonder of the city all over again, but this time it was mixed with fear.

"This is where Philomena Moffett has been headed back to all along," Archie said, looking out one of Buster's gun ports. "This is where she can get her ultimate revenge."

Freckles the giraffe had watched as Moffett hopped a train

bound for New Rome, the Dragon Lantern in hand. And Archie was sure she had come to the capital of the United Nations to use it.

"We made good time," Clyde called down through Buster's internal speakers. "She can't have gotten here much faster than we did."

"And I don't see any raygun fire or burning buildings," said Hachi. "So if she is here, she hasn't done whatever she's going to do."

"She's come for the Septemberist Society," Archie told them. "That's who she's been after all along. Alcatraz, the Shadow League, the Transcontinental Railroad dedication, the Monster Army, Gettysburg—they were all distractions. Opening acts. It's always been about Dodge City for her. It's always been about revenge."

"So, this Septemberist Society headquarters," said Gonzalo. "Where is it?"

"I never knew for sure," Archie told them. "But I always thought it was under the statue of Hiawatha in New Rome Harbor."

Standing just a little taller than Buster and made of copper that had turned greenish blue in the salty air of the bay, the statue of Hiawatha stood sentinel over the city he'd called home some two hundred years before. From the waist down he wore leather pants and moccasins; from the waist up he was naked, but for a leather strap tied around his left arm and the Hiawatha Belt that would become the flag of the United Nations draped over his right shoulder. A bear claw necklace hung around his neck, and the area all around his eyes and down under his ears looked painted, though still blue-green like the rest of the statue. Hiawatha's hair stood in a short Mohawk, and two eagle feathers stuck out from behind his head on the right side. Over his left shoulder he wore a quiver of arrows, and in his right hand he held a longbow as tall as he was, for the First Nations had then yet to rediscover the raygun.

"'By Hiawatha,'" Archie said. "Moffett said 'By Hiawatha, I'm going to punish the Septemberist Society.' She must have meant the statue."

"But everybody says 'By Hiawatha,'" Clyde said.

"No. She was telling me where she was going," Archie said. He was sure of it. "She wanted me to know. She couldn't help it. That's where she is."

"Well, the rest of you could take a ferry sub to get there, I guess," said Clyde. "But me and Buster are gonna have to sit this one out."

Archie had seen Clyde and Buster jump from the Golden Gate Bridge to Alcatraz Island in Don Francisco, but the tiny island where Hiawatha stood wasn't close enough to anything for him to jump.

"I can carry Buster," Martine said.

Archie gave Martine a skeptical glance. "Um, I can't even carry Buster," he told her.

Martine pushed a button on her harpoon, and an enormous steel squid broke the surface of New Rome Harbor, sending three ferry subs in its path into a tizzy.

"I sent *The Kraken* up the eastern seaboard, in anticipation of our arrival," Martine said. "My ship should be able to carry Buster across in its tentacles."

"Okay," said Fergus, "I am definitely riding in the submarine for that."

Curious airships hovered all around Buster as he traveled across New Rome Harbor in the arms of the squid-like submarine, and the big steam man whistled happily at them and wagged his tail.

"Not exactly keeping a low profile, are we?" Clyde asked via shell.

The rest of the League watched through one of *The Kraken*'s big eye-windows, but Clyde had refused to leave Buster alone on the journey.

"No," said Archie. "But I'm done keeping a low profile." He and Hachi shared a look, and she nodded. There were going to be changes to the way things were done. But only *after* Moffett had been taken care of.

The Kraken set Buster on Oyster Island as gently as a pneumatic elevator, and Clyde let the big steam man run free in the grassy area around the base of the statue while Clyde climbed into the sub.

"If I'm right, there's a secret submarine entrance to the headquarters somewhere below the surface," Archie said.

The Kraken rumbled, preparing to dive deeper, but Señor X told them to wait. "I've got it—the Dragon Lantern. I'm picking up its energy signal. It's here, but it's not underwater. It's higher up. It's . . . *inside the statue of Hiawatha.*"

The League of Seven spilled out into the park at the base of the statue and ran for the stone pedestal it stood on. A small ticket office and guard post were leveled as though they had

been hit by a tornado, and the door that accessed the inside of
the statue was blown off its hinges.

"*Moffett*," Archie said.

A tall spiral staircase inside the statue went all the way to
the top of Hiawatha's domed head.

"But what's she doing up there if the Septemberist Society's
headquarters are down below?" Fergus asked.

"Whatever it is, it isn't good," Hachi said.

"Guess it's time to cowboy up and climb," Gonzalo said.

"Buster can lift all of us up," Clyde said.

Fergus's gyrocopter popped out of his backpack. "I can give
at least one person a lift."

"We come at her from all sides," Hachi said. "We don't give
her a chance to run, and we don't give her a chance to do whatever it is she means to do."

"Which means she can't see us coming," Gonzalo said.

Philomena Moffett stood on a walkway along the outside rim
of Hiawatha's head, holding on to one of the two eagle feathers that stuck out from his head. Wind blew the curls of her
dark black hair into her face, and a tentacle pushed them back
so she could see. The city of New Rome stretched up Manna-
hatta Island to the north and into Breucklen and Queens to
the northeast, and she could see the longhouses and factories
of Hackensack territory off to the west, in Jersey. There were
hundreds of thousands of people down there, she thought, all
busily living their sunny, happy little lives, ignorant of the
untold horrors lurking under their feet and beneath the waves
and in the shadows.

For centuries, the Septemberist Society had kept the darkness from their doors. Hidden the truth about the world from the tribes of America. How many lives had been sacrificed to keep them from discovering the awful truth of the Mangleborn? How many people had died so that these stupid, oblivious people could turn off their gaslights at night and sleep in peace without fear of something monstrous going bump in the night?

Hundreds. Thousands. Philomena Moffett knew from her time as chief of the Septemberist Society. But there was only one life that had been given that she really cared about.

Not given. Taken.

Hers.

Philomena's mother had died, her good-for-nothing father had abandoned her, and the Septemberist Society had taken her. Taken her and experimented on her, hurt her in ways unimaginable, both physically and mentally, all to try to make her into a hero. A hero to protect a world that had never done anything for her, never loved her, never cared for her. A hero to beat back the evil at the heart of the world so these pathetic, mewling kittens could go on purring and preening and pretending the world was a bright, warm, beautiful place. She had given her life for theirs—*no, it had been taken!* she told herself again. Her life had been *taken*, just like the other children's lives at Dodge City. Sacrificed so these people could live in blissful ignorance. And now it was time to even the score.

Behind her, the Dragon Lantern hummed. Very soon now, she thought. Very soon now it would be over, and everyone who had ruined her life would pay.

"Mina," said a deep voice behind her.

Moffett spun, and gasped. On the other side of Hiawatha's bald head was Twelvetrees, the big Navajo boy the scientists at Dodge City had turned into a buffalo-man.

"No!" Moffett cried. "How could you—?"

"Mina, end this," said Renata, the New Spanish girl who'd been mutated into a feathery lizard by the Dragon Lantern.

They were all here. Twelvetrees. Renata. Henry, the Acadian horse-boy. Ivan, the Inuit who'd become a mute lobster-like monster with red claws and a hard shell. Ominotago, the Cheyenne girl who was so inhuman, so unlike anything of the Earth, that her organs floated in a semitransparent ooze.

And gliding in to land on one of Hiawatha's giant eagle feathers, the Illini girl who'd grown wings and talons. The girl who had been Moffett's only friend before the Lantern.

Sings-In-The-Night.

Horror slipped around Moffett's heart like a tentacle, but she knew in her brain it was a trick. The fox-girl who had stolen the Dragon Lantern. She was doing this. She'd met Sings-In-The-Night. She knew all about Dodge City.

But how did she know about the others?

"You're not real," Moffett said, trying to talk herself out of what she was seeing. "You're all dead. I saw you all die."

"I didn't die," Sings-In-The-Night said. "You *killed* me."

The Dodge City League wasn't real; Moffett knew that. They weren't really here. But what she was seeing meant that Archie Dent's new League *was* here, hiding behind the illusion. Distracting her. Moffett smiled. The fox-girl's tricks could hide them, but they couldn't protect them.

"I did kill you," she told the illusion. "And I'll kill the rest of you too!"

Moffett spun, took a deep breath, and screamed at the empty space around the Dragon Lantern. Kitsune's illusion evaporated, and suddenly Hiawatha's crown was full of Leaguers. Real Leaguers. The fox-girl, looking pale and tired. A Texian boy with a tin star and a wave cannon. Hachi and her clacking little toys. The little UN soldier and his giant steam man peeking up over Hiawatha's head. They surrounded her.

Two more of them—Fergus and a gray-skinned, tattooed Karankawan girl Moffett didn't know—were bent over the Dragon Lantern, trying to turn it off. And with them was Archie Dent, the boy made of stone. He leaped in front of Moffett's sonic scream, protecting his friends.

WOMWOMWOMWOMWOM! Moffett focused the sound waves on Archie, pushing him back. He tripped over the Dragon Lantern, tumbled backward down Hiawatha's round head, and disappeared over the side.

"Now," Moffett said to the others. "Who's next?"

36

Archie fell. Again. He was always falling off things. Airships, floating cities, giant underground machines. And now the statue of Hiawatha in New Rome Harbor.

"Slag," Archie said. He closed his eyes and waited for the thud.

Shunk. Something caught him long before he should have hit the ground. Buster! Clyde had caught Archie in the steam man's big brass hand!

"Need a lift?" Clyde asked.

Archie smiled. "Yeah. Thanks. I wasn't looking forward to climbing all those stairs."

Clyde put Archie back on top of Hiawatha in the middle of a free-for-all. Moffett stood over the glowing red Dragon

Lantern, fighting everyone at once. Hachi struggled in Moffett's tentacles, her flying circus trying to pry her free. Fergus, his leg brace broken from the sonic scream, knelt nearby and hurled lightning. Ghosts of the Dodge City League appeared randomly around Moffett, surprising her. Martine tried to jab her flaming green harpoon through Moffett's swirling tentacles. Gonzalo fired a blue beam from Señor X.

WOMWOMWOMWOMWOM! Moffett screamed at Gonzalo, deflecting the ray that would freeze her in amber. Archie used the chance to rush her. *Thoom*. He hit Moffett with all his strength, and she dropped Hachi and rolled backward toward the edge of Hiawatha's head. Her tentacles caught her at the last moment, and she pulled herself up to face them.

"Give up, Moffett," Archie told her. "You can't beat all of us at once."

"You're right," said Moffett. WOMWOMWOMWOMWOM! Moffett swept the top of Hiawatha's head with a sonic scream. Archie held his ground against it and Hachi ducked behind Hiawatha's Mohawk, but everyone else went tumbling off the roof.

"Kitsune! Fergus! Gonzalo! Martine!" Archie cried, but it was swallowed up by Moffett's piercing screech. When it died away, Archie took a step toward her, anger welling up inside him.

"There. That evens the odds a little, don't you think?" Moffett crowed.

Hachi leaped over the copper Mohawk and stood with Archie, her flying circus buzzing around them. Behind them, the Dragon Lantern's humming kept getting louder, its red glow getting brighter.

"She set it to overload," Hachi said over the wind. "She means to blow it up, taking Septemberist headquarters with it."

"Not just the Septemberist Society," Moffett said. "When that thing explodes, it'll destroy the whole city!"

Archie raised a fist to smash the thing.

"Go ahead," Moffett said. "Do it now and I won't have to wait!"

Hachi caught Archie's hand. "Don't! Smashing it could make it explode!"

Archie picked the Dragon Lantern up.

"Then I'll throw it! I'll throw it into the ocean!"

Moffett laughed. "It won't matter! You can't throw it far enough. You might save your precious Septemberist Society, but plenty more people will die!"

Buster's head appeared beside them, and he held up one of his big brass hands. Kitsune, Gonzalo, and Martine stood on his palm, and Fergus flew up alongside on his gyrocopter.

"Top floor: Dragon Lanterns, copper feathers, and lady supervillains!" Clyde announced.

Fergus fired lightning at Moffett, and she leaped out of the way.

WOMWOMWOMWOMWOM! Moffett screamed again. Fergus went spinning away, and Clyde closed Buster's hand around the three Leaguers he held to protect them. Moffett turned the scream on Archie and Hachi, and he grabbed her hand to keep her from flying away. Hachi kicked in the air like a wind sock, but Archie held tight.

Moffett's scream died away, and Hachi began to fall back to Hiawatha's head. Archie hurled her instead, throwing her right at the sagging Philomena Moffett. Hachi did a somersault in the air and hit Moffett feetfirst—*oomph!*—driving her back over the edge.

Clyde set the others back on Hiawatha's head. "Did she fall?"

Hachi inched toward the side, her flying circus flitting ahead of her to see. Hachi was almost to the edge when Mr. Lion, Jo-Jo, Tusker, and Freckles began chittering and fluttering around like mad. Hachi turned and leaped away, but a purple tentacle shot up over the edge of the statue and grabbed her, flipping her away into the sky.

"Hachi!" Fergus cried, diving after her with his gyrocopter.

Moffett pulled herself back onto the head. Behind Archie, the Dragon Lantern reached an ear-splitting vibrato.

"Why are you protecting them?" Moffett asked Archie. "How can you fight for a society that sacrifices children for their own comfort? They used you, just like they used me!"

"We're not the Septemberist Society," Archie yelled back. Behind him, Martine bent over the Dragon Lantern again, and Gonzalo and Kitsune spread out on Hiawatha's head, bent low against the thrashing wind. "The Septemberists have a lot more than Dodge City to answer for," Archie told her. "But not like this. Not this way. You're going to kill hundreds of thousands of innocent people!"

"Innocent!?" Moffett cried. She pointed at the city behind her, her long skirt whipping in the wind. "You think they're all innocent, just because they don't know? They're the ones who benefit from our sacrifice! They're the ones who allow it to happen so they can live their lives in blissful ignorance!"

KaPOW! Señor X fired a blue beam at her again, and she dove away. Archie pried one of Hiawatha's big copper feathers from the statue's head and swung it down in front of Kitsune and Martine, deflecting the sound waves as Moffett screamed again. WOMWOMWOMWOMWOM!

Fergus and Hachi landed to one side of Moffett as her scream ended. Hachi brandished her knives. Fergus glowed with lektricity. Gonzalo circled with his wave cannon. Buster peeked up over the edge. They had Moffett surrounded.

Archie raised the huge copper feather, threatening to flatten her with it.

"Tell us how to shut it down, Moffett," Clyde said. "It's over."

Moffett stepped back toward the ledge. "Never!" she cried.

"Leaguers, full steam ahead!" Clyde cried.

Fergus shot lightning. Hachi threw knives. Gonzalo fired his blue amber beam. Archie slammed the copper feather.

Moffett dodged them all by diving over the edge. She grabbed for the closest of the two feathers still sticking out of Hiawatha's head, but her tentacles passed right through it. *Whoosh.* The illusion vanished, and with wide-eyed horror Moffett fell three hundred feet to the ground below. She hit the ground in a squall of writhing tentacles, and was still.

Kitsune limped up behind the others on Gonzalo's shoulder. "Funny," she said. "All those times she saw the statue of Hiawatha, and she didn't remember he only had two feathers, not three."

"The Dragon Lantern!" Clyde reminded them all.

The ancient Mu device trembled and glowed redder, the pitch from its overloading circuits almost deafening. Martine still sat staring at it as she had been for minutes.

"I'll throw it in the ocean!" Archie yelled over the wind and the whine. "It's all we can do!"

"Nae," Fergus said. "I can get it farther carrying it on my gyrocopter!"

"No! You'll die!" Hachi yelled.

"If I don't we're *all* gonna die!" Fergus yelled back.

"I'll freeze it in blue amber!" Gonzalo cried.

"It won't help!" Hachi told him.

"Well somebody do *something*," Señor X said.

"All right, here's what we're gonna do—" Clyde told them.

Martine reached out and touched the claw of one of the four silver dragons that snaked up the corners of the lantern. *Feuuuuuuuw.* The awful screeching and shaking stopped all at once, and the Dragon Lantern's dangerous red glow faded away into nothing.

"Or we could do that," Clyde said.

Archie pulled Martine to her feet, and she stood bewildered and ramrod straight as everyone hugged her and clapped her on the back and congratulated her.

"Let me guess," Hachi said. "That was the friendliest dragon."

"Actually, no, he wasn't," Martine said. "But he did tell me where the off switch was."

Archie went to the edge of Hiawatha's head and looked down while the others laughed and celebrated their victory. Moffett's body was still there. She wasn't getting up again. Ever.

Hachi came up beside him, holding onto Archie's arm against the strong winds.

"She always did like climbing up on things," Archie said.

"Yeah," Hachi said. "But she wasn't as good at falling off them as you are."

Archie chuckled.

The others joined them, huddling around Archie for protection from the wind.

"I think I can see *mi casa* from here," Gonzalo said.

"You can't see anything from anywhere," Kitsune said, still on his shoulder.

Archie couldn't take his eyes off Moffett's broken body. "I know she did terrible things," he said. "I know she hurt people. Killed people. But she had a good reason to be mad."

"Aye, but that doesn't excuse what she did," Fergus said.

"No. I know," Archie said. "It's just—she wasn't born a monster. Somebody made her into one. The same people who made me into a monster."

Gonzalo shook his head. "Meanness don't just happen overnight."

"He's right," Hachi said. "They did awful things to bring you to life, Archie. Made you into a boy of living stone. But only you can make yourself a monster."

Archie nodded. Still, he felt sorry for Philomena Moffett. She'd never asked for any of this. Neither had he.

"I guess we oughtta go put that lantern back on top of Cahokia in the Clouds," Clyde said.

"We will," Hachi said. She looked at Archie, and he knew exactly what she was thinking.

"There's one last thing we have to do here first," Archie said.

37

The Kraken surfaced in a gaslit cave where two more small submarines sat at an ancient stone dock. Martine slid her ship up alongside, and six Leaguers, all of them but Clyde, climbed out, with Mr. Rivets not far behind. They followed Archie up the stone steps from the dock and into a big round room where seven life-sized statues stood guard beside seven doorways.

The great hall of the Septemberist Society. It was underneath the statue of Hiawatha in New Rome Harbor after all, just as Archie had always suspected.

Underground, Archie thought to himself. *It's always underground.*

The Leaguers spread out in the room, marveling at the statues. Fergus stood before Wayland Smith, the tinker.

Gonzalo stood before Maat, the Aegyptian weigher of souls. Martine stood before Daedalus, the Greek scientist. Kitsune, on crutches, stood before Anansi, the Afrikan trickster. Hachi stood before Hippolyta, the Amazonian warrior.

Archie stood between Heracles, the brooding, half-naked hulk, and Theseus, the neat, dashing Athenian hero. Once he'd longed to be the hero, but now he knew he was the hulk.

Archie marched past the statue of Theseus into the Septemberist Society's offices, and the other Leaguers followed. At the end of a long corridor stood the closed doors of the Septemberist Society council chambers. Archie remembered running up here in a panic the last time, screaming about a Manglespawn in the catacombs below. It seemed like forever ago, but it had really only been months. He felt so much older now. More experienced.

And so much more sure of himself.

A polished Mark II Machine Man stepped in his way and put a hand up.

"What a pleasure it is to see you again, Master Archie," Mr. Pendulum said. Mr. Pendulum was the head Tik Tok for the Septemberist Society. "But I'm afraid the council is in session at present."

"Good," Archie said. "Tell them the League of Seven is here to see them."

"Oh. Yes. Well. How extraordinary," Mr. Pendulum said, his glass eyes studying them all. "But I'm afraid the council gave strict orders that no one should disturb them."

"Lucky for us then," said Fergus. "We no longer take orders from the Septemberist Society."

Archie picked the thousand-pound Mr. Pendulum up and set him aside like a potted plant.

"Oh, I say," Mr. Pendulum muttered as the League of Seven pushed past.

Ka-THOOM. Archie punched open the council chamber's massive wooden doors, and the seven council members jumped from their seats at the big round table in the center of the room.

"What's the meaning of this?" demanded Frederick Douglass, the head of the Society's Lawbringer Guild. He stood behind the council chief's seat; he'd apparently been voted the Society's new leader after Philomena Moffett had gone rogue.

Around the table were the other current members of the Septemberist Council: Sally Tall Chief, the actress; Hellcat Maggie, the slumlord; John Two-Sticks, the lacrosse star; General Lee, the soldier; Hevataneo, the inventor; and Archie recognized Ellen Swallow, the scientist, who must have taken the guild leader position from Moffett in his parents' guild.

"We're in the middle of a very important report from General Lee here," Douglass told them. "We understand you've accomplished great things. But if you'll just wait until we're finished, we'll see you then."

"You'll see us now," Hachi told him.

"I beg your pardon, young lady!" Tall Chief said.

"Gonzalo?" Archie said.

The Texas Ranger stepped forward, pointing Señor X at the council from his hip. "By the authority vested in me by the great Republic of Texas, you are each and every one under arrest for the kidnapping, torture, and murder of children at the secret facility known as Dodge City."

The council stared at the League, gobsmacked.

"You—you can't be serious," Douglass said.

"Dead serious," Archie told them.

"This is preposterous!" Two-Sticks said.

"That was twenty-five years ago!" the Cheyenne inventor told them. "None of us were even on the council then!"

"You are also charged with conspiracy in the 1864 murders of one hundred men, thirty-seven women, and fifteen children at Chuluota," Gonzalo told them.

"And just who's going to try us?" Hellcat Maggie snarled. "Who's going to convict us?"

"We are," Hachi said darkly, drawing her knives.

Frederick Douglass threw up his hands. "The September-ist Society *may or may not* have had a hand in your creation," he said, sounding like the lawyer he was. "But if we did, it was necessary. Just *look at you!* You are full and truly a new League of Seven! If General Lee's report is to be believed, you have saved the world!"

"From the menace *you* created in the first place," Kitsune said.

"A new League arises whenever the world *needs one*," Archie told them. "Not when *you* choose to make one. If we exist, it's only to clean up your mess!"

"So arrest us then," said Sally Tall Chief. "Drag us off to the courts of New Rome. Who will believe you? Who will believe any of it? No one knows the Septemberist Society even exists."

"There is no more Septemberist Society!" Archie roared. He slammed his fist down on the huge round table with the Society's all-seeing pyramid eye carved into it. *Kra-KOOM!*

The table split in half and crashed to the floor. The council members jumped back again with real fear in their eyes.

"You're finished!" Archie told them. "We're shutting you down."

"But—but who will safeguard the secret of lektricity?" Miss Swallow asked. "Who will protect humanity from the Mangleborn?"

The room shook, and rock and dust streamed from the ceiling.

"An earthquake?" Two-Sticks asked, backing away.

The roof crumbled. Rock and dirt thundered down on the broken table. Sunlight streamed into the room through a giant hole in the ceiling, and the council put their hands up to shade their eyes.

"*Arf! Arf arf!*" Buster whistled happily, his big brass hands covered with dirt. He and Clyde had dug down from the park above.

Clyde waved hello from inside the giant steam man's head. "Man, Buster's got a full year's digging done in one week, and that's a fact!"

"We're starting a new society," Archie told the council. "And it's not going to be a secret anymore. No more working underground. No more operating from the shadows. Before we're done, everybody in the United Nations is going to know about the Mangleborn and the League of Seven. Everybody in the Americas. Everybody in the *world*. No more secrets. No more lies. And no more hurting people to save the world."

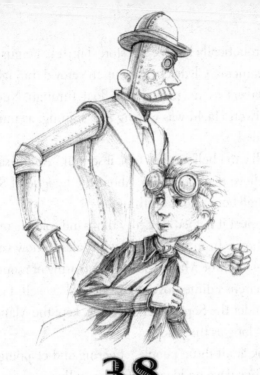

38

The New Rome crowd along the parade route roared as the airship carrying the League of Seven floated down Broadway. Ticker tape streamed from windows, and confetti fluttered in the air. Brass bands played "Seven Heroes True" and "Keep Them Monsters Down," and kids with toy rayguns and home-made bandoliers and cardboard steam man costumes chased through their parents' legs.

Mr. Rivets poked his head inside the float's cabin, where Archie was hiding.

"Master Archie?" Mr. Rivets said. He came all the way inside. "Why aren't you with the others?"

Archie watched the rest of the League through one of the float's portholes. Gonzalo and Kitsune, holding hands. Martine waving robotically like a cigar store Tik Tok. Fergus mugging for the cameras. Clyde chatting up the crowd through Buster's loudspeakers as he pulled the float through New Rome's streets. Even Hachi was waving and smiling, as much as she ever smiled.

"I still can't believe they took it so well," Archie said. "I still can't believe they believe it. About the League of Seven and the Mangleborn and everything."

"I suspect it helped that fifty thousand soldiers recently returned home from Gettysburg with tales of how you helped them defeat three Mangleborn and an army of monsters. And Mr. Senarens's dime novels have helped as well. Frankly, sir, it's a wonder the Septemberist Society kept the Mangleborn a secret as long as they did."

"Look at all those people, cheering and clapping," Archie said. "They have no idea what we're really up against."

"I suspect not," Mr. Rivets said. "But you were right—knowing what darkness lies beneath is far better than pretending it isn't there. And when the time comes, you and your friends will be there to help them again." Mr. Rivets paused. "But you still haven't answered my initial query. Why are you hiding in here? I seem to recall you telling the former Septemberist Council you would no longer be working from the shadows."

"I wanted to be a hero, Mr. Rivets," Archie said. "I wanted to be Theseus. Remember? The guy out front. But that's not who I am. I'm the shadow. This is where I belong."

"You belong with your friends," Mr. Rivets told him. "You belong with the League of Seven."

Archie nodded. "I *will* be with them. I'll be with them in

the new headquarters we're building downtown, and I'll be with them whenever, wherever we need to be to stop the Mangleborn, day or night. I can still be a hero, but I can't be out there now, smiling and waving at people. Not that kind of hero. Not the way I was born. Do you understand, Mr. Rivets?"

"Yes, sir. I think I do."

Archie was quiet for a long moment.

"About that, Mr. Rivets," Archie said at last. "About the way I was born. I've been thinking."

"Yes, sir?"

"I have the strength of a hundred men, right? Because I've got the blood of a hundred men inside me."

"As I understand it. Yes, sir," Mr. Rivets said.

"Well, if it took a hundred lives to create me, and that gave me the strength of a hundred men, maybe I've got a hundred lives to live as well. A hundred lifetimes. You understand?"

"I think so, sir."

"I mean, I don't know if it's true, but—"

"But if you are correct, sir, you would live for somewhere between eight to ten thousand years," Mr. Rivets said.

Archie looked at Mr. Rivets in the dark.

"All my friends, everyone I know, they'll all be dead. Nobody I know will be around when I die."

"I will be, sir," said Mr. Rivets. "No matter what may come, I shall be there with you. Always."

ARCHIE

HACHI

FERGUS

CLYDE

KITSUNE

The League
of Seven

MARTINE

GONZALO

ACKNOWLEDGMENTS

To my own League of Seven: Susan Chang, Ali Fisher, Kathleen Doherty, Brett Helquist, Bob, Wendi, and Jo. Full steam ahead!

Reading & Activity Guide

THE MONSTER WAR
A LEAGUE OF SEVEN NOVEL
by Alan Gratz
Ages 10–14; Grades 5–9

ABOUT THIS GUIDE

The questions and activities that follow are intended to enhance your reading of *The Monster War*. The material is aligned with Common Core State Standards for Literacy in English and Language Arts (www.corestandards.org); however, please feel free to adapt this content to suit the needs and interests of your students or reading-group participants.

ABOUT THE BOOK

The Monster War is the third book in Alan Gratz's action-packed, steampunk League of Seven series. In Gratz's alternate nineteenth-century America, a secret organization known as the Septemberist Society works to prevent ordinary citizens of the world from realizing that deep in the earth live terrible monsters known as Mangleborn, and that there are technologies, such as electricity, that can awake and excite the Mangleborn to destroy the world.

Into this scenario comes young Archie Dent who learns that he is part of the newest incarnation of the League of Seven, a group of exceptional individuals called by the Septemberists to defeat onslaughts of Mangleborn. Archie and his newfound League associates, Hachi and Fergus, track down the thief of a dangerous device known as The Dragon Lantern. In doing so, they realize that the Septemberist Society which called them into being may also be responsible for some great horrors.

As Archie's adventures continue, more League members are found, and each must grapple with painful truths about their pasts, their friendships, and their terrifying mission . . .

Pre-Reading Discussion & Writing Activities

1. Read aloud these opening lines from the three LEAGUE OF SEVEN stories:

   "The secret entrance to the headquarters of the Septemberist Society could only be reached by submarine."—THE LEAGUE OF SEVEN

   "Archie Dent dangled from a rope twenty thousand feet in the air watching the blue ribbon of the Mississippi spin far, far below him."—THE DRAGON LANTERN

   "The chain that shackled Archie Dent to the boy beside him rattled as the steamwagon bounced down a rutted road, and they swayed into each other."—THE MONSTER WAR

   Point out features in these texts which suggest that the LEAGUE OF SEVEN stories do not occur in a real time and place. What expectations do these opening sentences set up for the stories to come?

2. *The Monster War* is set in an alternate nineteenth-century America. "Alternate histories" are works of fiction in which recognizable historical figures have experiences different than those recorded in history books, and notable events have different outcomes. Alternate histories beget the question: Is

history inevitable? Consider current problems, such as gun violence in America or global warming, and discuss what you have read in newspapers or online resources covering the ongoing debates as to how these problems should be handled. Informed by your class discussion and current events research, write a short essay addressing the question: "Are historical events inevitable? Why or why not? And, if not, how can individuals have an impact on the history of their world?"

Supports Common Core State Standards: L.5-8.5, L.9-10.5; SL.5-8.1, SL.9-10.1; W.5-8.1-2, W.9-10.1-2.

Developing Reading & Discussion Skills

1. In the opening chapters of the novel, Archie has been tricked into a captive situation by Mr. Rivets. Why does he resist helping the kidnapped children? What fears does he have about himself?

2. What does Archie come to realize about Gonzalo and Senor X in Chapter 5? Do these realizations change his relationships to these characters? Do these new insights affect your reader's perspective on Gonzalo and his "weapon"?

3. What is "lektricity" and why is it dangerous? How might you respond to Hachi's words on page 138: "Isn't *everybody* who messes with lektricity a madman?"

4. Archie and his friends find Martine both amazing and frustrating, especially in instances such as their argument over whether a "knot's a knot" on page 83. Does Martine remind you of anyone from real life, film, or television? In our world, might she be considered *non-neurotypical* or *autistic*? Why might this be important to the story?

5. What is a "proper League of Seven"? Who comprises the League? List the names of *The Monster War* characters who

are members of the League and the roles they play. (Hint: Reread Chapter 10.)

6. Recount at least two instances in which League members must persuade others that (a) they need to be saved and/or (b) the League of Seven, young and strange as they appear, can save them. What do you think is important about this recurring dynamic?

7. What is the relationship between Mangleborn and subterranean oil? What other resources, landmarks, or other "ordinary" things readers take for granted, or believe they understand, in their world are, in the story, the result of actions by—or reactions to—Mangleborn?

8. On page 215, Kitsune says, "It's funny how fear makes you do things you never thought you could do." Do you agree? Can you recall a time in your own life where fear impacted your actions? How might this help you better understand the motivations of characters in *The Monster War*?

9. In the first chapter of the novel, Archie tells Gonzalo that he doesn't have any parents, "which was true and wasn't true." As you read the novel, how many ways might you interpret or understand this early observation?

10. Who is Philomena Moffett and why is the League so intent on achieving her capture? How does this goal require the League members to divide and how do they do so? Compare and contrast the ways the League teams defeat the Mangleborn they encounter.

11. Throughout the novel, human characters, such as Hachi and Fergus, humanlike (or partially human) characters, such as Archie and Martine, and technology-based characters such as Mr. Rivets and Senor X, interact. How might readers see *The Monster War* as a story about the limits of the way ordinary human beings can understand history? What insight and value might artificial intelligence or other types of per-

ception lend to our world view and to keeping peace in the future?

12. Describe the relationships between Archie and his friends as the story progresses. What forms the core connection between each of these characters? Do you think the other League members fear Archie "most"? Why or why not?

13. On page 264, Hachi says of Archie that his "weakness" is his human brain. Do you agree? Is this a weakness? What do you think the author is trying to show about humanity's relationship to technology and to the powers of nature and the planet on which we live?

14. On page 296, Archie observes that, "There didn't seem to be a great deal of difference sometimes between the Mangleborn and the heroes who fought them . . ." If this is the case, how might you define the difference between a villain and a hero?

15. Why does Archie feel sorry for Philomena Moffet? How can he relate especially well to Moffett? Why do you think Hachi, who has had to forgive Archie for so much, seems to be the friend who most empathizes and most helps Archie see the differences between himself and Philomena?

16. At the close of the novel, what does the League come to realize about the Septemberists and their own role in history? How do they decide to change the future? To what risks might they be subjecting the world by deciding to make this change?

17. Early in the novel, Hachi tells Archie, "You have to live a life worthy of a *hundred* lives. You have to fight for all the people who died to create you." (p. 112) How might this be viewed as a central theme of the novel? Do you find this instruction to be valuable to readers today and/or to your own life? Explain your answers.

Supports Common Core State Standards: RL.5-8.1-5; RL.9-10.1-5; SL.5-8.1, 3; SL.9-10.1, 3.

JOURNAL. Archie often feels like an outcast, although he is also an integral part of the League. From the perspective of Gonzalo, Hachi, Fergus, or another character, write at least three journal entries, including one reflecting on your history with Archie, one considering your feelings about being part of the League of Seven and its mission, and one discussing both the dangers and values of befriending Archie Dent.

BIOGRAPHY. From Harriet Tubman to General Grant to Jesse James, Alan Gratz brings real historical figures to life in fictional ways throughout his story. Go to the library or online to discover the real identities of these historical figures. Create a "Biographical Guide to *The Monster War*," identifying at least five historical characters with facts about their real contributions to history and brief explanations of why you believe the author chose to include them in his novel.

DESIGN. Select a scene in which Archie and/or his League friends encounter a Mangleborn creature. Study the text for clues to the creature's appearance. Then, using a computer design program or traditional art materials, create a portrait of your selected Mangleborn. If desired, create a larger display of portraits made by friends and classmates.

SYNESTHETIZE. Martine senses relationships between letters and colors which might, in our world, be interpreted as a form of *synesthesia*. Learn about the concept of synesthesia. Discover famous synesthetes from the worlds of art and literature. Imagine that you are a character in *The Monster War*. Using your research, write a speech in which you explain Martine's unusual perceptions, and their potential value, to the other members of the League.

MYTHOLOGIZE. Go to the library or online to learn about the legend of Uktena. Review chapter 23, in which Senor X describes First Men who were "... the first to understand that everything that happens ... will happen again and again, like a snake eating its own tail." What is the relationship between Uktena and this observation? Write a short essay answering this question and explaining why the snake image recurs in discussions of this topic.

RHYME WITH SCIENCE. What is the relationship between Humpty Dumpty and the Second Law of Thermodynamics? Go to the library or online to find the answer to this question. Is Archie's existence as the *Jandal a Haad* connected to this nursery rhyme-scientific theory metaphor and, if so, how? Share your answers via a poster, PowerPoint, or other visual presentation.

ADDRESS YOUR CLASS. Go to the library or online to learn the true history of the Gettysburg address. Read it aloud in your class. Discuss how the address changes for the events and characters of the League of Seven world, and how its message remains valuable to readers in both contexts.

ROLE-PLAY. Archie struggles with his role in the League because he feels different, unworthy, and like an outsider. Have you ever felt this way in your own life? When and how? Invite a friend or classmate to play the character of Archie. Role-play a conversation between "Archie" and yourself in which you share your own perspectives on feeling different and brainstorm ways to handle these feelings.

WRITE A SEQUEL. *The Monster War* is an alternate history, mixing historical facts and real people with fictional characters and outcomes, particularly 19th century American history and Native American legends. Go to the library or online to learn about a famous Native American from this period who has not already appeared in a *League of Seven book*. As author Alan Gratz fictionally turns Jesse James from outlaw to hero, what "alteration" would you make to your historical character, and how might you connect him or her to members of the *League* to begin a new book in the series? What title would you give the book? Write 2-3 paragraphs describing your ideas, followed by an outline of the first 5-10 chapters of the story.

REFLECT & CELEBRATE. On page 315, Hachi tells Archie that ". . . only you can make yourself a monster." Create a poem, set of song lyrics or visual art composition interpreting this statement as it might apply to the lives of people throughout literature, history, and even yourself.

Supports Common Core State Standards: RL.5-8.1-5; RL.9-10.1-5; SL.5-8.4-6; SL.9-10.4-6; W.8.1-4, W.8.7-8; W.9-10.1-4, W.9-10.7-8.